# UNDERTOW

## THE UNDERCITY CHRONICLES

## S.M. STELMACK

Copyright © 2013 by S.M. Stelmack
Editing by Alyssa Palmer
Cover Art by CrocoDesigns
Interior Book Design by JT Formatting

**www.smstelmackauthor.com**

Printed in the United States of America
First Edition: September 2013
Library of Congress Cataloging-in-Publication Data

Stelmack, S.M.
Undertow: The Undercity Chronicles / S.M. Stelmack – 1st ed

ISBN-13: 978-0991869862

1.Undertow—Fiction. 2.Fiction—Romantic Suspense
3.Fiction—Action & Adventure

*For those who walk in the shadows*

(Authors Moira and Serge Stelmack)
http://www.smstelmackauthor.com

## A Note from Serge

My father came from a criminal background, and several of my friends were once members of the police and intelligence community. Though my personal background has been pretty vanilla, I've had the opportunity to rub shoulders with real thieves, conmen, hackers, enforcers, detectives and spies. As such, I've always been aware of the secrets and subcultures that permeate our world, and just how bizarre and far-reaching they can be.

In the early 2000s, my knowledge of the underworld was further broadened when I volunteered to work with street people in my home city of Vancouver. They too had their own sub-cultures. Communities of addicts and sex workers and radical political activists, alliances of people with mental health issues, bands of wild-eyed conspiracy theorists and even street shamans. They fascinated me, though the mental instability of many I met didn't give me cause to want to join their world.

It was with this background that I read Jennifer Toth's 1993 book *The Mole People: Life In The Tunnels Beneath New York City*. Though I have no way of confirming the veracity of Ms. Toth's investigations into New York's underworld, much rung true. There were echoes in her book of the legends and rumors I'd heard since I was a child, stories known to those who walk the wrong side of the law or otherwise reject the rules and order imposed by mainstream culture. The more I read the more connections I made, and almost of its own accord a story revealed itself to me.

Many of the people in *Undertow* are strongly based on actual people I've known, including Detective Monroe, Reggie, Mr. and Mrs. Moore, Shamba, Tocat and even the vile Mr. King, and I have done my best to weave their stories and personalities into the canvas provided by Ms. Toth.

*Undertow* is, of course, a work of fiction. It carries no agenda or political message. But I have done my best to make it reflect the very real shadow world that touches all of our lives, a little glimpse into the dreams and horrors lurking right beneath our feet.

# PRoLoGUE

LINDSAY DESPERATELY WANTED to hold Jack's hand. Her breath came fast and shallow, and her every muscle had stiffened into near rigor mortis. And still the elevator dropped beneath the city streets, down into the dark guts of New York, its metal lattice floor the only barrier between her and the shadowy depths below.

She wasn't about to admit her fear of heights to Jack. Sure she had a crush on him, as bad as any fifteen-year-old could have, and would've considered herself the luckiest girl in the world to hold hands with him. Yet, she also knew he hung out with her because she could keep up with him. To confess her vulnerabilities now would make her no better than all the other girls, and she was determined that he would remember her as someone exceptional.

Sam Cole, Jack's father, gave her a lopsided smile. "This crate's on the slow side, but we'll be there in a minute. That hardhat fit okay, Lindsay?"

She managed a nod, and the oversized yellow helmet slipped over her eyes.

The other side of his smile shot up. "Good. I'm glad Jack invited you. Another couple of weeks and we'd be finished down here. Not many people ever get to see the real underground."

As if on cue, the elevator reached the bottom, making Lindsay's already queasy stomach lurch.

"You okay?" Jack asked.

Great, she probably looked like the vomit she was trying to keep down. "Yeah. I'm—I'm a little nervous of heights."

His golden eyes shone. "So I noticed." He looked down. Her hand had his in a death grip.

Lindsay gasped and let go, her face burning. "Oh, jeez. Sorry. I didn't even realize that I...sorry."

She hurried off the elevator—and stepped into a fresh hell. The subway tunnel was dark and filthy and reeked of grime and oil, and she could feel claustrophobia begin to crush her. The halogen lighting created a pool of civilization in which the workers called to each other, and there were the strong noises of steel striking steel and generators throbbing out energy. Beyond that, in the world Jack was going to take her, there was only darkness and silence. Yet he and his father looked content, as if this dank scene was a veritable wonderland.

Jack had used that very word when he was talking her into coming. A wonderland. She described it the same way to her parents, and to her brother, fifteen years her senior, and his wife around the dining room table. Her niece, two going on irrational, wanted to go right away, and when Lindsay explained that wonderland didn't mean Disneyland, she said it was okay, that Jack could lift her on his shoulders and take her to the playground there. Due to her gender, Seline adored Jack. Lindsay's mother melted when Jack came over and ate through the fridge and pantry, and Lindsay had the distinct feeling that it was Jack's charms had played a large part in her mother had giving her permission to go underground. Her father, being male, had only given the go-ahead once he knew Jack's father was going to be nearby. Then her brother, male and bossy beyond belief, had called up Jack's father to confirm the dos and don'ts. Gracie, her sis-in-law, had winced in sympathy. "You should see him with the babysitter. The poor girl is stiff with worry before we've even left, and then she's got an evening of Seline. I always give her an extra ten as stress pay."

Sometimes Lindsay envied the casual bachelor relationship between Jack and his father. Sam Cole was pretty laidback as far as parents went, and actively encouraged his son to explore the tunnels. He'd done the same thing in London when he was a boy, and was overjoyed that his only child shared his lifelong passion for places deep and dark.

"Be back within the hour, and no taking Lindsay off the track," he said. "I don't want to go searching for you again."

Jack laughed, sharing an in-joke with his father. "We'll be careful. Let's go, Linds."

He flicked on his helmet light and waited long enough for her to do the same before leading her down the tunnel, away from the swarm of tradesmen and engineers. Jack was always ready to chart unknown territory, and he wasn't one to check if anyone was following. He was always the first to take a dare, not to show off but because he couldn't resist a challenge. That she was his regular buddy filled her with pride. That he was leaving for Hong Kong in a month, and likely never coming back, filled her with a profound sadness.

Right now with him so real and solid beside her, Lindsay wasn't going to worry about the future. The immediate present was freaky enough. She could feel the darkness here. It had a kind of smothering thickness to it, so alien to anything on the surface.

"What's this about sending out a search party for you?" she asked off-handedly, as if this was no different than walking the streets above.

"They did, but I made it back on my own and they got lost. In the end, I was part of the group that found them."

That was Jack. Total master of his surroundings. Lindsay looked about, her light cutting a pale swath over wet concrete walls, iron rails, graffiti. "Sounds like you know these tunnels pretty well."

"No, I've barely scratched the surface. One day I want to come back here and map the whole underground."

He wanted to come back. Okay, not to see her. Still, there was no way he wouldn't look her up. She squashed down her excitement. "How long do you think they'll take to map?"

Jack gave a short laugh. "A lifetime."

She stopped in her tracks. "You want to spend your life in tunnels? Don't you think that would get old after a while?"

"Not for me. Come on, I want you to meet someone."

"What?"

"There's this guy who lives down here. Name's Tim."

"Who the hell lives in a tunnel?"

"People with nowhere else to go, Linds," he said quietly and, to her ears, reproachfully. "Used to be a lawyer or judge or something. When the transit authority kicked him out of the tunnels, I got him a copy of the keys so he could get back in."

Lindsay wondered what the men in her family would say if they knew Jack was taking her to visit a bum. Or that he'd done something shady for that bum. Maybe she'd skip this part.

"Tim knows everything about the tunnels. My dad told me they've had people down here since the 50's. Tim says there were people underground before that. Way before. You wouldn't believe the stuff that goes on down here."

Lindsay looked over her shoulder, uneasily noticing how

far they were getting from the work crew, and bumped into Jack, who'd stopped immediately ahead of her.

"Sorry…"

Jack didn't seem to notice, his gaze focused down the tunnel on some point beyond the beam of his helmet light.

"What is it?" she whispered.

"I thought I heard something up ahead. Like a yell or… something."

Lindsay strained to hear anything. Nothing but the faint dripping of water. "One of the workers?"

"No," he replied hesitantly. "They'd be wearing a light." He started forward again. She couldn't stop herself. She caught his arm.

"Shouldn't we go tell your dad?"

Jack kept his eyes on the darkness. "It's probably just Tim. He said he has nightmares sometimes. Sees things that aren't there. Come on. There's nothing to be afraid of."

Then why had his usual confident pace slowed? Wordlessly, she followed on Jack's heels down the tunnel for what seemed like a mile, each step taking them further into the gloom of the underworld until the lights behind them had almost faded to nothing. Cold crept over her, a vapor that twined about her limbs.

She was about to suggest again they return when Jack pivoted to face a small side passage that branched off the subway line. The opening didn't reach Lindsay's shoulders and was barely as wide as her body, and it was so obscured by pipes and cables that she never would have noticed it on her own.

"In here," he said, and crouching, disappeared inside.

Fear rooted her feet to the ground. Something was wrong here. Very terribly wrong, and though she trusted Jack, her intuition screamed at her to run back to the safety of the surface, away from whatever lay beyond. But Jack was waiting for her, and she'd never abandon him even if she knew that disaster lay ahead. Especially then. She took a deep breath and followed.

She stayed right on his butt so she was beside him when the cramped passage emptied into a chamber the size of Lindsay's bedroom.

It was the smell that hit her first. Warm, metallic. Blood. Jack's hand clamped around hers, the beams from their helmets skittering about as they frantically scanned the room. Lindsay took in scattered newspapers and paperbacks, an overturned folding cot, pop bottles and a kerosene lantern.

Then Jack made a soft pained noise, and she turned so that her light ran alongside his. Blood was smeared along the wall by the entrance, left by hands that had clawed futilely at the concrete before being dragged off into the darkness.

"Oh my God," Jack whispered. "They're real."

# CHAPTER ONE

*Eighteen years later*

LINDSAY SAT ALONE in Captain Monroe's small, drab office and tried not to be sick all over his desk, a mishap that might not have mattered much since it already looked as if raccoons had been set loose on it. The fluorescent lighting flickered, emitting that mosquito-like frequency as it prepared to burn out, though it wasn't loud enough to drown out the death rattle coming from the computer hard drive. On the printer sat a delicately balanced styrofoam cup of cold coffee, perched there like a bad deodorizer. She might've opened the window with its view over the slate gray waters of the Hudson River, except he doubted that would be appreciated given the freezing temperatures that had gripped the East coast during the past week.

Deep down she knew it wasn't her environment that was making her nauseous. It was why she had to be there. Her eyes drifted, as they did every time she visited, to the maps plastered on the walls. Faded from long years of use, they were, except for the one of the New York subway, all byzantine in their complexity. They depicted tunnels and sewers, air ducts and water mains, forgotten train lines and long-sealed garbage pits. There were maps of cable, gas and steam lines, each representing vast labyrinths buried deep beneath the streets, systems that joined and overlapped, multiplying their complexity. If that were not enough, many of them were incomplete, inaccurate or both, rendering navigation in some sections of the city's bowels virtually impossible. She'd learned as much from several private investigators, all of whom had turned down her case.

After an eternity, Captain Monroe entered, steaming cup of coffee in hand, and sat across from her without a word of greeting. She bit back the urge to tell him about the precarious position of the abandoned cup. She wasn't here to regulate his coffee consumption.

"Thank you for seeing me, Captain," she said as evenly as she could. "Again."

He grunted, and began shuffling through the papers on his desk, clearly searching for something. "You here for an update?" His dismissive tone made it clear he wanted her out the door as quickly as possible.

She tried to keep the frustration out of her voice. "Yes. I'd like to know why nobody is searching for her."

Monroe examined a sheet, frowned, tossed it back and kept rooting around. Lindsay itched to jump in and make square corners and open spaces on his desk.

"Ms. Sterling, do you know how many miles of tunnels there are beneath New York?"

"No. I don't."

Monroe squinted at another scrap of paper. "Neither do I, or anybody else. They run for hundreds of miles, and go down as deep as twelve stories. What I do know is how many men I have to patrol those tunnels, and that number is exactly thirty."

There was a stapled sheaf of papers suspended over the edge of the desk, and the way the Captain was bulldozing around it was going to slide off. "Nevertheless, it's your duty to search for missing persons."

He pinned her with a look no doubt reserved for punks and do-gooders. "I don't need you to remind me of my job. I've been on the force for thirty-four years. I know my responsibilities."

Clearly being nice wasn't going to work. "Then, why aren't you doing anything?"

"Ms. Sterling, how many times do I need to repeat myself before you get it? The people down there are not like the people up here. Most of them are drug addicts. Many have extreme psychological problems. Unless we get some kind of solid lead on this investigation, I'm not sending my men down in a blind search. It's too dangerous."

"But you're the police!"

The captain's face reddened in anger. "Last year we had an officer knifed to death down there. Another one was beaten so badly he'll never walk again, and do you know what he was beaten with? His own nightstick. And that's in subway and maintenance tunnels we regularly patrol, not in the lower levels. We'd need an army to conduct a thorough search, and —surprise, surprise—we don't have one. I explained this to your niece before she went down. She decided she knew better."

Lindsay sucked in her breath to snap back, and then slowly released it. If she was going to find Seline, she needed his cooperation, no matter how unwilling he might be to give it. She rescued the slipping report and set it safely on his desk. He peered at it, then snatched it up.

"Well, at least you found something that you were looking for," she commented with emphasis. "Look, I understand my niece was no great friend of the NYPD. I understand she was conducting her research despite your warnings, and despite *my* warnings, to be frank. I understand that you're undermanned and don't want to place your men in danger. But Captain, I can't just forget about her. There must be something we can do."

Monroe stared coldly across at her. She held it. "Ms. Sterling, I really don't think I can help you…" he began, but his eyes darted to a battered old Rolodex tucked against his computer. She pressed for the advantage.

"Please, Captain," she pleaded, "if you can think of anybody who could find her, anyone at all, I need to know."

Monroe stared back, setting his jaw as if weighing his options. "There is one guy," he said after a moment, though by his expression he was already regretting his words.

"Who is he?"

"His name is Jack Cole. Used to be a professor."

Lindsay froze, went as stiff as the bodies of the homeless that turned up every day now on the city's icy streets. "Did you say Jack Cole? Jack Andrew Cole?"

Monroe's hand hovered over the Rolodex. "You know him?"

"Yes," she replied, fond memories softening her initial shock. "We used to be best friends back in high school. I haven't seen him in"—she did the math—"eighteen years. He's a…a scientist?"

"Anthropologist. Expert in urban subcultures." Monroe set the Rolodex in front of him and began flipping. "Did a lot of work around the world. London, Paris, Rome, Moscow and here in New York. Nobody knows more about the underside of cities."

Lindsay shook her head in wonder. "That's the kind of work he always said he was going to do. He could find Seline, couldn't he?"

"If he wanted, though I doubt he will," Monroe said. "I guess you could say he's retired."

"Retired?" Lindsay echoed.

"About three years ago, Dr. Cole went missing in the underground during one of his expeditions. We searched for him as best we could. After a couple of weeks, we simply didn't have resources to keep it up. He was presumed dead, and that's the way things stayed till early last year when he finally surfaced."

"He spent two *years* underground? What happened to him?"

Monroe eyed one of the cards, then shook his head and kept flipping. "He didn't say."

"What do you mean he didn't say?" Lindsay asked. That wasn't the Jack she'd known. He would've popped up, those lion-like eyes of his bright with enthusiasm, and begun telling the world of his adventures.

"I'm saying he didn't say," Monroe growled. "End of story."

Not for her. She'd find him and he'd help her. He wouldn't let her down. She knew that much about him.

"Yeah, here it is." Monroe stopped at a card and began patting the papers in the hunt for a pen.

Lindsay produced her own pen and paper.

Monroe smirked as he jotted down the address. It was a few blocks from Gates Avenue, in Bed-Stuy. Though parts of Bedford-Stuyvesant were wonderful places to live, featuring beautiful tree-lined rows of century-old brownstone homes and tight-knit communities, Gates Avenue was infamous for its poverty and crime rate. She didn't need to be a psychologist to see Monroe doubted that a professional white woman, dressed like she'd stepped off the pages of a fashion magazine, would dare set foot there.

"You have his phone number?"

"No," Monroe said flatly. "Now if you'll excuse me, I have a lot of work to do today."

Lindsay had the address memorized before she reached the door. As she was leaving, the captain called out to her.

"Make sure you go yourself."

She turned in the doorway. "I beg your pardon?"

"I said you'll need to go there yourself. Cole isn't likely to help you, Ms. Sterling. He definitely won't if you hire someone to go talk to him."

What did he take her for? Thirty years on the force and he hadn't figured out that appearances meant nothing. "I learned long ago that if I wanted anything done, I'd have to do it myself. Today you just reminded me of that."

At that precise moment, the fluorescent light burned out, leaving Monroe in twilight. It was her turn to smirk. "It's hell being left in the dark, isn't it?"

---

SELINE WOKE TO a sudden squeal, letting out one of her own as she bolted upright in the blackness, the sleeping bag provided by her captors twisting around her legs. She unzipped it, the opening of the nylon teeth sawing on her ears. She tried to determine the direction of the noise, or if there had been one, and not yet another hallucination. The chain that stretched from the thick collar around her throat to a concrete pillar clunked and scraped against the floor with her every move, messing with her ability to gauge sound. God, she hated the chain. Early on she'd measured it using her hands and estimated it to be fifteen feet long, not long enough to reach any of the walls in the tiled room, walls she knew existed because if she stretched her legs her feet barely brushed against them. She craved to have a wall at her back.

She sat cross-legged on the bag and breathed deeply, the smell of cold iron and stale air filling her, and willed her racing heart, the beats impossibly loud, to slow. It took longer each time the panic attacks hit, but she calmed herself enough to allow for rational thinking. She'd been down for about a week, though time was fast becoming a shredded concept in this world of perpetual night. She'd tried using the number of times she slept to gauge the passage of days, until she realized that the lack of light and noise made her sleep too often. Or maybe not. All she knew was that she was far from the surface, in the lowest levels of the tunnels, and that despite the silence that surrounded her, she wasn't alone.

She could only guess how many captors there were. She hadn't even gotten a glimpse of them before they'd pulled a sack over her head and dragged her through endless passages, her screams muffled. There were at least two of them to start with—one had held a knife at her throat while the other had bound her wrists behind her back. She now sensed that there were more. Many more.

"Hello?" she called, her voice echoing through the chamber. She always called out after waking. It was a way of establishing contact with her captors, of reaching out to possible rescuers, of proving her humanness. She'd heard somewhere that the best thing to do if kidnapped was to try and make friends with your captors. If they saw you as a person, as opposed to just a hostage, it made it harder for them to harm you.

"Hello?" she tried again. As usual there was no response, and it was the silence that made her more afraid than anything. She wished she'd listened to Lindsay, to that Jack Cole, to everybody. They all said the tunnels could kill. She'd gone down before, twelve times, and nothing had happened, not a whisper of anything. And then this. For the thousandth time she thought of Lindsay's story about when she and Jack went into the tunnels as teenagers. Was she going to be ripped apart like that poor man?

No. No. Against all odds she was alive. They would've killed her outright, if the stories were to be believed. Whoever or whatever was keeping her prisoner actually seemed intent on keeping her alive. She hadn't been beaten or raped. While she slept, the provided bedpan was emptied. A stringy meat stew, palatable after hunger had hollowed her out, was regularly provided along with a bottle of fresh water.

Only they hadn't uttered a single word to her.

"Listen," she called out, repeating once again her offer. "If you contact my sister, she'll ransom me. If you let her know that I'm alive, she'll pay for my release."

Silence.

"Her name is Lindsay Sterling," Seline continued. "You can reach her at Sterling Restorations. Or you can call her home." She rattled off the numbers.

Behind her she thought she heard the slightest rustle and twisted around.

Blackness.

"Please. I'm no threat to you. I'll go away and never come back if that's what you want. I won't tell anyone about you, promise. Please let me go."

Silence.

"I only came down here to help. I'm not with the police. I'm not even a real social worker, just a student. I wanted to make the people who run this city realize that you're down here. To make them stop ignoring you."

Then, a sound. It came in hushed vibrations all around her, making her heart thump wildly. From every corner of the pitch-black chamber she could hear her keepers. Ever so quietly, they were laughing.

---

THE STREET WHERE Jack lived was all but deserted when Lindsay reached it, the rows of cheap shops and slum housing standing stiff and battered in the chill morning. A bunch of young men gathered around a junker turned as her Lexus cruised by, their expressions sullen and calculating. All seemed too cold to do more than look.

Jack's address turned out to be a dilapidated grocery store, its barred windows smashed and brick facade layered in crude graffiti. Pulling over to the curb, she double-checked the address. Had Monroe played some kind of cruel trick on her? Surely to God, Jack couldn't be living in a place barely fit for a rodent.

She locked her car and wondered if she would ever see it again. Oh well, that was why she paid the outrageous insurance premiums. You shouldn't have what you can't afford to lose. It's what her father had always said, and she'd made it her personal motto. She walked across the street and was about to step onto the curb when the heel on her right Blahnik got wedged in a pavement crack. She tugged with her foot, and nothing happened. The heel was sensible, a full inch across, and still this.

"Fine," she muttered. She unzipped the boot, slipped out her nyloned foot and hopped on the other as she began prying out the heel. From down the street, she heard the men snort in laughter.

Yes, she could afford to lose her six hundred dollar boots. Her pride was an entirely different matter. She was not going to meet an old high school friend with one shoe. Besides, it was freezing. She went at it again with renewed vigor.

The heel popped loose which sent her hopping madly about in all directions to keep her balance. The crowd laughed raucously, and Lindsay jammed her foot back into her boot, closed it with a most satisfying zip, and straightened. Then gasped.

She was looking up at the biggest black man she'd ever seen in all her New York life. He was a tree, a building, a mountain. He wore a knit hat, a parka that could've covered her car, and tundra boots that had to have been custom-made to fit him. A brown paper bag full of groceries hung from his bear paw of a hand with no more effort than she'd hold an empty envelope. Down the two-lane bridge of his nose, he looked at her with the mild disdain normally reserved for pigeons.

He took in her boots, her coat, her car, and no doubt, her skin color. "You lost?"

Lindsay tried for a friendly, brisk tone. "Not at all. I'm meeting a friend. He lives right here." She attempted to skirt around him. "I mustn't keep him waiting."

The giant pulled a face and narrowed his eyes. "Here? What's his name?"

She dropped the friendly and kept the brisk. "Why would I tell a stranger my friend's name?"

His eyes widened and apparently conceding the point, he stepped aside to let her pass.

"Thank you," she said. "Have a nice day."

She got past him and headed up to the rusted metal door of the shop. She tapped on it, then banged on it. Nothing. Aware that her every move was being watched, she tried the handle. It was unlocked—didn't, she realized, even have a lock. She glanced back to where the winterized wall of humanity stood watching her. He smiled, flashing a set of gold teeth, clearly not intending to walk on.

"Uh, looks like he left it open for me. Must be home, then."

His smile glittered. "Must be."

"I'll have to remind him not to leave his door open." She paused deliberately. "Who knows who might wander in?"

"Yeah. Good idea."

Lindsay didn't know what to do, so she pushed open the door and tried to close it quickly behind her. It took a couple of goes as the door didn't sit square with the frame. She waited, listening for the Yeti of Bedford to follow. Nothing happened, and she turned back to the shop's interior. Or what there was of it.

Crumbling white plaster exposed wires, and the floor was stripped straight to the plywood underlay. A patchwork of old linoleum tiles, mud-stained carpet rolls and cardboard trailed from the front door to a reinforced metal one at the rear.

"What the hell happened, Jack?" she said under her breath. She crossed the gutted store and knocked on the metal door.

No answer. Lindsay went straight to the door knob. It was locked. She knocked again, harder this time. Behind her, the shop door crashed open and in came the giant.

"You ain't getting past that one," he said, nodding.

"Wha—?"

He strolled towards her, shifting his bag to one arm, while his hand dug around in the pocket of his parka. "Locked it on my way out." He pulled out a set of keys so full that they formed a stiff three-quarters arc and selected one.

He stepped forward and she stepped aside.

"You live here? Not Jack Cole, then?"

"That the name of the friend who's waiting for you?"

The game was up. She sighed. "Yeah, it is."

Again the man's mouth broke into an amused smile. "He'll be back soon. You want to, you can come down and wait." He moved sideways to hold the door open for her.

Lindsay tried not to look as scared as she was. What the hell had Monroe gotten her into? The cop had warned her to talk to Jack herself, but hadn't mentioned anything about his living in the basement of some abandoned building with Bigfoot. Perhaps it was a kind of test. After all, if she didn't have the guts to go down there, how could she expect others to face New York's real underground?

"Sure. Sounds good." Carefully she walked down the stairwell, him clumping behind her, filling the one escape route. They emerged into a clean, spartan apartment. No, not spartan. Spartan was its own kind of style. This was absence, the kind of deprivation found in a prison cell. There were no bookshelves, no television, no phone—not even a single picture on the cracked plaster walls. The only illumination was the weak beams of sunlight that fell through a pair of small street-level windows high on the back wall. Lindsay had no sense of Jack in the bleak apartment, nothing to make it seem as if this was where he belonged.

The black man kicked off his boots, carpeted the floor

with his coat. "Sit down. He'll be back soon."

Her seating choices were two chairs, an uncomfortable-looking plastic one by a small formica kitchen table, and a worn mud-brown leather armchair pushed into the far corner. Lindsay crossed the room to take up the latter.

"So...my name's Lindsay."

The man took two cartons of eggs from the paper bag, placed one on the counter and the other in the rusted fridge. "That right?"

Lindsay was tired of being played with. "Yeah, that's right. Now could you stop with your I-know-something-you-don't-know game and act like a normal human being?"

His eyes positively gleamed. "Man, I can't wait for Jack to come back and see what I brought home."

"You make it sound as if I were a bargain at a garage sale."

He gave a soft hoot. "More than what Jack bargained for, I'll bet." He turned to the sink and began washing his hands under a sputtering tap. "Reggie," he tossed over his shoulder. "I'm Reggie."

"I take it you're a friend of Jack's?"

Reggie dried his hands on a towel that Lindsay wouldn't have washed her floor with and took a large frying pan from one of the small cupboards. "Yeah. Something like that."

Lindsay took in his familiarity with the place, and had to ask, "You and Jack are...roommates?"

"Yeah." Reggie scrunched his forehead in sudden thought. "You asking if I'm gay?"

The directness of his question threw her, and she reacted with her own bluntness. "I don't care if *you* are. I'm just wondering about Jack, is all."

Reggie let out a whoop of laughter, and he fell back

against the ancient yellow fridge, rocking it and holding his gut. He chugged out a succession of long motor-like guffaws. "Oh, man, I can't wait. I can't wait." Gradually he subsided and began cracking eggs into the pan.

He was on his seventh when he theorized, "Might explain why he's so off women, but I doubt it."

Lindsay watched as Reggie broke all twelve eggs into the pan and proceeded to scramble them on a two-burner hot plate, his back to her.

"How do you know him?" Lindsay said, shedding her jacket and folding it over the back of the chair. The place wasn't as cold as it looked.

"How come you say you're a friend of Jack when you've never come around before?" he asked right back.

He had a point. "We were friends in high school, then he and his dad moved away, and I haven't seen him since. I didn't know until today that he was back in New York."

"You're here to say hello?"

Lindsay wasn't about to go into it with Reggie. "Yeah. Something like that."

He snorted at having his line thrown back at him. "I like you, girl." He shook his head. "I can't wait."

When the pan had heated to a steady hissing, he tipped half of the yellow globby contents onto a plate, and ate the rest out of the pan, staring off into space as if he were by himself.

"You live alone?" he suddenly asked.

This time Lindsay was prepared for Reggie's abruptness, maybe because he was a straight-shooter like her. "No. I have a niece."

He stopped chewing. He looked ready to ask another question when the door at the top of the stairs opened. The light from the store above briefly cast a man's shadow down to the dim apartment. Gold teeth appeared in anticipation. "Must be him now."

Lindsay stood automatically. Her hand fluttered to her pale hair and she wished she'd thought to check herself in the mirror instead of watching Reggie shovel egg into his face.

Not that she was here to rekindle a high school crush, her ears tracking the descent of the booted footsteps. Still, there was no denying it. She was looking forward to seeing Jack Cole again.

# CHAPTER TWO

IT WAS JACK, but not the boy from her memories. He was a man now, of course, taller, filled out, with a rough, angular face and dark hair grown overlong. What made Lindsay stop, however, were his eyes. The amber had brightened and hardened, become the eyes of a bird of prey. Powerful and intimidating, they instantly locked on hers. Lindsay felt herself caught, held at bay. Then he looked to Reggie, snapping the connection.

"What's she doing here?" he asked, zipping off his parka and dropping it on the floor with Reggie's.

Reggie shrugged his massive shoulders. "She came looking for you."

Annoyed at being referred to in the third person, Lindsay found her tongue. "I'm Lindsay. Lindsay Sterling. Remember, from high school—"

He cut her off. "I remember."

His hostility stunned her, and despite her normal eloquence, Lindsay stumbled over her words. "Oh...yes... well..."

"What do you want?"

"I need your help."

His mouth twisted. "This about your niece?"

What was going on? "You know her?"

"She came to me about four months ago. Dropped your name. I take it she's in trouble."

Seline had gone to see Jack—four months ago!—and hadn't said one peep about it. "She came to you? How did she find you?"

"She met Reggie at Grand Central and my name came up. Said she heard all about me from you." He made it sound as if she'd spread slanderous gossip.

"All I ever said about you was the time we visited the tunnels when we were kids and...and what we saw. I told her that to try to stop her from going down." That had backfired. It had only made Seline sit bolt upright on the couch and demand what Jack had meant by 'They're real.' Lindsay hadn't been able to answer, because Jack had never told her. Whenever she'd brought up the subject, he'd always become distant— and then fall quiet. During her last few weeks with him, he last thing she'd wanted was a silent Jack. She had wanted him full of life, wanted him happy around her and *because* of her. And if that meant not talking about their experience in the tunnels, then so be it.

Jack brushed at his face, as if ridding himself of a crawling fly. "Looks like it didn't work."

"No, it didn't." At twenty, Seline had more courage than brains; she assumed that a knack for dealing with street people gave her impunity in the tunnels. The people who lived beneath the city's streets were steeped in dark urban legend, and even the most ignorant New Yorker knew that the world beneath their feet was one of danger.

Jack had his eye on Reggie's pan of eggs. "Leave any for me?"

Reggie pointed his thumb behind him at the plate on the plank-wide counter. Jack slid past him into the narrow kitchen and practically disappeared behind the black man. The grocery bag rustled, a drawer opened and then the draw of a knife through bread.

Lindsay crossed the room to him and raised her voice to make sure she was heard. "Seline's been missing for the past week. Eight days, to be exact. She's in the tunnels, I know it."

"She could've come up and not come back home," Reggie suggested.

"No. We had rules."

After the first time Seline had gone down, Lindsay had kicked her out but had relented a week later, when she spotted her niece outside Grand Central with an empty guitar case and singing about paving paradise for a parking lot. Two weeks after that, Seline went down again. So ground rules were established. "She couldn't stay for more than two days, and she had to call within an hour of re-surfacing. She always did." Lindsay didn't add that each time she'd picked up to her niece's cheery voice she felt as if she were drawing breath for the first time in two days. Eight days now, and every breath was an effort.

Reggie scanned Lindsay up and down through a squinted eye. "You don't look old enough to be her aunt."

Her eyes locked on Reggie. "She's my brother's kid. He and his wife were killed in a car accident twelve years ago. So were my mom and dad. I'm not Seline's aunt. I'm her whole fucking family."

There was dead silence, Lindsay's chest tight with the ache of her chronic grief. She wrapped her arms around herself, an instinctive act that had she'd developed into a deliberate, self-comforting one. It was a way of recognizing the pain without giving in to it. And this was absolutely one of those times that she couldn't let it run the show. Reggie blew out his breath in a long gust and slowly pivoted on his heel, like a door opening, so that nothing stood between Jack and Lindsay.

There was the Jack she'd known, the real Jack. The sympathy in those deep golden eyes was unmistakable, and hit her to the core. Lindsay suddenly felt more weak and vulnerable than she had in a dozen years, and more than anything wanted to walk straight into his arms. Then hardness crept over his features and the imposter was back.

"Heard about that from Seline. Sorry." He might as well as have laughed at her for all the tenderness in those trite words. "So your niece went down into the tunnels." He was changing the subject because he didn't care about her tragedy. And why should he? There had been twelve blank years between them. He was now someone she'd once known.

"Yes. Monroe said you might be able to help me find her."

Reggie shook his head in disgust, obviously offended by the very name of the police captain. Jack's expression remained neutral. He dished the eggs onto a slab of bread, covered it with another and took a bite. "I warned her what might happen if she went down there. I'm not responsible for her stupidity. You neither."

Lindsay's mouth went dry. What had happened to that kind, adventurous boy? For the first year after he'd left, they'd fired postcards and letters back and forth, Lindsay marking down a different address every time as Jack and his father moved so much. They kept it up for five years with phone calls on their respective birthdays. They'd even talked about her flying to London after her graduation from design school.

Then the accident had happened, and she'd known that her old life was over. She didn't call on his birthday, left a couple of postcards unanswered, and after the sale of her family home, she herself changed addresses. No, she couldn't blame Jack for losing touch. It was she that had shut the door. She had changed. Only—only she hadn't expected him to.

"Look, Jack, I know I'm the one who dropped the connection with you. I can see my showing up here today isn't what you wanted. And I know you're not responsible for my sister. But I need your help. The police don't have the men to search for Seline, and none of the private investigators I've contacted will take the case."

"Can't spend the cash if you're dead," Reggie interjected grimly.

Lindsay ignored the comment, took a step towards Jack. "I can pay you well for your time. I can hire a search party for you to lead. Anything you need. Anything at all."

Jack laughed, a dry, derisive sound. "Didn't you hear Reggie? I value my life more than money, too."

Irritation spurred by disappointment shot through her. She swept her arm around the barren place. "Looks to me as if you don't value either."

Reggie let out a low whistling breath, as if his favorite boxer had got a blow to the midsection. For a long moment, Lindsay and Jack glared at each other, then without breaking eye contact, Jack spoke fast and clipped. "A search party wouldn't be any use unless it was huge, and you're never going to get enough experienced people underground to make it worthwhile. I spent twenty-three months under this city. I know what I'm talking about when it comes to the tunnels, and odds are excellent your niece is dead. The chances of finding her remains are slim to none, and very good that you're going to get yourself killed looking for them. You need to face the truth."

Lindsay felt her stomach twist, and it took a huge effort to keep her voice firm. "I'm not a bimbo, Jack. I know damn well she's probably dead. But if there's a one percent chance that she's still alive then I need to try. I've done my best to get help over the past week, and you're my last option. If you won't go then my only choice is to go down there myself."

Reggie looked aggrieved. "Then you'll die."

"We all do. Better that it be for the right reason," Lindsay snapped.

Jack shook his head. "Reggie's right. No sense getting yourself killed, too. There are people who need you alive." His eyes skimmed over her. "Like the shops on Fifth Avenue."

It was a calculated dig, and Lindsay struggled to keep her temper in check. With as much grace as could pass through her clenched jaw, she asked, "Do you know anyone who would help me, then?"

"No. And if I did, I wouldn't tell you."

"Because?"

"Because you'd go to them, sucker them with your money or your looks, and they'd go down and that's the last we'd ever hear of them." Jack finished his egg sandwich in two more bites and one swallow and sent the plate clattering into the sink. He rounded on her again.

"People like you have no idea what's living under their feet. Not even the street homeless know the truth. There are things down there that you wouldn't believe, and I'm not talking about ghosts or bogeymen. I'm talking about *monsters*. Real flesh-and-blood monsters."

If he intended to frighten her, it was working. She remembered the blood, the animate darkness that had shadowed them, and a chill descended on her colder than the New York winter. Under Jack's anger, she felt his fear, as palpable as if it rippled through her own soul.

She spoke softly. "Jack. You found out who got Tim, didn't you?"

Jack's face became inscrutable, and he stared off into some nameless place. After a long while, his answer came low and final. "I sure as hell did."

She closed her eyes and drew a deep breath. "Is there any way you could still help me, Jack?"

He slowly came back from wherever he'd gone and looked at her, his eyes fierce and empty. "No, Linds. There isn't."

———————————

LINDSAY UPENDED THE contents of her shopping bags in front of her Christmas tree—still up two days past New Year's. Finding the things she'd needed in post-Christmas, post-Black Friday New York had been a challenge, and the weary shop staff had been less than helpful. Nobody cared, which seemed par for the course.

As aggravating as trying to mobilize the cops had been, at least they had had good reasons for not going down in search of Seline. But Jack's refusal—. She could understand him not wanting to be trapped in the tunnels again. Still, couldn't he have asked around on her behalf? Would it have been too much for him to have given her a lead or advice, or even acted as if he cared? He must've known he was her last real hope.

Now *she* was Seline's last hope, and she'd be damned if she was going to let her niece down. Lindsay sorted the equipment, snipping off tags and reading through her list to make sure she hadn't forgotten anything.

"Halogen flashlight, pepper spray, low-light goggles, first aid kit, an extra pair of boots, climbing rope, extra flashlight, batteries, survival rations, road flares, canteen, matches, pocketknife...."

The phone rang out 'We Wish You a Merry Christmas'. It was Janice, her office manager, and a call she so did not want to take. Janice was her employee, although they both knew she was more, much more. Lindsay's mother and her had been best friends. After the accident, Janice had glided in and helped Lindsay with Seline and the legalese of guardianship and transfer of property, and the day-to-day effort of looking after a bewildered and needy eight-year-old orphan. She'd co-signed the loan Lindsay had needed to start her business, and when the company blossomed into a success, Lindsay hired her to help run it. If there was one person who cared about the small Sterling family, it was Janice.

"Lindsay. I didn't hear back from you today. You holding up okay?"

"Yep." Lindsay injected perkiness into her voice, because that was what Janice wanted to hear. "I'm all right."

Lindsay had no intention of telling anyone what she was going to do before she did it. She would email all the details to the office, along with the name of the attorney who handled her will. Janice would find out tomorrow morning, too late to stop her.

"How did the meeting with Jack Cole go? Did you manage to track him down?"

"He's turned into an asshole. Told me flat out he wasn't interested in helping."

"Really? Your mother would be so disappointed." Janice made it sound as if Jack's obnoxious behavior was a deliberate insult to the memory of her departed friend. "She had such high hopes for you two. She was thrilled that you had plans to visit him, you know."

"Yeah, I know." Her mom's affection for Jack had been part of the reason she broke her connection with him back then. Lindsay had been such a mess that she would've ruined their relationship and she couldn't have borne to have one more thing fall apart. As it turned out, it had been a good call. Jack wasn't the sympathetic sort.

"Are you sure about him, Lindsay?" Janice said. "I found an article on him on the internet. He seemed very promising."

Trust Janice to check out Jack. She'd regularly googled both Lindsay's and Seline's dates. "What does it say?"

"It says he's been beneath cities all over the world. 'The ultimate urban spelunker' is what they call him."

"Does it mention how he got lost under New York for two years?"

Janice made soft clucking sounds as she presumably scanned the article. "No, nothing. The article is from four years ago, though. From the magazine put out by the Royal Geographic Society. Do you want me to dig around for something more recent?"

Lindsay grimaced. "No, my meeting with him today brought me about as up-to-date with him as I want to be." Seeing how Jack had turned out had been like saying goodbye to him all over again.

"Do you want me to come over? It might help to talk. To have someone around."

Lindsay eyed the pile of survival gear on the floor. "Janice, I think I need to be alone tonight."

"Okay. You call me if you want to, though. Anytime."

Lindsay wondered if it was Janice that needed the

company more than her. Seline's disappearance must be killing her, too. "You take care, and try not to worry. One way or another we'll get her back."

She opened her new backpack and loaded it up, trying to make every item easily accessible. Giving up, she zipped it close and slung it over her shoulders. She stood and adjusted her balance to the weight on her back. She forced her attention away from the glowing Christmas tree. It landed on Leo. She'd found the fifty-pound stuffed lion at a novelty store, outrageously overpriced, and had instantly bought it, forgetting to even bargain. Seline had squealed in undiluted excitement when she'd first seen it, and would lie down alongside it on the couch and stroke its mane. There'd been many a night that she herself had stretched out along its length and felt comforted.

The lion stared at her in friendly abstraction. Its golden eyes, Lindsay realized with a jolt, bore an uncanny resemblance to Jack's. The damn man was tagging her every thought.

She cut through the Chelsea apartment she'd spent the last three years and every spare penny making over. She and Seline had replaced or redone nearly everything else, and except for the finishing carpentry, all by themselves. She'd scoured stores, auctions, and newspaper ads for the absolutely perfect rug, perfect sofa, perfect dining set. She'd wanted to make an ideal home for them, a perfect home like the one she'd grown up in.

She found herself looking at it through Jack's eyes. His crack at her wealth stung more than she cared to admit. She loved beautiful things, because they were beautiful and not because she was materialistic. Didn't she give to charities? Didn't she pay her employees generously? Hadn't she put her heart and soul into every project she'd ever worked on? Yes, yes and yes. So fuck him.

Anyway, Seline had been the one to take on good causes. From the time she was a little girl she'd been interested in social work and was determined to make a difference in the lives of New York's poor and homeless. Charismatic, honest and caring, she had earned the trust of addicts, derelicts and petty criminals that many seasoned social workers were afraid to deal with.

Through it all Lindsay had been worried for Seline—and so very proud. Perhaps her niece's attraction to things grim and gritty stemmed from her own aversion to them, but the point was the girl was blazing her own trail. Now Seline was the one who needed help, and here, only a few days into the New Year, she found herself about to gamble her life in the hopes of staging a rescue.

*That ought to count for something, Jack Cole.* She hadn't seen the man in eighteen years, he was living in some hole in the wall with all the success of a garbage picker and the sweet attitude of a cornered rat, and here she was worried about what he was thinking of her. "Fuck you, and the box you came in," she added aloud for good measure.

She pulled out pen and paper from the coffee table drawer. *Seline, I've gone into the tunnels to find you.* She was about to sign it 'L' when she added, *Wait for me and we'll take down the tree together, like always.*

She tucked it between Leo's front paws because if, by some miracle, Seline came home, that's where she'd go first.

———————————

LINDSAY HAD LEARNED from her niece that there were countless ways into New York's underground—manholes, subway tunnels, maintenance hatches and the basements of certain condemned buildings. Since Hurricane Sandy, even more had been created by repair crews drilling new holes to pump out water. Her route would be the same as the one Seline had chosen, however. Via Grand Central Station.

The place was a kind of gateway to the underground, where both the common citizens of New York and its homeless mixed, often unknowingly, with the tunnel dwellers. According to Seline there were about a thousand people living beneath the marble floors and arched windows of Grand Central, colonizing its tunnels, ducts and passageways, and the safest and simplest way to gain access to the lower levels was through an unmarked door off one of the platforms.

This particular door was controlled by a gang of sorts, who had somehow gotten hold of a copy of the transit authority's key. Anyone who wanted to descend merely had to pay them a toll, which varied in amount depending on the apparent wealth of the person and how much the gang liked them. Her niece had described these gatekeepers as 'friendly' and 'pretty reasonable, considering', which Lindsay took to mean that they might not rip her off too much.

Rush hour was over when she arrived at the Terminal, and being a Thursday evening, it wasn't crowded. She spotted a few rumpled businessmen, a handful of Japanese tourists, and a chattering gaggle of teenage girls. None of them seemed to pay her the least bit of attention.

Wandering down the platform she spied what she took for the correct door, an innocuous steel portal, no different from others in the station, located exactly where Seline had said it would be.

Lindsay hitched up the backpack, where it was already cutting a groove into her shoulders. This was nuts. Jack and Reggie were right. She had about as much street smarts as the

Pope. She had no idea how to talk to people down here or how to find her way around. She'd get lost or robbed or murdered. Then an image of Seline rose in her mind, buried alive beneath the frozen streets, cold and starved. It was as she told Jack: she had no choice but to go on. Besides, if a whacked-out crackhead could survive down here, surely she could. She suppressed the niggling voice that said that perhaps you *had* to be a whacked-out crackhead to survive in the tunnels.

Or Jack Cole.

A train arrived, and she watched as people shuffled onto it. The doors closed, and with a rush of stale air the subway cars moved on, leaving her momentarily alone on the platform. Time to do it. She strode to the door and banged her fist against it. There was a pause, then it unlocked and opened a crack, giving her a glimpse of the tall, shadowy figure behind it.

"Hi there," she smiled, doing her best to appear confident. The door swung wide open, and her smile vanished. Staring down at her, his brow furrowed, stood Reggie.

"You!" they said simultaneously.

Reggie launched in. "What the hell are you doing here, woman? This ain't no place for you."

Lindsay gave back. "I told you I was going to look for my niece. What, you thought I was kidding?"

"Sheeet. Come over here." Closing the door behind him, he dragged her by her arm to a nearby bench.

"Let go of me!" she demanded, digging in with her heels. It was as if she was hitched to a moving truck. He plunked her down, the weight of the backpack easing off but its bulk arching her back so bad her butt perched on the edge of the seat.

"Lady, you gotta be as blonde as you look. You're like

34

your niece. You don't listen to nobody."

"You knew her. You let her go down there. Why not me?"

Reggie was already looming over her and now he bent until he was a foot from her face. It was like having a falling building suspended above her. "Because it's *my* fault. I should've turned her back, like Jack said to, but I didn't. She was a good person. Came here to help people who ain't got nothing. And now I gotta live with that."

Guilt twisted his features. Lindsay understood because it clawed away at her, too. She also understood something of what hadn't been said during their last conversation. "Jack doesn't know you let her through, does he?"

Reggie straightened, crossing his huge arms across his steel girder of a chest. "A man makes mistakes."

"And a real man does something about them."

Their gazes locked in a fearsome stare-down. He looked away first. Lindsay smothered a triumphant smirk. " So how about you open up that goddamn door and I'll pay you double the toll."

The whites of his eyes stood out against his dark skin. "You think you can bribe me? That's an insult. I run an honest business."

"Then let's do business." She started to stand, but Reggie blocked her way.

"I ain't helping nothing by letting you go down there. If Jack was with you it might be another story. Things the way they are, it ain't happening."

"I asked him and he said no!"

Reggie shrugged fatalistically.

Lindsay struck at his pride. "Are you going to let some white man boss you around? He's half your size, with a peach pit for a heart. What's he got over you?"

Anger swelled his enormous body, his arms lifting away from his side as the pressure of the emotion ballooned him. "Jack Cole is twice the man that anyone could hope to be and just because he don't want to do what you asked ain't no reason to diss him."

This time Lindsay didn't even try to stare Reggie down. The man obviously had his loyalties screwed up. Not knowing his story, however, she couldn't argue against his having them. She looked fixedly at the door, then up at the man. Once again he had his arms folded like a stubborn bouncer.

"Okay, then. Care to suggest how I might sway your hero into going with me?"

Reggie rolled his gaze upward as if seriously thinking about it. "Jack's his own man. Won't be easy."

"I tried money."

"Yeah. He don't care about that."

"No doubt, given his lavish lifestyle," she remarked.

Reggie grinned. "You haven't seen his bed, have you?"

"No occasion to."

Reggie whistled lowly. "The man's got one nice bed."

"I'll take your word for it." Lindsay frowned. "You trying to give me a hint?'

"Huh?"

Lindsay drew herself up. "You suggesting I sleep with him?"

Reggie's eyes brightened. "I can guarantee that wouldn't work on Jack—he's off women. You could always try it on me."

"Would it get me anywhere?"

He gave her another golden grin. "No. But I'd let you down easy."

Another time she would've grinned back. "You don't think I've got a snowball's chance in hell of getting his help, huh?"

Reggie shook his head. "Not even."

Jack had said as much. Had she really thought the answer would be any different from Reggie? What she'd hoped for was that he would open the way to Jack the same way he manned the entry to the underground. Reggie was right: desperation was making her stupid.

And yet—. She hoisted her backpack and got to her feet. "You aren't the only way down, Reggie. One way or another I'll get a door to open for me."

# CHAPTER
# THREE

USUALLY LINDSAY IGNORED street people and if eye contact was inadvertently made, she'd toss them whatever was in her pocket—gum, change, soap samples. Now that she needed their help it felt more than a little awkward.

To the first few panhandlers she gave a few dollars, asking them straight out if they knew of a way into the tunnels. That approach only garnered suspicious looks and shrugged shoulders, so to the next down-and-out person, a man with straggly gray hair and old boots with no laces, she offered fifty dollars to take her to an entrance.

He looked up at her with bloodshot eyes. "You need to talk to tunnel folk, ma'am," he said in a slow southern drawl, running a hand through his greasy mane. "I can take you to 'em for the fifty."

Beggars couldn't be choosers. After tucking away the fifty in the many folds of his clothing, he led her on a circuitous journey through the station, gradually descending to the lower platforms. "Gotta find 'em," her guide explained.

Lindsay was about to conclude that the man was taking her on a wild goose chase when he brought her to a platform where he pointed out a couple of rough-looking Hispanic teens standing with the commuters. "Them guys are tunnel folk. Y'all stay here while I talk to 'em, okay?"

Without waiting for her answer he shuffled over to the boys, gesturing to her when he caught their attention. The arrival of a train created too much noise for her to catch what was said, she could see the teens watch her coolly as they listened. She felt like a T.V. they were looking to lift. The doors of the train opened, people came and went, and when the train moved off, her fifty-dollar guide waved her over.

"Okay, these here are Chase and Stray," he said, by way of introduction. "They can take you where you want to go."

Chase gave her a predatory smile and ran his tattooed hand over his shaved head. Lindsay stood straighter and looked him in the eye.

"Why you want to go down?" he asked as the older man faded away.

"I'm looking for my niece. Her name is Seline. Seline Sterling."

Chase glanced at Stray picking at a sore on his chin. "Oh yeah, we know her."

"You do?"

"Yeah. We can take you to her friends. They'll know where she is. Fifty bucks for each of us should do it."

Forget the T.V. She was an ATM every low-life knew the PIN for. Just punch in 'Seline'. Though Lindsay was almost positive the boy was lying to her, there was only one way to find out for sure. "Okay," she answered, sliding her hands into the pockets of her jacket, one of them curling around the pepper spray. With the other she pulled out a small money clip, flashing it like a badge. "You get the hundred when we reach them. Let's go."

Chase and Stray looked at each other, shrugged, then led

her to the far end of the platform where there was a small metal gate, the sign on it warning of danger and an alarm. Not a peep sounded as they pushed past it. She followed them down a short flight of concrete stairs where they emerged into a tunnel. Both Chase and Stray pulled flashlights out of their pockets, and Lindsay did the same.

"Watch that third rail." Chase laughed, looking back at her in the dark. "Six hundred volts. Fry you like bacon."

Lindsay shone her light on the subway rails, including the electrified third one, and edged closer to the wall.

They walked on, flattening themselves against the concrete whenever train cars whipped past. In the narrow space the violent gusts ripped at her, threatening to drag her under the wheels. The kids saw her fear after the first train and laughed as if it was the funniest thing they'd ever seen.

"Don't worry, baby. We'll protect you," Stray wheezed, his taunt ricocheting through the tunnel.

Twenty minutes later, they were deep underground, the light from the station having long since faded to nothing. The only illumination came from the flashlights, and what they revealed was nightmarish. Lying along the tracks were scattered needles and crack vials, garbage and human feces. The walls were sprayed with graffiti of the crudest kind, and above them ran a tangle of hissing steam pipes and decayed catwalks too dense for their lights to penetrate.

The smell was nauseating, a mixture of oil and piss, rot and mold. The only living occupants she spied were diseased-looking rats, scurrying to avoid the flashlight beams.

This was worse than with Jack eighteen years ago. Had time so crumbled the tunnels or was it because being with him had made it better?

"Where is everyone?" she squeaked out.

"They're all over the place," Chase said in a hammed-up spooky voice. "You just don't have the eyes to see 'em. Don't worry though. Almost there."

The three came to a fissure in the tunnel, a sort of subterranean alley flanked by rusting pipes and two oversized electrical boxes.

"Down here," Chase directed her, and following the two, she stepped into a chamber so small that their combined beams fully lit it.

Six-inch blades appeared in the boys' hands, and they circled to cut off her escape.

"What the—?"

"Stupid blonde bitch," Chase grinned. "Now give us your fucking money."

Dammit, she should've known. She pulled out her can of pepper spray and took aim, then realized that with them blocking the only exit, she couldn't push past even if they were blinded.

They knew it, too. "Ooooh," Chase said in mock fear.

"Back off you bastards or you'll be sucking down this whole can." She held it up a little higher.

He snickered. "Baby, you're the only one who's going to have something to suck."

"The hell she is!" The voice boomed from behind the two boys, and out of the darkness of the passage came Reggie. The kids spun around, jaws dropping at the sight of the giant.

"This got nothing to do with you, Reggie," Chase said, his blade wavering between Lindsay and her rescuer.

Reggie grinned. "That a fact, Chase? Says who? You?"

"Look, we don't have no problem with you," Stray interjected, his reedy voice quavering.

Reggie swiveled his head toward him. "You do now,

41

bitch! That's Cole's woman you got there. Better be glad I found you. Least now you die quick."

At the mention of Jack's name, Chase and Stray looked as if Reggie had pulled out a flame-thrower.

"We didn't know that," Stray whined. "We'll leave, okay? We don't want no trouble."

Reggie's golden smile disappeared. "Too late for that, Stray. Way too late."

With a kamikaze yell, Chase dropped his flashlight and leapt at the man, the wild play of the beam momentarily blinding Lindsay. There was a meaty thud, followed by a sickening crack and a howl of agony. Lindsay recoiled as she saw Reggie holding Chase's arm at a highly unnatural angle.

Reggie hurled the boy against the brick wall, the impact cutting off the wailing. Plastered against the other side of the room Stray held up his hands in surrender, the knife clattering to the floor.

"Please, Reggie. Please...."

Turning from the limp Chase, Reggie seized Stray by his shirt collar and dragged him down the narrow passage back to the tunnel.

"Man... Reggie...please... no...." Stray begged.

Picking up the dropped light, Lindsay followed them out to the tunnel. She gasped at the sight of Reggie hauling the boy toward the third rail.

"Time to die, bitch," Reggie growled, heaving the boy up by his shirt until he kicked the air.

"No man... oh God, no...."

Reggie brought his face up against Stray's. "Scared to die, huh?"

The kid's head vibrated in frantic agreement.

"Then you better be spreading the word 'bout Cole's

woman. I find you, or any other man, messing with her then I'm going to have myself a third rail barbecue. You get me?"

"I get you, man, I get you."

Reggie tossed Stray aside, letting the youth sprint off into the darkness.

"Thank you," Lindsay said, as she slid the can of pepper spray back into her pocket.

Reggie turned on her. "Those were *kids*, woman! You still think you got what it takes to find your way down here?"

Lindsay shook her head. "But I still have to try."

The shoulders on the big man drooped, and he let out a long sigh. "You're one dumbass blonde. Even a blind man could see you're going to need help."

---

"YOU TOLD THEM *what*?" Jack demanded of Reggie.

They were in the kitchen of the basement apartment, Jack leaning against the counter beside a full cup of coffee, Reggie on the wooden chair holding a half-drunk one.

"I had to tell 'em something. Nobody's going to mess with her if they think she's yours. She even looks like your type, y'know? Kind of classy and…clean."

Jack rubbed his eyes. It had been a little past midnight when Reggie had shown up. Not that it mattered. As usual he hadn't been able to sleep, though this time it was from thinking of something new. Lindsay.

Although it hadn't been the first time he'd thought of her in eighteen years, it had been the first time he'd let himself think of her—really think of her—since the disaster of his return nearly a year ago. Even when Seline had turned up all those months back, he'd kept memories of Lindsay at bay. Her showing up at his piss-poor place, looking so damn good and so damn needy—it had shook his already precarious purchase on sanity.

The New York girl who'd been his best friend had grown into the woman he always knew she'd become: smart, tough, beautiful. And successful. She wore those designer clothes as if they'd been made for her alone. She made success seem as if it were her right, that failure wouldn't dare cross her path. Even that heart-wrenching accident had made her stronger.

And then Reggie had pounded his way in hours ago and told him about what had nearly happened to her, and he got the shakes so bad he'd had to set down the coffee cup. To have all that bright, bold beauty, all that made Lindsay so…exclusive, to have all that wiped out by those punks, sent jolts of fear through him every bit as bad as when he'd been trapped beneath the city. He wished to hell she'd never shown up. He couldn't give her what she needed. There were things that could crush a person, things worse than death that could snap even the strongest spirit. Once he would have marched into hell itself to help her, but a big part of him had died on just such a journey. He'd been broken, and he was beyond fixing.

"I know where you're heading with this, Reggie, and I'm telling you right now, I'm not going down there."

Reggie sucked in his lips until there was a thin dark line. "And I'm telling you, that woman's not quitting. Even after tonight, she's still going back down there. Not many people would do something like that. I only ever met one other."

"And look where it got me," Jack said, reaching for his coffee. This time he got it all the way to his mouth and down again steady enough.

Reggie looked down at the floor. "I know a lot of people who lost everything. Lost 'em to meth, crack, booze…you're the only one who lost 'em for another living soul."

Jack shook his head. "Shit. Don't go there."

"She gave me her number, and promised she wouldn't go down till I called." Reggie paused. "She also said she'd be trying again tomorrow night if she don't hear from us. Don't think she won't."

"She always was pigheaded," Jack muttered.

"Yeah? High school, she said. She an old girlfriend or something?"

"No. We were...good friends. Then I moved and we lost touch." Patching it together, he realized she'd stopped answering his letters around the same time as the accident. Now he could understand her need to move on. Back then, he was filled with hurt. He'd looked forward to her visiting him, and he'd entertained fantasies of them taking their friendship to a whole new level. "I had heard she'd gotten married."

"Uh-huh. Well, I don't think she is anymore," Reggie observed. "No wedding ring. No talk of a husband. You'd think if she had a man she'd have said something."

Jack had noticed that, too. He didn't want to think about why his eye had traveled to her bare finger twice, to confirm. He wondered what the lousy cretin had done to screw up a life with Lindsay.

Reggie rubbed his stomach as if thinking of something warm and good. "All I'm saying is she'd be someone I'd be getting back in touch with, if you know what I mean." His hand stopped under Jack's glare. "You know I'm in deep with Cassie. It's you I'm thinking of, man."

"If you were thinking of me, you wouldn't be here," Jack retorted, then breathed out. "Look, I'm sorry. Can we just stick to the topic?"

Reggie regarded Jack, then tactfully did what he was

asked. "Thing is, you and I know Seline could be still breathing. Maybe taken to Seneca, or—"

"No, we don't," Jack snapped. "For all I know, Seline got hit by a train or murdered by some methhead or tripped on the third rail. Maybe she's lost, or she's hanging out at one of the camps. Anyway, it's not my goddamn problem. What am I, the patron saint of stupid people?"

"You're Jack Cole," Reggie replied, holding Jack with his gaze. "Everyone beneath the streets knows who you are. Maybe even better than you do."

Jack slumped against the counter. "I know, Reggie." His voice dropped to a near whisper. "I'm afraid that if I go back down I won't have the strength to make it back up again."

His friend's faith wasn't shaken. "You did it before."

Jack looked at him wearily. "That was…different."

"This time it would be for a woman, too," Reggie said quietly.

Jack shook his head. "Not incentive enough."

Reggie continued quietly. "Then try this. Try this woman gang-raped and hung over the third rail. You try holding onto your coffee cup, then."

Jack winced.

"Listen," Reggie added, "you don't want the guilt. Trust me on that one, man."

Jack frowned. "I've never blamed you."

Reggie lowered his head and gazed into his cup. "Don't need to be blamed to feel guilt."

They fell silent, each lost in their own harsh memories of the underground. For Jack, it went deeper. For him, there was one more memory of a moment that happened neither in the darkness of the underground nor the light of the surface. It was an elevator ride with Lindsay and his dad, down into the underground. He knew Lindsay was scared stiff. At the first jolt of the elevator downward, she'd reached for his hand, pulling back at the last moment. He'd waited, hoping, and then at a scraping of steel against rock, she grabbed his hand like it was a lifeline. Her grip was hard and painful, and he was pretty sure there'd be permanent damage. He never felt so happy. He let her hold on as she made small talk with his dad, and when the elevator stopped, and he finally mentioned her hold on him, he felt the sting of loss as she released his hand, and a weird satisfaction that in times of fear, her instinct was to seek him.

Today, she'd done the same thing, reached out to him. And he'd set her aside. Now, through Reggie, she was doing it again. This was his second, and final, chance. He flexed his left hand, the one she'd held. There'd been no damage, of course. But eighteen years on, her grip on him was as strong and painful as ever.

Jack poured his coffee down the drain and went for his parka. "Give me her number. I'll make the call."

Reggie was right behind him. They headed to the nearest working payphone five blocks away. The sidewalks were poorly shoveled if at all, meaning at times they had to trudge through the darkness in knee-deep snow.

At a point when they were up to their balls in a snow bank, Reggie called out, "Shit man! You know, having a phone is no sin."

Jack plowed on. "I hope you're not complaining about the good deed we're performing here."

There was silence from Reggie as frigid as the weather. At least there was, finally, silence. When they reached the phone booth, Jack dialed the number Reggie gave him, his numbed fingers stabbing the keypad.

"Hello?" Lindsay answered. He hadn't even heard the line ring.

"This is Jack. Heard you didn't get your money's worth this evening."

Lindsay's reply was quick and cold. "Jack, I need your help, not a lecture on subway safety. Which you planning on giving?"

Jack pulled the phone away from his ear. Of all the arrogant, ungrateful, bitchy....

"Hello? Are you still there?" Her voice came down the line faintly. He pressed the freezing plastic back against his ear.

"Yeah, yeah. Listen, you seem to have made quite the impression on Reggie, so against my better judgment, I'll go look for Seline."

Jack heard her breath catch, and then let go in a soft sigh that erased his every nasty thought about her. "Thank you, Jack. I can't tell you how much I appreciate that. We need to leave ASAP."

"What?"

"I said, we need to leave as soon as possible."

"What's this 'we' stuff? I said I'd go and look for her. Me. Alone."

"I appreciate your help, Jack," she said all sweetness, like she was breaking bad news to an oversensitive employee, "and I know you don't think I should be going down into the tunnels. I get the feeling that you're just telling me what I want to hear."

Jack's teeth ground together. "You saying I'm lying to you?"

She carried on, apparently ignoring his tone. "Seline has already been down there a week, Jack. Thus far nobody's wanted to help me, including you when we met. I can't take the chance that you're handing me a line, even if it is for my own good. I have to be sure that someone's really looking for her."

"I'm not a tour operator, woman!"

"As you might remember, my name's Lindsay," she said pointedly. Gone was the sweetness. "And I know you're not. Yes, I'm stubborn and unreasonable and it's dangerous down there and yadda yadda yadda, so let's cut to it: I'm heading back to Grand Central, and I'm going to find Seline. You coming?"

He should hang up right now. If all his loss and pain and misery had taught him anything at all, he should hang up. Hang up on the memory of a long-ago time when his life was much happier, and she was the first girl he'd ever really wanted.

"You know that big clock at Grand Central. On the main level?" he asked.

"Yes."

"Be there by seven in the morning. Seven sharp."

He slammed down the receiver, stared at nothing. Nope, he hadn't learned a damned thing.

"You okay?" Reggie asked.

"No." And nothing more was said as they trudged back to their basement home.

---

GRIPPING THE HAND-rail above him in the swaying train, Jack was packed so close to Reggie's back he could see the nylon weave of his friend's parka. Butted up behind him was a woman who, from the smell, was likely heading for a day behind the perfume counter at Macy's. He was suffocating, caught up in this press of dead end people heading for dead end jobs in a city where nobody cared about anything except their own dead end interests.

Reggie was right. Up here he was nobody—poor, unemployed, forgotten by virtually everyone. He'd gone through jobs as a security guard, a taxi driver, a janitor, every low-level job possible. The pattern was always the same. He'd show up for the first shifts all spit and polished, but then a day would come when he couldn't even open his eyes to the gray light of his room. He'd arrive late or not at all, and not surprisingly, he was soon reading the want ads again. Right now, he was, what the employment counselor termed, 'between jobs'. He should be ashamed about his situation. The problem was that he couldn't bring himself to give a damn. All that had ever really interested him lay beneath the surface.

For below the streets his reputation spanned the city. He was a legend to be respected and feared. But it wasn't the people that called him back. It was the tunnels themselves with their sudden twists and dark openings. It was as if he were traveling through a great, troubled mind that held the secrets and terrors of all humanity. He was forever drawn to this labyrinth, even though he knew it scarred his soul.

Perhaps if he could help Lindsay he could prove to himself that, at his core, he was still the same man he'd been, though he scarcely knew who that was anymore. Like one who fumbles to recall a fading dream, he felt that once he must've been someone that Lindsay would hold hands with. Someone who could walk both worlds and not feel lost in either.

As the train neared Grand Central, Jack became aware of uncharacteristic nervousness building in his hulking companion.

"It's okay, Reggie," he said, "You're right about helping her. I'm glad you did."

Reggie turned awkwardly to Jack, and seemed about to say something, then didn't. Instead, he looked away in grim contemplation.

They swayed in silence as Jack turned the situation over in his mind.

"You let Seline in, didn't you?" he asked suddenly.

Reggie snapped his head around. "Who told you that?"

Jack's face was expressionless. "Nobody," he replied evenly. "When you've got guilt in you, Reggie, you don't hide it well. Too honest for your own good."

The man shifted on his feet. "Shit. You gotta know, Jack, I didn't think it would go down like this. I gave her my name to drop. She blended in. She made friends easy. Never went too deep. How'd I know she'd go off and do something stupid?"

Jack stared straight ahead.

"Bet you're pissed, huh?" Reggie asked.

"Very," Jack said, his voice impassive. "But I'll get over it."

His response nudged a nervous smile out of Reggie. "Guess that's two I owe you."

The train began to slow, preparing to stop at Grand Central.

"Damn right you do," Jack mumbled.

Making his way topside, Jack quickly spotted Lindsay. She was sipping fancy coffee by the information booth, her bright hair in a ponytail, her long legs parted over a backpack between her feet. He felt his heart suddenly pound hard, and he stopped, unused to the hard beat here on the surface. Must be nerves about going underground for the first time in a year. As the swell of commuters expanded and contracted around him, he waited for his heart to calm. Waited so long that it was Reggie who reached her first and him playing catch-up.

"Thank you for changing his mind," he heard her say to Reggie. To him, she gave a quick nod of acknowledgement.

His life and sanity on the line for her, and he got a nod. Figured. "You and I need to get some things straight."

She rolled her eyes. "Please, Jack. Don't waste your breath trying to talk me out of this again. You know what I'm going to do."

"Wouldn't be here if I was going to talk you out of it," he said. "Set down the double latte and show me your backpack."

"What for?"

Jack clenched his jaw so hard it hurt. Reggie slowly backed away. "I'll be over here...."

Lindsay stared after Reggie like a puppy after its departing owner, then she toed her backpack his way. "Have at it."

He forced himself to release a long breath and then knelt to rummage through it. "Not bad," he said, pulling out her low-light goggles. "though mostly junk."

Lindsay dropped beside him. "Junk? That night-vision thing cost me eight hundred bucks."

"Uh-huh. How long is the battery life?"

"Eight hours."

"Not long enough. You know this thing only intensifies light, right?"

"Well, yeah."

"Too bad there won't be any where we're going. You won't see shit unless you're carrying a light, in which case you might as well be using a ten-dollar flashlight to make your way. If this thing had an infra-red illuminator you might be okay. Even then, not in high humidity areas. You know this thing can't see in color?"

Jack was a little gratified to see it was her jaw that was now hard. "Yes, I know."

"So how you going to spot water-damaged floors before you fall through them? By the way, these things glow, so anyone with a gun can see where your head is, and they'll blind you under sudden bright light." He dropped the goggles into her pack and handed it back to her. "Like I said. Junk."

Lindsay zipped the bag closed and stood. "Fine, Jack. I get it. Can we get going now?"

He rose, too."Sure. Right after I tell you the rules."

"Rules?"

Was everything a question with her? "Yeah, rules. As in the non-negotiable ground rules for me helping you. Get it?"

"Okay. What are they?"

"The first one is keep your mouth shut and your footsteps light. It won't matter so much when you're close to the station. The deep tunnels are a different story. Sound travels there, and it carries your age, your gender, your size, and your numbers with it—valuable information to anyone wanting to ambush you. I'll tell you when it's safe to talk."

"Okay." He was pretty sure he could hear her teeth grind.

"Second rule. No whining. You complain about the filth, damp, cold, vermin or danger just once, and I'm taking you right back to the surface. As it is I'm going to have to babysit you, so don't think I'm going to put up with any gripes or attitude."

"You know I'm not a complainer, Jack."

She wasn't, but it was important she concentrated on proving it to him. "We'll see about that. When we're down there you do what I say, because I'm the expert. I've survived in the deepest tunnels for days without food, water, clothing or weapons. You can't make it a mile out of Grand Central without being robbed."

Jack paused here. She was not going to like this next part. "And that brings me to the final rule. Reggie introduced you as my woman, and we're going to stick with that story. That means that when we're down there you defer to me completely, because as far as the tunnels go you can forget women's lib. Under the streets a person's either predator, prey or property, and until you're ready to be the first you're going to be the third. Got it?"

"Got it."

No questions? No backtalk? "You do?" Jack challenged her. "Then tell me the rules."

Lindsay twisted her mouth unhappily. "Be quiet, no whining and do what you say," she replied without hesitation and then sighed before adding, "and that property thing."

She looked so damn annoyed, Jack nearly smiled, and to hide it he spun and started toward Reggie. Over his shoulder, he risked saying, "Great. I don't own much. You're my biggest ticket item."

He could hear her scramble after him. "Yeah? Well, hope you got a warranty. Maintenance on me is high."

Didn't he know it.

# CHAPTER FOUR

BEYOND THE DOOR that Reggie guarded was a long, dim hallway. From it branched stairwells and service hatches and, at its end, was an oversized manhole held in place by a pair of weighty padlocks.

Reggie squatted and undid them. "This here's the fastest way down," he explained to Lindsay. "Past all the meth heads that hang around the station. Right to the core of the City."

Although the cover was designed for a pry bar, Reggie's fingers were strong enough to pull up the thick metal plate unaided. He rolled it aside, revealing a sturdy steel ladder descending into a seemingly bottomless concrete pit.

Lindsay felt her stomach heave. Her first step on this adventure was straight into her greatest fear. She glanced at Jack. He had clearly read her mind.

"Still not good with heights, huh?"

A small part of her was flattered that he'd remembered. A bigger part, and the one that kicked in, was determined to keep up with him, like all those years ago. She batted her eyelashes and honeyed her voice. "My answer might be construed as whining, and I wouldn't want to break your rules before we've even started, Jack."

"Uh-huh. I see why Reggie never stood a chance with you."

Reggie pretended to look affronted. "You saying I'm a sucker?"

Jack frowned at Lindsay. Not quite at her, she realized, but her hair. It was back in a ponytail. What was his problem? "That would be the pot calling the kettle black," he answered, reaching into his backpack which was about half the size and weight of Lindsay's. He shoved a black knit hat into her hands. "Here, stick your hair underneath this. Blondes stand out in the tunnels."

Lindsay clamped her mouth shut and did as instructed, twirling her hair into a knot and jamming on the hat to hold it in place. She tilted her head at Jack for inspection and caught in his tawny eyes a strange watchfulness.

He abruptly turned to Reggie. "I won't be back until tonight. Probably late."

Reggie nodded. "Najib will be here, then."

The two men regarded each other for the length of a deep breath with the kind of stalwartness that might pass between departing soldiers. There was a whole lifetime she was missing here, and as unjustified as she knew it was, it rankled.

"Ready?" Jack asked, and without waiting for the reply, edged past her and started down the hole, pausing after a half-a-dozen rungs to look up at her. He gestured with his head for her to follow.

She presented him her backside and gingerly reached for the first rung with her foot.

"Don't think of this as heights, Linds. Think of it as depths." He was barely holding back his laughter.

"That really helps, Jack. Thank you. That and knowing that you're there to break my fall." Lindsay felt for the next rung, her gloved fingers closing over the cold, oily bars. One more and her head was below the platform.

"Good luck," Reggie said, and dropped the manhole cover into place with a heavy thud that jolted Lindsay despite her expecting it. Aside from the weak light that filtered through the small holes in the metal, Lindsay found herself in pitch-blackness.

"Don't turn on your light," Jack whispered below her. "Keep coming down." The mocking had left his voice, as if the closing of the manhole shut down what passed for his lighter side.

Lindsay continued her descent, feeling for each steel rung and doing her best to be quiet. Beneath her was silence, and she wondered how Jack could move so soundlessly. She didn't know how far he was below her, or even if he was there at all. Obviously, it was a skill picked up in the tunnels. Chase and Stray had said people were all around them, and perhaps they hadn't been lying.

After what seemed a lifetime on the ladder, Lindsay's boots touched concrete. Other than the rumble of a subway in the distance, no sound met her ears. The darkness was more an oppressive force than the mere absence of light, and it was only the low timbre of Jack's voice at her ear that steadied her.

"I'm going to give you just enough light to see. Don't turn your flashlight on unless I say so, and if my light goes out, don't move."

She nodded, before realizing he couldn't see her. She was about to speak when a penlight clicked on, casting a pale circle at their feet that moved along the floor ahead of Jack as he guided her down a narrow corridor.

The hall branched after about a hundred feet, then did so again and again, each time Jack leading her in a different direction. The air was cold and stale. At least it didn't stink, and as her eyes adjusted to the gloom, she began to pick out details of her surroundings beyond the small ring of illumination.

Above them was a featureless concrete ceiling broken now and then by the underside of manhole covers, and once by a dark shaft that rose to some nameless place.

Along the walls were thick pipes and cables, coated with dust and the sporadic cobweb. There was the occasional access panel or vent, along with intermittent graffiti unlike any she'd seen before. The art of the streets consisted of stylized names, messages and images borrowed from a familiar alphabet and popular culture. Here, it was applied in bizarre, twisted patterns and caricatures, as if the creators had based their work on some dark, tormented mythos. Lindsay wanted to examine them more closely, but she didn't dare call out to Jack.

That this labyrinth extended for so many miles, on so many levels, humbled her. The place was a city beneath a city, and as they continued onward she began to appreciate the magnitude of the task Captain Monroe had in policing it.

She stumbled over something invisible in the dark, and caught herself against a pipe. Jack's light swiveled to her as she straightened, the eye of its beam settling on her midsection. He was a few seconds ahead of her, though he appeared as no more than another shadow in the gloom. Even so, she felt comforted. Jack, whatever he'd become, was with her. She gave a small, apologetic wave. The light lingered, and then turned away.

On and on they walked, twisting though the endless maze until Lindsay was certain she nor any other normal person could find their way back. They crept down spiraling stairwells with banisters of antique iron, and squeezed through openings scarcely wider than vent holes. They threaded their way though dank halls made foggy from cracked steam pipes, and past a large chamber piled high with rusting, unmarked oil drums. Their silent passage wound on for hours, with pauses lasting only long enough for Jack to refresh the batteries in his penlight.

At last he motioned her to a small alcove in a concrete wall. She slumped down on its chilled floor, her legs aching. He squatted beside her, his warmth as strong and vital as the sunshine, and she instinctively tilted towards him until their shoulders brushed. He leaned away, and Lindsay bit her lip. If Jack was a source of comfort, it was of the cold variety.

"Tired?" he whispered.

"No," she lied.

He carried on. "We're coming up to a large cavern now. A place called 'Sumptown'. There's a community of people there, and they might know what happened to Seline, but it's going to be very important that you don't offend them."

"Right," she said obediently. "What offends them?"

"Don't contradict them or challenge their beliefs. They really hate that."

"Okay, I can do that. Falls under Rule One, right?"

She thought Jack gave a fleeting smile. "You always were a quick learner, Linds."

Linds. A few people had used that short form over the years. A boyfriend or two. Janice. Her ex-husband. With them, it was a name. With Jack—. With Jack, it was invoking a relationship, a history, an understanding. An intimacy. Not that he saw it that way. She needed a drink, and dug into her bag for her bottle of water. She took a swig, and pulled out a power bar. Jack gripped her wrist.

"Don't open that here."

She looked into the glitter of his eyes. "Why not?"

"The smell will attract rats."

Lindsay cocked her head. "So?"

"In some parts of the tunnels, people eat rats," he explained. "In this part, the rats have been known to eat people."

Lindsay swallowed hard, dropped the bar back into her pack. "Why the hell does anyone live down here? I mean, even the worst part of New York has got to be a hundred times better than this."

Now Jack leaned into her. He was warm and strong, and intense—really intense. "You say that because you're used to the surface. To the people here, the tunnels are a sanctuary. Most of them came down because the world above *was* worse. To them the surface is where they were abused or neglected or where people wanted to take their children away from them."

"People bring their *kids* down here?" Disbelief pitched her voice up an octave. "That's insane!"

Jack sighed and stood. "No, Linds. What they're running from is."

---

ABOUT A HUNDRED feet beneath Manhattan was a small underground lake—a flooded cavern whose slowly churning waters were fed by an abandoned sewer tunnel and the constant dripping of condensation from the stalactites above. Pulling out his flashlight, Jack shone its beam upon the water, reflecting an oily rainbow of toxins leeched from the city streets, then raised it to illuminate the only way across—a floating bridge fashioned of rope and oil drums that stretched off into the blackness. Its length was reinforced by scavenged cables, topped with rusting sheet metal, and decorated with dozens of little tin bells that looked as if they had been pilfered from a department store Christmas tree.

Lindsay eyed the structure and was relieved Jack had forbidden eating. Her stomach was roiling like the waters below.

"Sumptown is on the far side of this lake," Jack explained. "We have to cross the bridge to reach it. It doesn't look like much but it'll hold. You can turn your flashlight on too, if you like. Just don't go shining it in anyone's face."

Switching on her light, she teetered along behind Jack's sure footing. The bridge swayed under their weight, setting off the bells to alert the residents to visitors. Across the water shimmered the glow of a fire, though not until they reached the far side was she able to make out what it illuminated.

Sumptown was located atop a steep embankment, its shore defended by coils of razor wire. Beyond this hostile barrier was an encampment of small huts and tents cobbled together from tarps, plastic sheeting, plywood and corrugated metal. At the center was a fire pit large enough to roast a bull, around which three dozen or so people were gathered, all of them with their eyes on Jack and Lindsay.

Lindsay glanced at Jack. He'd stopped at the end of the bridge, mostly shielding her from view, but she could still see the locked jaw, still sense his tension. They waited as a stocky man got up and approached, an automatic rifle in his hand. His bearded face was dark with grime, causing his eyes to shine brightly in the flickering light.

"Well, well, look what the rat dragged in." He slowly smiled. "How long has it been, Mr. Cole? A year? More?"

"More," Jack confirmed.

The man called over his shoulder, "Dee? Dee. Come say hello."

An older woman, around the man's age, broke from the others. Though her face was every bit as grimy as his, her hair was wrapped into an elaborate bun studded with rhinestone hairpins, and she was wearing an evening sweater with sequins that glinted faintly in the light. A line popped irreverently into Lindsay's mind: *A funny thing happened on the way to the opera.*

"Well, look at you," Dee said, coming straight up to Jack and peering into his face. She held out her hand and when Jack took it, her other one came over his in, what looked to Lindsay, motherly affection.

"You're looking as good as ever," she said, then caught sight of Lindsay over Jack's shoulder. "And who might this be, Mr. Cole?" The teasing innuendo was clear in her voice. Should be no problem convincing them that she was Jack's.

Jack turned so the women could face each other for introductions. "This is Miss Lindsay Sterling. Lindsay, this is Mr. Frank Moore, mayor of Sumptown, and his wife, Mrs. Dee Moore. As you can see, Miss Sterling's a topsider."

The Moores gave Lindsay a look of profound pity.

"Oh," Dee said. "Well, I suppose that can't be helped. Most everybody is, after all. Please, come and join us by the fire. You two are just in time for lunch."

Lindsay was shown to a backless kitchen chair beside Jack who was offered a padded office chair, complete with a back—clearly a place of honor. The entire community surrounded them, and Lindsay felt her anxiety ebb at their friendly appearance. Their demographic range surprised her. They were a roughly even mix of young and old, male and female, and they all seemed quite healthy considering their bleak environment. All had the same dull gray complexion and dark, glittering eyes, and from studying their faces, it was impossible to group them by race or creed.

Cooking over the fire was a large pot of oatmeal, the gray mush making great swampy belches. Dee ladled a generous helping into a chipped ceramic bowl, and handed it and a metal spoon to Lindsay. Graciously she took it, wondering how she was going to stomach the stuff. Dee gave one to Jack, and he began chowing it down.

Then again, this was a man who ate scrambled egg sandwiches on stale bread.

Jack's eyes narrowed on Lindsay, and taking up her spoon, she nibbled at the gunk. It was good, tasting of sugar and cinnamon, and kind of creamy, too. Lindsay's second spoonful was heaping.

The talk between Jack and the Moores was idle at first, revolving around tunnels that had collapsed or been discovered, and to residents that had moved on or found trouble. It was only when Jack had scraped his bowl clean that he got down to business.

"I'm looking for a lost topsider. Her name's Seline Sterling. Miss Lindsay's her aunt."

"Oh?" Mr. Moore slid Lindsay a wary look. "Tell us about her."

Lindsay opened her mouth, precisely as Jack cut her off. "She's a Samaritan. Came down here to see if she could help."

"One of those outreach people?" the mayor asked in disapproval.

"No, an independent. Like I started out."

"I see." Mr. Moore turned to a thin-faced youth crouched beside him. "Have you heard of her, Mr. Jarvis?"

"Yes, sir," he replied. "She's been in the subways for a few months, talking to the addicts. I heard she made contact with the APs, can't say for sure."

Jack winced at the mention of the APs, and it took all Lindsay had not to ask about them. "Are any of your other runners here today?" he inquired.

"No," the mayor answered. "They're all either fetching water or out on Mole patrol. They should all be back by supper. You're welcome to stay and wait for them if you like."

"I think we'll do that. Thank you, Mr. Moore."

The formal discussion between Jack and the mayor now over, snippets of conversation began amidst the others in the circle, though their voices remained hushed. Dee, who had been beside her husband, sat on an overturned pail beside Lindsay.

"This is your first time down here, isn't it?" she asked.

"That obvious, huh?"

"One glance at your eyes and you can tell." At Lindsay's confused look, Dee added, "They've got color."

Lindsay still didn't understand, then looking more closely she realized why all the tunnel dwellers appeared the same. The perpetual darkness had expanded their pupils so much that their irises had nearly disappeared, and it struck her that they could see things invisible to her. That was worrisome.

"I suppose if I stayed down here my eyes would become like yours," Lindsay said.

"Yes. Your skin would darken too. It takes a few months."

"I wouldn't get paler?"

"You would, except the grime down here soaks into you after a while," Dee said contentedly. "Turns everybody the same shade in time, which is good."

"It is?" Lindsay asked, eliciting a good-natured laugh from the older woman.

"Sure. Topsiders are always fighting over who's skin is

what color. Down here we're all the same. We're all human. Well, all except for the Moles."

Beside her, Jack shifted slightly and she knew that he'd tuned in. "The Moles?" Lindsay asked.

"They keep to themselves mostly, down in the pits, but they're awful dangerous when they want to be." She glanced at Jack. "I imagine Mr. Cole has told you more about them than anyone else ever could."

"Actually—" Lindsay began.

Jack reached across her lap and hooked his hand under her thigh. It was a small gesture of claim. Lindsay stared at the hard stretch of his arm nearly touching her breasts, the curve of his fingers on her leg, and she felt her insides warm at how good it looked. "Actually, Mrs. Moore, I don't trouble Miss Sterling with my tales given her present worry for her niece." His words were polite, yet both women knew better than to challenge them.

Lindsay gave Dee a small, helpless shrug, and the woman redirected the conversation. "Of course, Mr. Cole. So, what do you do for a living, Miss Sterling?"

"Oh, I'm an interior designer," she replied, awkward about her profession given the shabby surroundings, but Dee perked right up.

"You mean you decorate people's apartments and the like?"

Jack withdrew his hand, clearly satisfied with the change in subject matter, and Lindsay felt that same stab of disappointment as when he'd pulled away from her in the tunnels. She refocused on Dee. "Sort of. I mostly work on retail décor," she said. "I do restorations and renovations, create looks for stores, restaurants, boutiques...."

"Oh," Dee said brightly, "that's great. We'll need people

like you when we re-surface. It'll be important to make things beautiful again."

Lindsay blinked. "Um...."

"Sooner or later the world above will destroy itself," Jack interjected, the conversational lilt to his voice overlying a warning tone. "Then the people down here plan to re-colonize the surface."

Lindsay picked up Jack's signal and nodded gravely. "I see. Well, that would certainly provide, uh...plenty of opportunities for my business."

"Oh, yes," Dee bobbed her head, her glittery hairpins twinkling away. "One day New York will be as beautiful as the ruins of Pompeii."

# CHAPTER FIVE

AFTER LUNCH SOME of the Sumptown residents disappeared, drifting off to their tents or fading into the darkness that was never far away. Jack and the mayor stayed to visit over tea, and since Lindsay didn't know the protocol for excusing herself, she stayed as well. The conversation seemed interminable. They joked and gossiped about people and places she'd never heard of, their references too obscure for her to understand. Pipe-hand Joe and Gasoline Jane. Snakes and Ladders. The Pit Stop. The Black Door. Dyer Pass. Gutter Run. It was as if they were speaking graffiti; she understood the words, not the meanings.

She took to watching the people around the fire, and discovered that they, in turn, were watching Jack. The men, all skinny and stringy, stared at Jack as if he were a god. Though the women watched more circumspectly, Jack couldn't take more than three sips of his tea before it was topped up.

She herself began observing him. He'd hung his jacket from the back of his chair, his long legs were stretched in front of him, his booted ankles crossed. The flames danced shadows across the planes of his face, and every now and again, caught the golden glint of his eyes. He held an air of reserve and power, ideal qualities for the hero that everyone here saw him as. It made him seem alien to Lindsay, yet sexy as hell. All kinds of females shot her looks of envy and wonder, and Lindsay felt a kind of warped pride to be Jack's woman.

Try as Lindsay might to resist, her eyelids began to droop. She hadn't slept the night before, too wound up from her encounter in the subway tunnel and Jack's late night call. Her condition didn't go unnoticed. When Mr. Moore came to the end of one of his rambling anecdotes, Jack turned to her.

"You look tired."

It took a moment to bring him into focus. "I'm okay," she lied, in compliance with the second rule.

"Uh-huh." He turned to the mayor. "You have a place we can crash for a few hours, Mr. Moore? She's exhausted, and I could probably use a siesta myself."

The mayor nodded. "Of course. There're bunks in The Library."

Toting his gun, he guided Lindsay and Jack to the largest structure in the village: a pavilion tent, its entrance flanked by two small concrete lions. "Have a good sleep. I'll send someone to wake you when the runners get back."

With that he walked away, leaving them to settle in.

The floor of the library was made of plywood covered by a patchwork of old Persian rugs, the only furniture a pair of army cots pushed into a far corner, and a dozen overstuffed bookcases that lined the walls. Kneeling beside one Lindsay inspected the titles with her flashlight.

"Emergency Medicine... Anthrax, A Practical Guide for Citizens... The SAS Survival Handbook... Voltaire: Volume 5..."

Jack gave a thin smile, looking over his shoulder as he shoelaced shut the tent's entrance. "No television or internet down here, so people read a lot. You name it, they're ready for it."

"Is that why they're down here? Waiting for the end of the world?"

"That's the case with the Moores and a few others. Mostly they're here because their mayor takes care of them. He used to be in the Special Forces a long time ago, so he knows his stuff when it comes to survival. He's a good guy, but not someone to toy with."

"Wouldn't it be easier to buy a cabin in the woods somewhere? Isn't that what most survivalists do?"

"Maybe." Jack sat on a cot, loosening the laces on his boots. "Except then he wouldn't be helping people in the meantime. Besides, here he doesn't have to worry about the warrant for his arrest."

Lindsay darted a look at the entrance. "What's he wanted for?"

"Double homicide."

"Oh."

She propped her backpack against the other cot and dropped onto the thin polyester bed, her knees bumping Jack's. He swung his legs apart so that hers were loosely caught between his. His face, she could sense more than see, was inches from hers. And when he spoke, she could feel the warmth of his breath in the cool dimness. The scent of sugar and cinnamon.

"The runners travel around this part of the underground finding things to supply the town with. They trade too, so they often pick up bits of information that would be hard to gather otherwise. When they get back, we might learn something useful."

"How many communities are there like this?"

"Hard to say," he said, and she heard the rasp of his hand

running over his chin stubble. "Maybe a couple of dozen. Near the surface there was one called 'The Burbs'. Its people tapped into the power grid and piped in water. They had lights and showers, even had microwaves and refrigerators. Must have been about three hundred people living there. All they wanted was to be left alone."

"What happened?"

"The police found out about the place. About fifty officers went down with dogs and cleared it out. It was a bad scene."

"Were you there?"

"No, but Reggie was. The people were angry and tried to defend their homes. For a lot of them The Burbs were the only place they'd ever belonged. Many were raising families there. As for the cops, well, most of them were scared out of their wits. Only a handful had ever been in the underground before that night, and the sight of three hundred people threatening them with knives and pry bars didn't make them any calmer. It was a mess."

"I never heard about that."

"Of course you didn't. You think the cops invited reporters?"

"I don't get it. If the people were living peacefully down there, why did the cops evict them?"

Jack sighed. "Because it's their job. To be fair to Captain Monroe, he was under a lot of pressure from both the mayor and the transit authority to do something about all the 'homeless' in the tunnels, and that camp had grown too big to be ignored. Anyway, the people who lived there simply fled deeper underground. Splintered into smaller communities that were more difficult to detect, or too remote for the cops to reach."

Lindsay imagined what it would be like if the police were

to suddenly descend on Sumptown. While the residents were certainly hospitable, she doubted they'd abandon their little lakeside fortress without one hell of a fight. Not that authorities would risk a raid this far down.

"Who are the APs? Another community?"

"No. They're more like a... kind of like an organization. Their name is an acronym—short for 'aberrant psychology'. Basically they're a group of people who broke free from the state's mental hospitals."

"They're insane?"

Jack snorted. "Define insane. They have a kind of network they developed in the asylums. They help each other out. Watch each other's backs. That sort of thing. A definite method to their madness."

"That guy Jarvis mentioned that Seline had made friends with them," Lindsay said uncertainly. "You don't think they'd hurt her...do you?"

Jack tapped her knee with his, a quick touch, like a pat on the back. "Everyone down here will hurt you if you get on their bad side, but let's not worry about it for now. Jarvis wasn't sure, and to be frank it's rather unlikely. The APs stick to themselves."

"What if it's true?"

"Then we'll have to investigate it."

"You ever dealt with the APs before?"

"No," he admitted. "I know how to contact them if we have to. Now enough with the questions. Let's get some rest." He swung his legs away from hers onto his cot and stretched out, using his nylon bag as a pillow. Lindsay clicked off her flashlight and did the same. In the near dark, it took mere seconds before her eyes closed. Beside her, Jack began shifting about.

Lindsay murmured, "Bet you miss your comfy bed, huh?"

She could hear Jack twist to face her. "What were you doing snooping around in my bedroom?"

"I never went into your bedroom. Reggie mentioned it."

"Why would you and Reggie be talking about my bed?"

Lindsay suddenly wished she'd never brought the subject up. She could feel her face go hot—her whole body go hot. "Um...something to do with getting your help to find Seline."

There was a pause and then Jack gave a short bark of laughter. "You really are desperate, aren't you?"

Her eyes snapped open and she faced him. "You don't realize how much of a hero you are to these people, do you? The guys were clinging to your every word as if it were God's truth. And the women—Jack, you could whistle once and any one of them would gladly fill the spot with you that I'm pretending at."

His hand clamped down on her shoulder with a speed and accuracy that was eerie. "Shut up," he hissed. "Sound carries down here."

Lindsay hadn't realized her voice had risen. She blew out her breath and relaxed. As he let go, his fingers brushed her cheek, deliberate or not it was hard to tell.

"Yes, I do know that I'm treated like a hero here. But I'm like a bad movie, based very loosely on the truth."

Lindsay flipped onto her side. "So what happened to you, Jack? We haven't seen each other since high school."

His eyes glinted at her. "I've got a nice bed. That about covers my accomplishments to date."

Lindsay flopped back. "You're just trying to shut me up."

Jack folded his hands behind his head. "I thought you were tired."

"That's because I couldn't talk out there. Boredom causes

weariness."

"In that case, I'm bored."

"Oh, fine then. Sleep." Lindsay grumped. There was silence and Jack's eyelids began to close naturally. She should let him rest, she should rest herself. His life was not—repeat, not—her business."If you're so well-liked here in Sumptown why haven't you come to visit in a year?"

Jack said nothing. He was ignoring her which, she supposed, was his prerogative. Then: "Today is the first time I've come down since I made it back to the surface."

Although his voice was mostly even, Lindsay picked up on the raw, bleak undertones. She began cautiously, not wanting to intrude on his pain. "I knew about you being... trapped down here for two years, but until we came here I thought from where you were living that you were still coming down—"

"Lindsay," Jack ground out. "Shut. Up." Followed unexpectedly by "Please."

She did, though she had to bite her lower lip to do so. She finally understood why he'd been so reluctant to help her. From Jack's past love of the underground and his ratty lifestyle she'd assumed that he'd continued his adventures. His self-imposed exile meant that something terrible must have happened.

She licked her lips. There was still something he needed to know. "You should've looked me up, Jack. You know you could've. Especially when Seline came to see you. I can't believe she didn't tell me that she'd gone to you."

"Don't blame her. I asked her not to."

He hadn't wanted to renew their friendship. She pressed a hand to her abdomen and pushed on. "Jack. I won't make you go into what you don't want to talk about. Nevertheless, after we get through this, I want you to know I'm around if you'd like to do normal stuff. Like have a coffee or go to a movie, or buy a TV, a potted plant, a third fork—"

This time when he told her to shut up, there was a smile there, too. It emboldened her to ask one more question. A safe one that had nothing to do with him.

"Jack, who are the Moles?"

There was no answer. Beside her he'd gone still. She could feel him retreat from her. More than retreat because that at least would be a strategic move, this was a sudden absence as if he'd dropped into a black hole, and there was no way to follow him because she'd no idea where he'd gone. One thing was for sure. The Moles, whoever they were, had everything to do with him.

---

*JACK'S LUNGS BURNED as he ran the tunnel, the beam of his flashlight picking out the jagged chunks of concrete that littered the floor. He'd shed the weight of his pack and spent handgun, but he could hear the skittering footfalls of the Moles getting louder, closing in on him like wolves for the kill.*

*He leaped over a tangled mass of rebar and while airborne, his light caught a narrow opening in the wall. He zagged down it, into another brick-lined tunnel, and prayed it would soon join a path he knew.*

*Then, ahead, a cave-in. A wall of smashed masonry and oily black earth that cut off the way. Skidding to a halt, Jack swung around the beam of his light, searching for an escape route. There was none. He flung himself at the rubble, began to scramble up it. Something big and hard and cold slammed into him.*

Jack's vision exploded into stars as he tumbled, and his skull smacked against the corner of a cinder block. His flashlight was stripped from his hand and smashed against the tunnel wall. In the utter blackness, several of the things piled on him, and thin, iron-hard fingers curled around his neck, arms and legs, their grip wrenching as pliers. He heard the click of their teeth, and knew that in a second he'd be torn apart...or worse.

He found his feet, and, in a spree of punches and kicks, knocked three aside. He lashed out blindly at the others but they were too tough, too vicious and too many for him to escape. Their sheer weight in numbers dragged him down, and they wrestled a thick canvas bag over his head.

"Fucking bastards!" he screamed through the bag, his breath was cut off by the yank of a drawstring around his throat. His arms were folded back, wrists bound with raw wire that bit into his flesh. He continued to kick, then his ankles received the same treatment, and he was gripped by his tattered clothes and hauled off the floor.

Blood trickled over his face, sped by his frantic heartbeat as they transported him back the way he'd fled, deeper and deeper into the chasms of the underground. Bound and hooded, he still struggled, though it was no use. At least Reggie had got away. The tunnel fighter had been badly mauled, but it looked as if Jack had led the Moles off his trail long enough to afford an escape.

Their path twisted and turned, until at last they emerged into a place where their footfalls echoed and a chill, metallic reek filtered through the bag, burning his nostrils like acid fumes. He was dropped upon a cracked tile floor, the air knocked from his lungs. Limbs cramping, he flopped there like a dying fish, gasping past the cord tight on his windpipe. Then *something gripped him hard by the back of his neck, forcing it slowly around until his vertebrae were about to snap.*

*"Jack Cole," a voice beside him hissed and cracked like liquid nitrogen poured over naked flesh.*

*"You're...you're going to break my neck..." Jack choked.*

*His neck muscles were allowed to slacken by the tiniest margin. "Jack Cole," the inhuman voice repeated, bare of inflection or emotion. "You are Jack Cole. The one who has seen the roots of many cities."*

*Jack gritted his teeth in pain as its grasp tightened again. "Yes."*

*"No," it corrected. "Jack Cole is dead."*

*Nearby, Jack heard a heavy metal plate being pulled back, then a sickening reek of decay assaulted him, overpowering the burning acid stench. The wire that held his limbs was roughly untwisted, and he tried to stagger to his feet. No sooner did he move, then he was grabbed under the shoulders and shoved into a pit. He landed with a tremendous splash, and came up choking and sputtering, standing waist-deep in fetid water. He tore the bag off his head, the stench, asphyxiating, and doubling over, he vomited into the foul water.*

*Above, the metal lid was slammed shut, and he was sealed in the putrid darkness, gagging as he fumbled about. His hands met the slime-slick wall of the pit, then groping, his fingers closed over something soft and pulpy, like a swollen, rotten fruit. His hands trailed over it, then he recoiled, letting out a strangled cry.*

*It was a face—a human face.*

*And turning about, arms outstretched, he found it was not the only one.*

# CHAPTER SIX

JACK WOKE ON a great sucking gasp that lifted his head clear off the cot. He dropped back and shot a look at Lindsay. She slept on, thank God. Last thing he needed was her asking one more fucking question about himself, her voice all low and soft as if they were—as if they were something they weren't. He closed his eyes but she stole into his ears with soft, regular breathing and his nose caught her pure feminine smell. There was no way he was going back to sleep.

He opened his eyes to the blackness, so deep he might as well have been blind. What it hid, his memory generously found again. Her blonde hair blending with the clarity of her skin, her soft full pink lips, the high cheekbones....

He was acting like a hormonal teenager. When he was fifteen, that was excusable, not at thirty-three. Not when he'd been through the hell he had. He still wanted her, only not with boyish innocent lust. No, he wanted to pull her under him and pound into her, listen to her cry out and spill into her. And then he wanted to do it all over again. He wanted to use her like an animal.

An animal, like the fucking Moles had made him.

Returning to the tunnels hadn't been the gut-wrenching

experience he thought it would be. His memory had served him faithfully, guided him unerringly through the labyrinthine underground, and while he'd felt the pull of the tunnels, he didn't feel as though he was losing himself to them. Instead he'd once again felt the adventure of entering the flip side of New York City, once again saw on the walls and in the debris the stories of human resilience and despair.

It helped having Lindsay close. He'd been as nervous as hell approaching Sumptown. No matter how friendly, these people knew what had happened, and he'd feared they'd unwittingly say or do something that would unleash the terrors he'd worked so hard to lock away. With Lindsay right behind him, so sane and solid, he'd carried on.

The problem was that when he was alone with her she ransacked his emotions with all the recklessness and tenacity of a raccoon with a garbage can. He couldn't sleep and he couldn't take lying beside her. He'd go and talk with the tunnel dwellers. Play at being an anthropologist again. It beat what he'd been doing for the past year. Playing dead.

---

LINDSAY WOKE DISORIENTED, the everlasting night giving her no clue about how long she had been unconscious or if she was alone.

"Jack? You there?"

She reached across and patted the flat cot. "Guess not." She flicked on her flashlight and read her watch. 4:52. Were the runners back?

She shouldered her pack and whapped her way past the tent flap, almost bumping into Dee as she did so.

"Oh! Sorry."

Dee smiled at Lindsay's bleary-eyed look. "Mr. Cole is with the mayor by the fire. The last group of runners are back, so they're talking."

Lindsay started toward the fire, when Dee touched her arm. "Hey, if you have a minute, there's something I'd like to show you."

Lindsay hesitated. Whatever the woman had for show-and-tell couldn't compare to news about Seline.

"Come on. It won't take long."

Then again, not agreeing would break the obedience rule and while it might not apply to Jack's underground friends, better to err on the side of caution, and so she let Dee guide her through Sumptown. As they skirted the fire, Jack glanced up from his conversation with a couple of jack-shirted young men, and Lindsay gestured with her head toward Dee. He turned back without so much as a nod of acknowledgement. Jack was taking this property thing way too seriously.

Dee led her to a tent on the other side of the community, this one about half the size of The Library and lit by a kerosene lantern.

"Come in," she beckoned. "I wanted to show you this before you left."

Lindsay cautiously entered, then her jaw dropped at what Dee had on display. The tent was crowded with boxes and baskets, but at the back, space had been made for a weaving loom, and hanging beside it was a bright woolen jacket of an amazing pattern, recalling the strange images of the deep tunnel graffiti.

Dee slid it gently from its hanger and held it up for Lindsay to see. "Do you like it?"

"It's incredible. Did you make this?"

The woman's chest swelled visibly with pride. "I want to

give it to you. A present."

Lindsay didn't know what to say. "Mrs. Moore...thank you...it must have taken you ages to make that. Why give it to me?"

Dee laughed, the sound musical despite being hushed. "Because it's no use down here. It's far too bright and delicate to wear in the tunnels. I made it for fun, I thought you might like it, being a topsider and...and because it's good to see that Mr. Cole is no longer alone."

The woman was clearly fond of Jack, and Lindsay knew she didn't have much time. "Jack won't talk to me about the tunnels. Can you tell me what happened to him?"

Her kind expression still in place, she shook her head. "Oh, it's not my story to tell, dear." She shuddered. "Even if the telling of it weren't hard." She placed the folded jacket in Lindsay's hands. "I'm sure in time he'll talk to you. He's as fond of you as you are of him."

Which wasn't saying much. Then Lindsay remembered the squeeze of happiness she felt when Jack's hand was on her knee and his lips by her ear, and suddenly she didn't know what to think. She fumbled for something to say, and turned to the jacket. "Mrs. Moore, if you can create things like this you could make a good living on the surface...."

The woman gave a small gasp. "You topsiders are playing with fire, Miss Sterling, and one day it's going to catch. Sooner or later, it'll happen, and I don't want to be up there when it does."

Dee radiated a kind of serenity and faith that only came from those who were deeply at peace with themselves. Who was she to upset the weaver's world with her version of the way things were? Who was she to say that she had any better handle on reality? She'd spent her whole life not knowing what lay under her own two feet. She'd spent years thinking Jack was one thing when he was another.

"I'm sorry, Mrs. Moore. I didn't mean any offense."

Dee's dark eyes glittered like obsidian. "None taken, Miss Sterling. All I ask is that you enjoy it, okay?"

"I will, Mrs. Moore. Thank you."

Together they carefully folded the jacket into Lindsay's backpack, making space by removing several items that Lindsay gifted to Dee including most of her food packs and a large box of matches. Part of her felt guilty, exchanging such mundane items for a beautiful work of art, yet she got the impression that the mayor's wife was feeling much the same thing. To her the jacket was a useless hobby project, for which Lindsay was foolishly trading valuable commodities.

They had just finished when the tent door opened, and Jack stuck his head inside. "One of the runners was able to confirm that Seline was hanging around with APs in Grand Central, though whether she knew who they were is doubtful."

Lindsay gripped the handle of her backpack. What this news good or bad? "Then we have a lead?"

"I guess you could call it that. Let's get back to Grand Central. We're a long way from finding her yet."

The Moores and a good portion of Sumptown's residents came to see them off, and with a final wave goodbye, Lindsay and Jack exited over the floating bridge. When they had ventured a ways into the tunnels he motioned for her to follow him into a narrow fissure between two huge, mineral-stained pipes. Their fronts were nearly touching and their mouths inches apart. Close enough to kiss. He talked, in a low, rushed voice.

"This is the way it is: the people of Sumptown don't like the APs. They consider them spies and enemies."

"Why?" Lindsay asked, matching his decibel level.

"APs don't normally socialize with those outside their clique. Even here in the underground their relations with others are very limited. That's why the runner noticed when he saw them talking to Seline. It was very unusual."

"So you think they kidnapped her?" The thought of her niece in the hands of a bunch of crazy people chilled Lindsay to the marrow.

"Perhaps. I don't know," he acknowledged. "I do know that trying to talk to their members down here is going to be useless at best and dangerous at worst. The APs won't tell us a thing, and the people of Sumptown wouldn't be pleased to know we were dealing with them."

"So what do we do?"

"I am going to have to go and have a chat with their *representative*." He spat out the last word. "They have a person who serves as an ambassador to the underground communities and street homeless."

"You know where to find him?"

"Her, actually. Her name is MacMurphy. Randa MacMurphy." Jack spoke with distaste.

"I take it she's not one of your favorite people."

Jack shook his head. "She's what people down here call a dark angel. Someone who fucks with your head. Not exactly what I need right now."

She opened her mouth but it was covered by his gloved hand. "Not by her. And not by you, Linds."

She twisted her mouth underneath the rough fibers of his glove. "We're still in the tunnels," he said. "The rules still apply."

She stopped and glared at him, hoping her eyes conveyed her opinion of the rules. He didn't move his hand away. "You think if you ask enough questions you'll figure me out and fix me. Only what happens if you can't? You'll have taken me apart and left me in pieces, and I'm already broken enough without you making more of a mess. Considering you couldn't be bothered to stay friends with me, or even have the courtesy to tell me you didn't want me in our life, excuse me if I lack confidence in your ability. So how about you back off? Right. Now."

*No, Jack, no. I'm not making the same mistake twice.* Now was not the time to fight him. She nodded underneath his glove. His mouth thinned. He didn't believe her. She nodded again and mumbled "Okay" under his glove.

He dropped his hand and turned away, and she had to scramble to keep up.

---

IT WAS NEARLY eleven at night when they got back, and Lindsay couldn't remember ever feeling that physically tired. Her legs were wobbly, her lower back ached and her shoulders from the backpack felt as if a dull knife had sawed away at them. Jack went up the ladder first, and tapped his flashlight on the manhole cover without stop until there came a muffled voice, its accent distinctly Arabic. "Who's that?"

"Cole."

The locks clunked open, and Jack hoisted himself through the hole. He stayed in a squat position and reached for Lindsay. As he lifted her clear, he eclipsed his body between her and the overhead lights, casting her in his shadow. "It takes a bit for the eyes to adjust."

Lindsay's gaze lined up with the front of his chest, where the first couple buttons of his shirt beneath his jacket were undone, leaving the dim hollow of his throat inches from her. She took in the roughened texture of his skin, his unshaven jaw, the cords of his throat. He smelled of the tunnel, but also of him. Even a little of sweat, something she was drenched in, given the Olympic pace he'd set during their return.

All at once she felt a tug on her head and her hair tumbled free of the knit hat. She glanced up at Jack who had his eyes on her hair. "There, that's better," he said, with the satisfied concentration her hairstylist assumed when he'd finished with her.

Static from the hat had electrified her fine strands and Jack began smoothing them down with his hand. His touch was comforting and gentle. It also transmitted an unsettling current that tingled her every sex nerve.

Lindsay couldn't bring herself to break the contact, so she compromised by saying to his bare throat, "I think you need a shaggy pet."

His hand stopped and he stepped back, leaving her squinting into the lights. "That was unnecessary."

Lindsay, bereft again from another of his withdrawals, blinked at him. "What? I was only joking—"

"Exactly," he cut her off. Jack switched his attention to the tall Arabic man, who was discreetly standing a few paces away. "Najib, this is Lindsay Sterling. Lindsay, this is Najib Gupta, former mayor of the Burbs."

The man inclined his head. "Pleased to meet you, Ms. Sterling."

Though still annoyed with Jack, her emotions eased under the man's gentle manner. She gave him a genuine smile. "Likewise."

As Jack turned to go, the gatekeeper raised a hand. "Excuse me, Reggie said to tell you that he's going to use the apartment tonight. His lady friend is back in town."

Jack blew out a gusty breath. "Fine. When Reggie shows tomorrow, could you tell him that I've gone to the Mission?"

Lindsay scowled. That made no sense. "You're going to a homeless shelter?"

Jack gave her a look as if she were a junior officer speaking out of line. "Reggie's girlfriend only comes into town once every couple of months. I told him he could use my place. It's not a big deal."

"Why don't you just get a hotel?"

"No identification."

"What? How can you not have any ID?"

"I lost it when I was down in the tunnels. Haven't bothered to replace any of it yet."

Wasn't that a full year ago? He was deliberately keeping himself off the radar. She thought of Mr. Moore's warrant for murder—what had Jack done to make him hide from the world?

Lindsay trailed down the hallway after him, and they emerged through the door, her eyes watering from the lights overhanging the platform. Jack headed for the exit, not bothering to see if she was following or not.

She pressed her lips into a thin, determined line. She had said nothing wrong as far as she was concerned, and she wasn't about to indulge his moodiness any further. The rules didn't apply here.

She stuck her thumbs under the shoulder straps of the pack to ease its weight, and hurried to catch up, matching his long, quick strides with hers, despite her thigh muscles screaming for her to slow down. "Boy, those seem bright," she said conversationally, as if there'd been no sharp words between them.

Jack didn't say anything and she assumed that he was ignoring her, then he replied quietly.

"Live underground a few weeks and they're unbearable. That's part of the reason the people in the communities stay there. After a while you can't handle bright lights, let alone sunshine."

"It must have been hell on you after two years underground," she said, still keeping it light.

"Yes. It was." He bit out, then faced her, his eyes a warm, deep copper. "That's why your hair is no joke to me, Lindsay. There was a time not so long ago when I could never have stood to look at something so bright. I don't take it for granted."

He didn't touch her hair this time, but the way he focused on it seemed as immediate and real as his hand.

On impulse she asked, "Why don't you stay with me tonight?" Jack's expression slid into wariness, and she rushed to explain. "I mean, you can come crash on my couch. The shelter must be full in this weather anyway."

"You don't need to go to the trouble."

"Jack. I don't have to *make* the couch. It's there ready and waiting. How about it?"

His jaw went solid and she could see the stubborn ass was about to refuse again. "However, if you're into a communal mattress in a room with fifty other—"

"Dammit, Linds. *Fine*."

Lindsay suppressed a smile and they caught a cab. When she gave the driver her address in Chelsea, Jack raised an eyebrow.

"Posh area. You must be doing well."

Lindsay gave a noncommittal shrug. He'd already made it clear what he thought of her wealth. "More luck than money.

There was a foreclosure sale that I got wind of through my business. As it is, I've got a ridiculous mortgage. Still, it's a good investment, and the neighborhood is amazing."

"I know. I used to live on 24th Street. Remember?"

Lindsay recalled the small apartment he'd shared with his father. They lived like two stereotypical bachelors where everything was thrown but never out. It was a complete one-eighty from the way he lived now, though she didn't like his present circumstances either. He needed the proverbial woman's touch. On his apartment anyway. "So…what did you do after university in Paris?"

He shrugged. "Travelled around, got my doctorate at Oxford."

"Dr. Cole, huh?"

He gave her a dirty look. She persisted. "I heard you went on to explore all those cities, just like you told me you would when we were kids."

Jack turned to stare out his window. "My father loved to build tunnels. I loved to study them. There's nothing more." He shifted his head to look at the patch of seat between them. "Listen, Linds, I'm sorry to hear about your family. I was an asshole about it, and"—he lifted his dark gold eyes to her—"that was a hell of a responsibility you took on."

His unexpected tenderness sent her lips vibrating from emotion. Before she lost it, she spoke, "They were on their way to my graduation ceremony. They decided to all come in the same car. Seline was on a sleepover, so it was going to be a fun day. My brother told me that they were going to make it in the nick of time so when they didn't show I was more disappointed than worried. Afterwards when the caps and gowns were with their families, the police made their way through the crowd to me.

"A semi blew a tire changing lanes and plowed straight into the car. My Mom and Dad and my brother's wife were already gone, and my brother was barely alive. He lived long enough to have our family friend Janice arrange to have guardianship changed from my parents to me. Looking out for his family right to the end."

She let out a long steadying breath. "Long story short, Jack, it wasn't a responsibility. I needed my niece back then, just as much as she needed me. I still do." She shook herself free of the memories. "Ah, well. Sometimes that's what life is like, right? What about your dad?"

Jack's eyes stayed on her, searching. For what, she'd no idea. She was about to call him on it when he said, "He's living in London. Consults for the Department of Transport there, or at least he did when I last talked to him. It's been awhile."

"How long?"

This time, it was him who blew out his breath. "About a month after I came out of the tunnels."

Another question was forming on Lindsay's lips when the cab driver halted in front of her apartment block. Before Lindsay could rummage through her backpack for her wallet, Jack lifted his butt off the seat and pulled out a wad of bills from his front jeans pocket, paying the cabbie along with a generous tip, though Lindsay could see it almost cleaned him out. She'd make it up to him, whether or not he knew it.

Lindsay waved to the doorman who looked uncertainly at their scruffiness, until he recognized her. Then he looked very curious. Inside the mirror-paneled elevator, she inspected her face.

"My God! There's even dirt on my eyelashes."

Jack didn't look at his reflection.

After passing down a corridor of rich woods, they reached her door. As she inserted her key, she said in sudden nervousness, "You'll have to excuse the mess. I do my own cleaning, and I've kind of let it go the past week."

Jack said with utmost seriousness, "I think I can handle it."

Once in the tiled foyer, Lindsay dropped her pack and hung up her jacket. She took a hanger from the hall closet and reached for Jack's coat. He skittered a look at her leathers and neat row of painful footwear, and sent his parka wordlessly to the floor, his boots soon following. Lindsay grimly returned the empty hanger to the closet rod, determined not to let his opinion of her things get to her.

"Come on in. Make yourself at home." She led the way into the living room, making a wide, hospitable gesture. He stood at the entrance to the room in his sock feet, his amber eyes scanning her place in silence. She switched on a few lights, including the Christmas tree, casting her home in a soft glow. As she turned to face him, he was watching her with a strange focus. "Your husband die?"

Lindsay felt her jaw drop open. What business was it of his? "No, we're divorced."

"Why?"

She was about to tell him that her failed relationship was out-of-bounds when the irony hit her. If she wanted him to open up, maybe she should start with herself. "Dan and I never had one argument. Not even about our decision to break up. That was why we divorced. Our best conversation was when we admitted that we didn't love each other."

"You didn't figure that out before you got married?"

Lindsay shrugged. "There were no sparks, but we had lots in common. He was a director at an architectural firm. Still is.

We talked right before Christmas."

"You two still talk?"

"Sure. He and Seline are good buddies. I haven't told him about what has happened to her because I know he'll freak. He remarried and had a baby boy in September. Seline and I went to the baptism."

Jack stared. "You two still get together? What does his wife think of that?"

It was Lindsay's turn to stare. "I *introduced* her to him. After our divorce, she was a client and I thought they were perfect for each other. Turns out I was right. They're grateful to me."

Jack seemed to contemplate the floor for a long time. "Your business, Linds. I'm telling you, if you divorced me, I wouldn't speak to you again."

The finality of his words stunned her. "Why do you say that?"

"Because I'd marry for love. Why the hell would I want to be around someone who didn't love me back?"

Beneath the vehemence, there was a thread of sorrow Lindsay didn't understand. Then again, there was so much she didn't understand. "Well, seeing as how we're not married, I can't divorce you, so it looks as if we'll stay on speaking terms."

She thought her voice was light and calm, yet his eyes flared. "Let's get something straight. Just because we were friends half-a-lifetime ago, doesn't mean we're buddy-buddy now. I'm not Dan. I'm not someone you pick up and put down like"—he glared at Leo on the couch—"a stuffed animal. I'm here to help with your niece and that's it."

He was so cutting, so plain mean. She remembered the look in his eyes when he'd touched her hair, when he'd given his regrets in the cab over her parents' death. How could he be so different in such a short time? "Fine, then," she said, slow and precise. "I refuse to believe that you're really the bastard that you're behaving like now, but if you want to be one, I'm not taking it. I'm going for a shower. You can stand there and stew, or you can figure out what it means to make yourself at home and do that." She pointed at his parka. "And hang up your damn coat."

# CHAPTER
## SEVEN

IN HER ENSUITE bathroom Lindsay got busy with shampoo and conditioner, soaps and moisturizers. And steam. She let off a whole lot of that. Only after she bundled herself into pink flannel pjs, and her hair into a clip, did she seek out Jack. He was leaning against the kitchen counter, eating Cheerios from a large glass measuring cup, the open milk carton beside him. She peeked into the foyer. Parka and boots were gone.

She grinned. "See? You do know how to be civilized."

He scowled at her and kept spooning cereal into his mouth.

"And when you're done that," she sailed on, "it's your turn for the shower. There's a towel over the curtain rod for you." She moved into the living room.

He mumbled into his cup.

"Oh, you're welcome. I'll set up the couch for you."

The cup clattered into the sink, the fridge door opened and shut, and a moment later the shower was on.

She pulled open the couch into a bed and made it up exactly like when Seline's friends crashed for sleepovers, complete with soft white sheets, matching pillows and a down-filled comforter in burgundy and gold. Her lips twitched, and she arranged Leo so that he sprawled like a lounge lizard across the covers, belly-up, head on both pillows.

Humming now, Lindsay slipped into the bathroom and, diverting her eyes from what she knew would be a very clear outline of his body, she scooped up his clothes and tossed them along with hers into the washer. It was only when she was gazing into the soapy churning waters that she realized that she'd left him with nothing to wear.

She hurried into her bedroom and began rooting through her closet and drawers for something that might fit him and not make him seem a cross-dresser. Nothing. Seline would have something less fancy in her room, all too small. Then she remembered. Inspired she ran for the hallway storage closet and pulled out the box of Christmas decorations, which given that the joyous season had just passed, were thankfully near the front. What she wanted was right on top.

The shower shut off and Lindsay knocked on the door. "Jack, I put your clothes in the wash, but I found something for you to wear."

The door was opened a crack through which Lindsay wedged a pair of boxers. She held them out for an eternity. She gave them a shake. "Uh, they're new. They were a joke gift at the staff Christmas party. Long story. They haven't been worn before."

"Not by any self-respecting male, at least," Jack grumbled.

"It's either them or your birthday suit."

There was an even longer pause. "Jesus, Lindsay, have you looked at what these elves are doing to Santa? It's wearable pornography."

"Honestly, Jack, it's only you and me. And there's nothing else. You could wear a towel, I suppose, only as you can see they aren't exactly…er, masculine colors—"

Lindsay heard a low growl from a cornered male and then the underwear was yanked from her hand. She retreated down the hallway. Now would be a good time to check her messages. She reached for her smartphone on the kitchen counter, having deliberately left it there that morning.

Twelve text messages. All from Janice, each one peppered with more and more exclamation marks and unhappy faces. Lindsay grimaced. There was going to be hell to pay.

And it started halfway through the first ring. "Lindsay! Are you okay?"

"Yes, Janice. I just got back." She was fudging on that, though the upshot was the same.

"So you did go down there. What were you thinking?" She paused. "Did you find her?" Hope and fear were rushed together.

"No, we didn't, but we got a lead."

"What? A lead? Wait, no, who's 'we'?"

"Jack Cole."

"He came with you? You talked him into coming?"

That would've implied some sort of finesse on her part. "Sort of, yeah. Point is, he knows everybody who's anybody below ground, and the leader of a group down there connected us with people who know who Seline might've hooked up with."

"Hooked up with? Who?" Lindsay could sense Janice moving to her laptop to google them. That was Janice. Start with a google search and end with a coil-bound report.

"I don't think these people are linked into the web. They're…fringe types."

"Fringe? What do you mean? Lindsay. Please."

Lindsay heard all that was said in those last two words.

Forget about blood and names, Janice was part of their small family. "They're called APs. Short for aberrant psychology. They came out of mental institutions and there's one called Randa MacMurphy. We're going to meet with her tomorrow."

"Where?"

"I don't know. Jack will be getting in touch with her."

"You let me know and I can be close by. Okay?"

"Okay." The shower stopped. "Listen, Janice, I better go. Jack's almost done in the shower and we should head to bed."

"Jack's with you?" Shit. Why, why, why did she let that slip?

"Yes, Janice. He's sleeping on the couch. I'm sleeping in my bed."

"Why isn't he sleeping at his place?"

"It's occupied."

"Do you know that for a fact, or did he say so?"

"*Janice.*"

"Look. He seems like an intelligent man but he's down on his luck, and you're not doing badly and you were once good friends. He wasn't interested in helping and then he is. Sounds as if he did his own googling in the meantime and regrouped."

"Janice, it isn't like that."

"Then how is it?"

Lindsay did what she always did when avoiding pain. She got busy. There, for instance, was her pack which needed sorting.

"Janice, it doesn't matter what his motives are," she said, unzipping. "It only matters that he's doing it." The pack opened to Dee's jacket. A perfect distraction. "And like I said he's got lots of friends who can help. One of them even gave me a gift today, it's a gorgeous—"

Was this the same jacket? Under the foyer lights, its

colors were dull and mismatched, the mysterious symbols woven into its fabric lost. It looked as if it were cobbled together by a blind man.

"Pretty ugly, huh?" Jack's voice came from right behind her and she spun around.

For a man who'd lived two years underground and the past year only barely skimming the surface, he looked good. He was lean and muscled, with a natural athleticism. Water seemed to steam from his skin, and clung in droplets to his chest hair. Her eyes drifted to his midsection.

"No, not at all," she squeaked. "They're fine. Really."

Jack's eyes narrowed. "I was talking about the jacket."

"Is that Jack you're talking to?" Janice interrogated. "What's this about a jacket?"

Okay, she couldn't manage both Janice and Jack. "I'll call you tomorrow," she said into the phone. "Bye." She quickly disconnected. "That was Janice. A family friend. She was calling about Seline."

His answer surprised her. "I remember her. She and your mom were always together, cooking together, yapping together. My dad used to joke that it wasn't right that your dad had two wives and he had none."

Lindsay laughed. "Dad wouldn't have seen it that way. He always saw himself outnumbered."

"I can't remember your mom without remembering her, too."

"Yeah. When mom died, she really stepped up. I don't think I could have made it without her."

She paused, not wanting to drag her sad past out. Instead she held up the jacket. "Look at what Mrs. Moore gave me."

He accepted her cue. "Got a couple myself. Warm, but uglier than sin."

"It looked different there."

"Well, some things that look beautiful underground look ugly up here."

And vice versa, she thought, giving his body a sidelong glance.

"I'll show you some magic. You have any candles?" He walked into the living room and settled himself down on the couch-bed. He glanced at the playful pose of the huge plush lion, and then up at Lindsay. "You never give up, do you?"

She wasn't sure if he was annoyed or not. Either way she wasn't about to back down. "Not on what matters, I don't." She entered into a stare-down with him. Then deep in his eyes something flickered, and taking a pillow from underneath the stuffed head he began smothering Leo with it.

Lindsay gasped and pounced, landing on the pillow and tussling Jack for it. "That's cruel, Jack, and you know it."

He surrendered the pillow. "Has anyone told you that he's not real?"

"I know that!" She tossed aside the pillow and grabbed Leo, dragging his long bulk off the bed, taking him with her to the safety of an armchair. "It's just that...that Seline really liked him...and...and...haven't you noticed its eyes are exactly like yours?"

"What? Fake and unblinking?"

"No," she snapped. "Warm and bright and very nice."

He stared at her with eyes warm and unblinking. "Lindsay, get the candles."

She dropped Leo into the armchair and exited. The candles were in the bedside drawer as she'd expected, but she couldn't for the life of her find the holders, which should've been there, too. She rummaged through the drawer, bringing to the surface loose foil squares of condoms, a frustrating reminder of how sorry her love life had been lately. She had seriously wondered about going for her next birth control shot. It didn't help to know that a gorgeous, half-naked man was in the next room, sending off more mixed signals than a broken traffic light.

By the time she found first one holder, then another, she had become well and truly disgruntled. It didn't help her attitude any to see him stretched out by the Christmas tree, arm over his face, looking like a holiday centerfold. She unloaded the items on the coffee table with a deliberate clatter.

He lowered his arm. "I thought you'd wandered off completely. Where were you?"

Lindsay curled up with Leo and smiled prettily at him. "The bedroom, of course. Where else would I associate magic with candles? I brought a lighter, too."

She gloated over his suddenly wary look. *Good*, she thought, *no sense in only one of us being confused*. Jack swung himself into a sitting position and picked up the lighter. As he bent over the candles, she noticed on his left shoulder a crimson tattoo...no, a brand. It looked like one of the symbols she had seen in the tunnels, and on Dee's jacket. The mark was large, about the size of her hand, its shape vaguely resembling that of a spider.

She instantly rearranged her face into a mask of blandness the second he looked up, a hint of mischievousness playing across his features. "Turn off the lights. The tree, too."

She raised an eyebrow, but did as instructed, leaving the room in candlelight.

"Now look at the jacket again," he instructed softly. Jack held it up near the flames, and Lindsay grinned. It *was* magic. Dee's handiwork had reappeared in the dark, brilliant and beautiful.

"That's how it was made," Jack said, his voice still low. "By candlelight. It's not meant to be shown on television or in some store window. It's a work of subtlety."

She nodded, understanding. Without thinking she sat down beside him on the makeshift bed to better see the jacket. She became instantly aware that their bare thighs were only a handspan apart. To jump up would appear awkward to say the least, so she focused on her purpose for sitting down.

"What do all these markings mean?" she asked, running her hand over the woven symbols.

"They represent places in the underground," he answered, pointing. "That one is the MTA's 'money room', that's the gang tunnels under Chinatown, that's the labyrinth beneath Columbia University. Some are real, like Sumptown. Some, like The Burbs, used to exist once upon a time. And some are legendary, like Beach's City. They all carry a deeper meaning, too. Each place has a certain mood and history and imagery..." He trailed off. "Damn, I'm starting to sound like a professor again."

"You know, that's not a bad thing. You *are* a professor, Jack."

He shook his head, his profile dark and stony in the flickering light. "No. I'm not. Not anymore."

"Why not? What's keeping you from going back to work, or writing a book, or—"

"Maybe a talk show appearance?" he continued sarcastically. "Or perhaps an article in *People*?"

Any urge to wrap herself around his body was utterly gone. Unless it was her hands around his neck. "I don't get you, Jack."

"I know," he replied. "And trust me, that's a good thing."

She was about to give his attitude a dressing down when

her phone rang. Crap, she hadn't checked her land line. Maybe Seline—. She crawled across the couch bed and picked up the phone on the end table. "Hello?"

Silence.

"Hello? Anyone there?"

She thought she could hear breathing, slow and even, but nothing more. Despite the warmth of the apartment, a chill ran down her spine. She hurriedly hung up.

Jack was suddenly beside her. "Who was that?" His voice was low, sharp. His tension unnerved her. "Nobody. A crank caller, I guess."

"Check messages."

One look at his face and she did it. Thirteen messages. The first was silence and static. Same with the second. And the third. "There's no message. Whoever it is doesn't—"

Jack reached behind the table and yanked the cord from the jack. "You have other phones?"

"Yes. By the door and in the bedroom—"

"I'll do the one at the door. You do the bedroom." He was already walking away.

"Jack, what the hell is going on?"

"Move it! They're listening."

Fear and confusion tightening her gut, Lindsay hurried to her bedroom. When she returned she found Jack back at the couch, a brooding look on his face.

"Jack… what's going on?"

"I don't know."

"Bullshit!" she said angrily. "Don't you dare hold out on me."

When he spoke, it was in that same low voice he'd used underground, as if they were being spied on. "Every time you pick up the phone you make a connection, Linds, and it's not necessarily broken when you hang up. Someone's got your number, and they've been trying to eavesdrop on you."

"You're saying I'm being watched?"

"It's called a hook switch bypass," he explained. "They splice into the phone system and call you up. You answer it, get silence, hang up, and after that they can use your phone like a bug, listening in on you and all the calls you make."

"It's them isn't it? The people that have Seline."

Jack rolled his shoulders. "Perhaps."

"What do you mean 'perhaps'? How do you know about this phone stuff?"

"Calm down, Linds. It's probably nothing to worry about."

If he was trying to downplay the situation to not worry her, he was doing a shitty job. "Oh, right, of course. Someone's bugging my home, then you act like some guy from Homeland Security with all this unplugging, which is highly inconvenient. What happens if Seline calls? And you're telling me it's probably nothing to worry about? How about you humor me, pretend it *is* something to worry about, and tell me what the fuck is going on?"

"You wouldn't understand."

She lost it. Making a strangled noise, she lunged for Jack and knocked him back on the couch, her legs astride him, and pounded on his chest. "Fuck you, Jack. You talk to me. Talk!" she screamed into his startled face.

There was an inhuman snarl, and a second later her back hit the floor, the force of it crushing the air from her lungs. Jack was over her, one hand gripped around her throat, the other raised in a fist. Then, as fast as it had happened, he let go and yanked his body away, a sharp hiss of breath escaping his clenched teeth.

Her hand on her chest, she gasped for breath. He was at the window, his form silhouetted against the city lights, the muscles of his right arm trembling with unspent force—enough to have shattered bone.

He didn't move from there. "You okay?" His voice was hoarse as he choked out the question.

She could make out the flicker of the candles over the dark wood of the coffee table. Was she okay? What the hell kind of question was that? She drew herself up onto all fours and leaned against the couch bed. Only then did she make eye contact with Jack. He looked away and bowed his head. No matter that her neck was bruised from his grip, she wasn't the only one in pain.

"Yeah, Jack, I am," she replied as steadily as she could. "How about you?"

There was a long silence. "I know you have questions, Linds," he said from the shadows of the window, his voice hollow. "For now, I need you to trust me. I told you I'll help you find Seline, and I will, but we've got a long way to go, and I can't guarantee how this is going to turn out."

She sighed. "You didn't tell me how you were, Jack."

She heard the dull thud of his head as it hit the window frame. "I just attacked you after you invited me into your home. A woman who's already scared about someone else and now I've given her reason to be scared about her own life in her own home. How the fuck do you think I am? I'm sick. Fucking sick."

"Jack," she said, "you don't scare me."

He gave a short hitch of laughter. "I should, Linds. You've no clue what I'm capable of."

---

LINDSAY SLEPT POORLY that night, her dreams a nightmarish collage of the tunnels, Sumptown and Seline. She woke again and again, each time swearing she had heard her bedside phone ring, and when her alarm clock finally went off she felt more exhausted then when she'd gone to bed.

She wrapped her housecoat about her, and pulled back the curtains of her bedroom to reveal a dreary, overcast day. "Give me a break," she muttered and headed into the living room.

Jack was back in his own clothes, obviously having finished the laundry, and was leaning by the window, looking down at the streets below. In the exact same place she'd left him last night. She wasn't about to join him. She loved the view from her place, not the fact that she had to be ten floors up to get it. She got vertigo on a step stool, and would bribe Seline to wash the windows.

"Morning," she greeted him.

"You didn't sleep well," he responded, not taking his eyes from the scene below.

"No. I didn't," she said, surprised not so much by his observation, but that he would make it.

"I could hear you last night. Sounded like you were having bad dreams."

He was still not looking at her. She leaned her hip against the armchair, her arms crossed over her chest. "That why you have such a nice bed, Jack? You have bad dreams, too?"

"I need to go and see if I can find MacMurphy," he replied, changing the subject.

"How about some breakfast before you leave?"

He turned to her, and she saw that his amber eyes were as bloodshot as her own. "No, thanks. Not hungry."

"I think I figured something out last night," she said.

"What's that?"

"I think I know now why you don't have a phone. You were being spied on too, weren't you?"

He held her gaze for a long moment. They flashed with anger, and not a little anguish. He headed for the door, reaching it in a few strides. "I'll call as soon as I got news," he said, pulling on his coat and boots. "You can plug your phones back in. Disconnect them again if you get another one of those calls."

"Can I come with you?"

"No," he said, and the door slammed shut behind him.

Lindsay turned back to the living room. It was then that she saw it. Sprawled on his back, his head on the pillows was Leo, as she'd positioned him the previous night. Except now he wore the Santa boxers.

Perhaps the old Jack wasn't gone, just hidden beneath the surface.

# CHAPTER EIGHT

JACK WALKED THE cold streets alone, his mood as dark as the alleys around him. He'd spent the day asking around for MacMurphy, whose habit it was to roam New York transit like some modern day nomad.

He had gotten conflicting information. Rumor had it she'd knifed someone and been sent to Kirby, a hospital for the criminally insane. A call to the institution revealed that wasn't the case. He'd heard that she was hanging around at Columbus Circle, and South Ferry, and Queens Plaza. He hadn't found her at any of those places, either. Now it was nine in the evening, and his latest lead was taking him to a small coffee shop in the Bronx, a couple of blocks from the zoo, where MacMurphy was supposedly a regular.

He shoved his hands deeper into his coat pockets. All this day he'd been trudging around New York, but his mind had never left Lindsay.

His Chelsea home from when they were kids had been nothing like her apartment. He remembered the one time he'd brought her there. They'd stopped to pick up money before they'd headed out to the movies. While he'd rooted through the top ten places where his wallet could be, she'd stood inside the entrance and stared about with a pained expression. It opened his eyes to the stack of unwashed dishes, the toppled cans of pop, his jockey shorts on the back of the couch, the dust. He'd hurried her out and never brought her back.

The more things changed, the more they stayed the same. She'd turned up her nose at where he was living now, though it certainly wasn't because of the mess. It was as empty as he was.

One look at Lindsay's place and it was clear that he was in the presence of a warm, energetic and self-possessed woman. A woman who wouldn't normally seek his company, who was repulsed by the mean outcast he'd become. Sure, she'd go for coffee with him. That was a hell of a long way from wanting him like he wanted her, had wanted her even when—.

No. He wasn't going there.

It was a physical pain in his gut to know that he'd never be the man she'd want.

Nearly punching her in the face hadn't helped.

Of all the people in the world, the last person he thought himself capable of hurting was Lindsay. And yet he'd done it. He'd become his worst fear. A prodigy of the Moles. An animal that acted on instinct, ready to tear apart whatever got in his way. All he wanted to do was run from her, and yet it now had become even more important to restore Seline to her. To redeem himself, if only a little, in her eyes. Those clear blue eyes that had looked up at him as he held her in a stranglehold. Eyes that held no fear, nor even disbelief. Eyes that sought understanding, connection. They had pierced through his feral fury, called upon his higher self and he'd managed to pull away. She'd tried to reach out to him afterwards, only he hadn't trusted himself.

He didn't know what might happen if he touched her again.

He didn't know what might happen if he couldn't touch her again.

The softness of her hair and her cheek, the weight of her gloved hand in his, her knee tapping his—small incidents she would've thought ordinary but that had shaken him, awakened him to what it was to not feel caged and tormented.

And, in one savage moment, he'd blown it.

He pushed open the door of the tiny coffee house, and immediately registered the cool temperature. It felt almost as cold inside as it was on the streets. Aside from a couple of elderly men hunched over a chessboard at one table, and the bored-looking waitress padded in a sweater refilling their steaming coffees, there were only two other people in the place.

One was a huge man, noticeably bigger than even Reggie, whose combination of height, muscle and fat seemed to shrink the tables and chairs to kid-sized. The man's pale green eyes looked soft and bland, though from the prison tattoos on his neck and hands, Jack could tell this giant wasn't of the gentle variety.

As much presence as the brute had, however, it was to the woman beside him that Jack was pulled. She was thin, almost painfully so, with close-cropped red hair that made her sharp, weasel-like features seem even more severe. Her dark eyes contrasted with her pale, deadpan face, and were disturbingly wide. There was something in the stillness of her body, the watchfulness of her aspect that set her apart. She took in Jack's approach, no trace of emotion registering on her features.

The massive man rose before Jack like a human barricade. "It's all right, Hugo," said the woman, her voice carrying a strange sing-song lilt to it. "This man's a hero. You don't want to be getting in his way."

"MacMurphy?" Jack asked.

"Sit," she replied. It wasn't a request.

Jack wished he could refuse her, except she was his only hope and apparently she knew it. He was at the disadvantage, and he hated, really hated, the feeling of being cornered. But he'd given his word to Lindsay, and he'd hate himself even more if he couldn't keep his promise.

He took the seat across from the woman, pulling it away from the table, well beyond arm's reach of Hugo.

MacMurphy tilted her head. "You've been looking for me."

"Yes," he replied. "I need to find a topsider named Seline Sterling. She went missing in the underground about a week and a half ago."

The woman gave him a blank stare, then picked up her cup and sipped gingerly from it, as if it were scalding hot. When she set it down, Jack saw that it was empty.

"I understand," he pressed on, "that she made friends with some of your people at Grand Central. I was hoping you might be able to tell me what happened to her."

She flipped open the lid on her small metal teapot and swirled the teabag string. "Why are you still in New York, Cole?"

Jack wasn't surprised by the change of subject—one had to expect such things from APs—but he was irked that it had changed to him. "I live here."

"Why? A man like you could live anywhere. What keeps you in *this* city?"

"I'm not here to get psychoanalyzed. Can you help me or not?"

The trace of a smile nudged at the corner of Mac-Murphy's mouth. It wasn't a pleasant one. "You're in the dark, Cole. It's been a year since you clawed your way out of the tunnels yet you still can't see a thing. So, let me turn on a light for you. What is it that keeps you in this city?" She lifted out the teabag. It was dry.

He didn't want to answer her question, because to do so would only sink him further into his quagmire of churning emotions. "I'm not playing games here, MacMurphy."

"Neither am I," she answered.

For a long time there was cold silence between the two, each eyeing the other like predators standing over a kill.

"The tunnels," Jack said at last, spitting out his admission as if it were blood from a fistfight. "The tunnels keep me here."

The woman inclined her head. "That's right. You only thought you escaped. Really you're still down there, and you know why? Because that's where you belong."

Jack felt his muscles tighten, his hands twitch inside his coat pockets. He wanted to strangle her, make her wide, rodent eyes see that he was not what she'd reduced him to. Yet even in his anger he knew that what he really wanted was to strangle that tiny voice in him that forever whispered the same thing.

He forced himself to hold it together. "Where's Seline?"

"Connect the dots, Cole," MacMurphy answered, her lyrical voice quickening. "You know where she is." She tipped the teapot over her cup. Nothing came out. "You're a smart man," she continued. "A very smart man. You know what happened to the girl, so the only question left is the biggest one. Why?"

"Are you saying," Jack had to push the words past his anger, "that you helped them?"

"Helped them? Well, I figured out who your 'fantasy girl' was. It was a bit confusing... Lindsay, Tasha... but hey, ten years of being psychoanalyzed taught me how to unravel a few mental knots. We couldn't actually get Ms. Sterling underground, then what do you know? Her only flesh-and-blood turned out to be a bleeding heart, so anxious to help us poor downtrodden street people. All it took was a few sob stories and she was within their reach. No, no, I wouldn't say that we helped *them*."

MacMurphy's smile grew into a wide, maniacal grin.

"Don't you see, Cole? We helped *you*."

---

LINDSAY CRAWLED THROUGH Manhattan's rush hour, her hands gripped on the steering wheel, her body rigid with frustration. It had been almost two days since Jack had walked out of her apartment, and not a word from him.

On the first day she reasoned that he was busy pounding the pavement, looking for MacMurphy. She'd gone to the office, met with clients, contemplated cabinets and fixtures.

She'd slept last night, comforted by the thought that he'd probably call in the morning. Today had come and nearly gone in silence. Again she'd gone in to the office, except this time she hadn't been able to concentrate on anything. She was frustrated, she was angry, but more than anything, she was scared. Scared that the underground had swallowed up another person she cared about.

And she *did* care about Jack, something she wouldn't have thought possible a mere three days ago. Her teenage crush had turned into a brooding stranger, yet he still fascinated her, filling her heart with a cacophony of emotions.

"I must be going crazy," she muttered, and the fact that she was talking to herself proved it. "At this rate I'll be ready to join the APs myself."

Her cell rang, and in a fraction of a second it was at her ear.

"It's me."

Relief washed over her so hard and fast her every muscle turned to jelly. She hadn't realized how tightly she was wound, how much she had feared for him.

"You there?" He sounded annoyed. Her cranky Jack was back.

"Jack! I've been worried about you. Where have you—"

We have to talk, Lindsay," he interrupted her. "I need you to meet me."

He didn't sound well.

"Where?"

"I'm about a block from your apartment. A coffee shop called 'Big Cup'. You know it?"

"One of my favorite places," she replied. "I'll be there as soon as I can."

She was there in less than half an hour. The establishment was large and colorful, both its staff and customers trendy and upbeat. As a result, Jack stood out like a sore thumb, even though he'd consigned himself to the back of the room, nursing his coffee below the sign for the washrooms.

He sat slouched, his face shadowed by a couple days' worth of stubble, and now had dark rings to go with his bloodshot eyes. He looked even worse than he had sounded on the phone.

He must've learned something terrible. Her heart contracted. She took wooden steps across the floor and slid into the seat opposite him.

"I found MacMurphy," he said, his voice raw. "The APs lured Seline into the tunnels. They were the ones that told her about Reggie's door and about the communities. They set her up to go down there."

"Is she—?" Lindsay stopped. She could not breathe.

"She's alive. That's the good news."

Lindsay closed her eyes and let Jack's words flow through her. For the second time in an hour sweet relief softened her limbs. "Thank God." Seline was alive. She hadn't been searching in vain. She opened her eyes. "What's the bad news?"

He glanced away. "The situation isn't as clear-cut as we thought it was."

"Talk to me, Jack." That's what she'd asked two nights ago and it hadn't ended well.

He locked his gaze on hers, and she knew he was thinking the same thing. His bloodshot eyes were full of anguish and desperation. "I will, Lindsay, but you have to believe what I tell you. I didn't say anything earlier because I didn't want you thinking I'm crazy, only now you have to know what we're really dealing with. You have to believe. If not for me, then for Seline."

She didn't even blink. "Okay, Jack."

He leaned forward in his chair and she followed suit, their faces inches from each other. His voice lowered to a near whisper.

"I've spent my whole life exploring tunnels, Linds. Beneath London and Paris. Rome and Moscow. I've gone deep beneath all those cities, and I've found…things. Things I never wrote about. Things nobody at the universities would ever have accepted.

"The symbols in New York's tunnels, like the ones

embroidered on Mrs. Moore's jacket—they're under all those cities, too. I took pictures of them to show linguists and cryptographers, but they're not related to any known language. They're unique, and they represent a global subterranean culture."

He hesitated for a moment, his eyes boring into hers.

"I was fascinated by the idea that a world-spanning culture of tunnel dwellers might exist. In each city, Lindsay, there are legends, some going back hundreds of years, about people who live far underground. In Italy they're called *Latente*. In France they're *Ombres*. In England, the Rawheads. That's what brought me back to New York. Here they're known as Moles, and every tunnel person knows about them."

She, too, was now leaning forward. "And you found them, didn't you?"

"Yes. In the deep tunnels. I wound up getting captured by them." Strain lined his face at the memory. "They dragged me into the dark, and I didn't see light again until I escaped almost two years later. When I made it to the surface I was practically blind, and when I went home...."

He trailed off, his mouth pressed into a thin line of sorrow. Lindsay ached to touch him. He would hate her for it, though.

"What?" she prompted softly.

"Never mind...the thing is, Lindsay, the Moles exist. The whole world might think I'm crazy, but it's a fact. It's them that are holding Seline. They're the ones that kidnapped her."

"Why?"

His gaze shifted slightly upwards. Her hair. "Because of you," he answered quietly. "I told them about you, Lindsay, and they wanted you, but settled for Seline. They're trying to lure me back down, and your niece is the bait."

Lindsay was in shock. "I don't...." She already had so many questions for Jack before this meeting, and now that he'd finally told her something, her mind was ready to explode. She tugged free one question from the mess. "Why did you tell them about me?"

He looked at her bleakly. "Linds, I went half-insane down there. I lost all sense of time, of place. My memories were like a deck of cards. They became shuffled and after a while, a few went missing, others got bent out of shape." He gave a quick, bitter smile. "I wasn't playing with a full deck.

"I don't know exactly what all I told them, Linds. I do know that I told them about you and me going together into the tunnels when we were kids. I probably told them what you looked like—though the description would match Seline now more than you. We...we only went down that once, right?"

Lindsay nodded.

"Yeah, that's what I thought. And...and what exactly happened that time, Lindsay?"

She tried not to appear alarmed at Jack's confusion. His face was dangerously pale. "You were going to take me to meet some homeless guy you knew. When we got to his place, it had been trashed...and there was blood on the wall and floor."

"Was there...was there anybody there?"

"No, not that we saw. We got out as fast as we could. We told your dad, only he—"

"—didn't believe us." Jack finished flatly. "Still doesn't. Still wants me to forget about it all and get on with my life."

"Oh." Lindsay wasn't sure what to say. She knew that Jack and his father had been close.

"He remarried, my dad. A few years back. To a French woman, I can't even remember her name. She didn't understand English very well and he doesn't know French. I don't know how they got married."

"Maybe it was a mistake," Lindsay said. "Maybe he was only asking her out to the movies."

Jack's mouth crooked into a smile, and Lindsay felt good that for one moment she'd taken away a little of his pain. It was only for one moment. His face fell back into its drawn lines. "The thing is, Lindsay, is that what you said happened down there is not what I told them. Not after a while, at least. In my mind it seemed as if we went down there an awful lot, that we had all these bizarre adventures. We were down there for a week at a time, we painted murals, we discovered un-heard-of communities, you name it, we did it.

"It was only when I came up that I realized that it couldn't have happened that way. It was like coming out of a dream. This is the thing, Linds, the Moles must've known that I was making up stories. The underground is their world, so they would've known when I was lying. Yet they encouraged my delusions, built on them. Why? Because they were trying to make me into a new person. They were feeding me new memories."

"I don't get it."

"You saw my brand."

"Yes, did they—?"

"Yes. They marked me as theirs. It's a symbol found in all the undergrounds that I've been to. It's linked their race together for centuries, maybe millennia. We topsiders never realized it. No one had made a study of it the way I did. In me, they'd finally found someone to carry their messages from one underground to another.

"I was supposed to become that spider, spinning a web between them all. They were going to make me anew, make me into a hybrid of the surface world and theirs. They slowly recreated my past to make it seem that I was more and more like them. Did it to make me sympathetic to their cause."

"I'm their hope, Linds. Their experiment. I found a way out, and now they're trying to get me back down there. Into the lab, so to speak." He seemed so lost and defeated. Lindsay felt a surge of hatred for the Moles, for what they'd done to him. She felt horrible asking him anything more, but she needed to know...and oh hell, he knew how to tell her to shut up.

"Jack. What—what exactly are they?"

He fell back against his chair. "Not human," he replied, wincing even as he said it. "They're intelligent, so maybe they were human once. Now they're more like"—he seemed to struggle for words then shrugged—"they're like nothing on the surface. Nothing I've ever heard of anywhere."

"Do they look human even? Like the way chimps look human?"

"There's nothing I can really compare them to," he answered, rubbing his eyes. "They don't stay in one form like normal creatures. They can compress or extend their bodies, lock their joints, switch between being stocky or lanky, a biped or a quadruped. Some are even born with more limbs, or maybe they grow them as they age. The things live in total darkness, yet they can alter the texture of their skin, squeeze themselves through tiny spaces. Whatever form they're in, they're always like something out of a fucking nightmare."

He grimaced. "Shit. This is why I never told anyone, Linds. Who the fuck would believe something like that, especially from someone like me?"

She frowned. "What's that supposed to mean? 'From someone like me'? You're a professor. You've done groundbreaking research and published papers. Why wouldn't you be believed?"

"Look at me, Linds!" he snapped. His outburst drew looks from some of the other patrons, and gritting his teeth he lowered his voice. "Tell me what you'd think I was if you didn't know me. Go on. Tell me."

She wasn't standing for this. "Don't you try that bullshit on me, Jack Cole. You want me to tell you that you're a pathetic loser that no one in their right mind would give a dime to, much less five minutes of their attention. I'm telling you that what you need is"—she began tapping a list off on her fingers—"a shower, a hot meal and a long sleep. And I know a place a block away where you can get it all." She reached for her purse.

He didn't move. "It's too late for that, Linds," he said quietly. "I'm going back down now. I'm going to get Seline."

Lindsay's grip on her purse tightened. "You mean *we're* going to get her back."

Jack shook his head. "Don't even go there, Lindsay."

"So you're going to waltz down there and rescue her by yourself?"

His expression was grim. "This is my fault. All of it. So I'm going to damn well try."

With that he got up from the table. She had to stop him. "Wait till tomorrow."

"I've got to go. I'll have Reggie get in touch with you if there's any news."

"Jack, come home with me. Get cleaned up. I'll cook you a meal and you can get a good night's sleep. If you're going down there, at least get yourself together first."

He looked at her, pain in his amber eyes. He was going to refuse her, even though she knew he didn't want to. A different tactic occurred to her.

"Fine. Go. Only don't think I won't follow if you don't come back, and you can bet Reggie will be with me. You're not the only one who knows the underground."

The pain in his eyes switched to anger. "You leave Reggie out of this."

"Why? You think he wouldn't work with me to get you back?"

"Because it would be suicide! Reggie feels guilty over something that happened years ago between us. He doesn't need to but he does, and he doesn't need you talking him into something stupid."

"You two were friends before your capture?"

"Yeah."

"And you're friends now?"

"Of course we are. So what?"

She stood. She had to make him see right now, because she knew that if he walked out the door without her, she would've lost him, and if the fear of the past two days were any indication, it would be like losing her family all over again. "The Moles messed with your mind, not with mine, not with Reggie's. We've still got the real Jack. We know who you are better than you do. That's why you asked me about our time in the tunnels, because you know I know the truth about you. That's why Reggie is in your life, because he knows who you really are, too. And because he knows who you are, he's not going to abandon you any more than I will."

She and Jack were as close together as two people could be without touching. Another inch and their chests would be touching, another two and she could hold his hand, another three and they'd be kissing. If her words didn't work, she'd move onto doing that, right here in public. She didn't care. "If you think you can walk out that door alone, Jack, then you really are deluded, because Reggie and me have a claim on you that beats anything those Moles have. We're in you as deep as those tunnels are. You might want to do this alone but you can't."

She let out a long breath. She was done, though she wasn't sure she'd gotten through. His body had gone still during her speech and his expression was flat. It was his move and she could stand here until he made it.

When he did, when he whispered his answer, it was a good thing she'd said all she'd wanted to because she was suddenly too choked to have said anything.

"Take me home, Linds. I can't be alone, anymore."

# CHAPTER NINE

*JACK WATCHED THE Mole through the bars of his cage. There was not enough space to comfortably sit, lie or stand, so over time he'd adjusted to a hunched crouch.*

*It approached, its reeking metallic scent no longer bothering him, and held out a squealing rat in its claw. It slid the animal between the bars. Wordlessly, Jack accepted it.*

*The vermin struggled to sink its incisors into his hand. Jack tightened his grip and crushed the life from it, blood seeping between his fingers. He skinned it with his teeth and nails, then began to eat.*

*"What day is it?" came the Mole's voice, cracking and cold as the ice of the Hudson.*

*Jack gulped down a lump of stringy flesh, gore hanging from his ragged beard. "I don't know," he answered hoarsely.*

*"How did you get here?"*

*Jack shuffled in the cage. More than one question was never good. "I...I'm not sure. I followed someone. I don't know."*

*"What is your name?"*

*He set aside the remains of the rat. Questions made his mind hurt too much to eat.*

*"What is your name?" the keeper repeated. It wasn't going to wait much longer for a reply.*

*"Jack."*

*"Wrong."*

*Jack rested his head against the bars, his face screwed up in pained concentration.*

*"What is your name?"*

*"Jack...my name is Jack."*

*His keeper reached forward with a key, undoing cage's padlock. Swinging open the door, it took Jack firmly by the arm, pulling him forward. He shuffled out, remaining in his ape-like posture.*

*The first time he'd been let out he'd tried to run. That only made things much, much worse. They'd thrown him in the pit till his feet had swollen, his skin had peeled, his wounds had run with pus. In the end he'd been screaming, clawing at the slimy walls, weeping to be let out. Only then had they hauled him up, buckled him down, and fed something into his veins that had allowed him to survive.*

*Now he obediently loped after the Mole, down the black corridors where even his razor-sharp night sight failed. It didn't matter. He knew all too well where he was going. He'd been through this countless times. It was inevitable, and anything was better than the water pit. Even this.*

*Pushed onward he fumbled till his fingers met the cold metal of the gurney. His heartbeat quickened, his breath came in ragged gulps.*

*"Get up," hissed the voice.*

*His body began to shake, even as he did as he was told. He was strapped down, thick leather bands tight around his wrists, ankles and chest. He waited, trying to slow his gasping breaths. Still a whimper escaped and his lips trembled.*

*A rubberized cord was tightened painfully around his arm, a needle was stabbed in, then withdrawn. There was a dab of antiseptic, then again his keeper hovered close.*

*"What is your name?"*

*He'd tried lying before, tried guessing what they wanted to hear. It never worked. The injection dropped him fast into a fevered delirium, robbing him of the ability to invent anything believable.*

*He could feel his body warming, a toxic cloud spreading over the folds of his brain, and the darkness before his eyes swirled with forms and faces that couldn't possibly be there.*

*"Jack..." he whispered.*

*There was a pause, then the sharp metal teeth of a clamp bit down on his right nipple. He gritted his teeth, fighting against the fear and pain, but tears began to stream from his eyes as more clamps were attached to his naked body. His other nipple. The skin between his fingers. His earlobes. His testicles.*

*"Open your mouth."*

*His head ached with fever as he complied, and a thick rubber mouth guard was shoved inside and strapped behind his head.*

*Then the shocks began.*

*His body lurched and twisted at his restraints, the metal bars of the gurney rattling as he slammed his body against them. Shock. Rest. Minutes maybe, or perhaps seconds. Shock. Repeat. Again and again till his muscles twitched spasmodically.*

*After a time he lost what could have been called consciousness, and when he regained it, he was on the floor. His body was curled into a trembling ball, choked sobs bubbled out and his mind still sizzled in poisons.*

*"What is your name?"*

*It took him a minute to make his mouth work, to utter anything more than a pitiful gibbering through his cracked lips. "I...I...I don't know."*

*There was a long pause. "Good," came the emotionless reply. "Now we can begin to find the answers to these questions together."*

*His arms were gripped and he was dragged back to his cage. Inside he coiled himself up, his naked body thin and shaking, long filthy hair obscuring his sunken face. His name was the last thing that could be taken from him. The last mark on an otherwise blank slate. His last crumbling hold on identity—except for her.*

*His bony fingers curled around the thin steel bars, long blackened nails biting into his palms.*

*Tasha, he whispered to himself. Her name is Tasha.*

---

HE WOKE WITH a scream still on his lips. All was quiet in the darkened room, and moaning, he pressed himself flat against the white sheets on Lindsay's bed, taking deep breaths to calm his pounding heart. He hoped to God he'd gotten away with it as he had in Sumptown. For a moment all was quiet and he began to relax.

"Jack?" came her voice from outside the bedroom door.

Dammit. "I'm okay...just a dream," he called, trying to keep his voice even. The bedroom door cracked open. Of course. Had he really thought she would go away? Despite what he'd told her earlier in the coffee shop, there was a huge difference between not wanting to be alone and knowing how to be with others.

"I brought you some water," Lindsay said.

He sighed. Might as well as let her in because there was no keeping her out. "Sure."

The door swung fully open, and Lindsay appeared with a large glass of water in her hand.

He sat up in bed, taking it from her. "Thanks."

"You're welcome," she replied and watched as he downed it.

He handed the empty glass back to her. Rather than leaving, she seated herself beside him, her form gently illuminated by the moonlight filtering through the window. When he'd gone to bed she was fully clothed. Now she was in a thin, silky nightie that glided over breasts and behind.

Her lips curved. "Guess even a good bed doesn't always help."

Not without a good woman in it. He tugged his gaze away from her front and it collided with the bright mass of her hair. He tried to focus. "I told you to let me take the couch again."

"How is it that you could sleep down in Sumptown, and not here?"

"I didn't. You never woke up, that's all."

She leaned back on one hand, causing her body to curve so nicely before him, presenting a place on her hip where his hand would fit perfectly. "Sounds like you don't get much rest."

Her hair swept about her shoulders and his fingers twitched to reach for it. "Insomnia becomes a lifestyle after a while," he said.

"There are cures for it, you know."

His cock hardened in agreement. He needed her in bed or out of the room. Her being *on* the bed was killing him. "If you say so."

She gave a soft growl of annoyance. "I know so."

He gave in. He touched her hair. It was meant to be a quick, one-time gesture, but his hand slipped through her hair again and again, lifted the strands upward until the moonlight caught them, then filtered them through his fingers. Lindsay tilted her head back, sinking into the simple caress, and Jack automatically cupped his hand around her neck to give support. His thumb began gently stroking the softness of her throat. She made a low purring noise.

Too far. Don't make this painful.

"Linds—" he whispered. Her palm passed over his mouth in a gentle request for silence, then traveled downward past his throat and across his chest.

"Linds," he repeated uncertainly. "What are you doing…?"

Her lips moved dangerously close to his own. "What would you like me to do?"

Jack could not have her this close and not do something. "Stop me," he said, then curling his fingers back into her hair he closed the gap between them.

The kiss was hard. Vital. And as it deepened Jack was spurred by a raw need that sent his heart racing with fear as much as lust. Again, he tried to pull back. She followed him, leaning her body over his, the soft weight of her breasts upon his chest.

"Don't run from me, Jack," she whispered into his mouth.

"I don't want to hurt you, Linds."

"You won't. I want you, Jack. I want you."

His fingers tightened in her hair, his other hand moving over the curve of her breast, and not gently.

His mouth still on hers he pushed her onto her back, then grabbing hold of her nightgown, he pulled it up, breaking the kiss only long enough to bring it over her head. It caught around her wrists, and straddling her Jack looked down. Her arms were bound over her head, her chest heaving, breasts bare and nipples hard.

She looked up at him in the darkness, trusting, wanting, begging him to give into his carnal instincts. He felt the rise of the caged animal inside him, the dirty inhuman thing that tore at flesh. In an instant he was off her, away from the bed, slamming his hands against the wall and leaning there, eyes shut tight.

Silence.

"Jack..."

"I can't, Linds...I can't undo what they did. I won't hurt you. Not you."

He stood there, facing the wall, teeth clenched in frustration. In humiliation.

He heard her slide from the bed. *Go, Linds. Go!*

But when had she ever listened to him? Her arms slid around him, and she pressed her naked torso against his toughened back, her head resting against his shoulder blade.

"Hey," she said softly. "Back when we were teenagers, did you know that I had a huge crush on you?"

He remembered her smiling up at him as he came up alongside her locker. "No. No, I didn't."

"Or, for that matter, that practically all eight hundred girls in the school did?"

He felt the hard lump inside him ease. He turned inside her arms until he was facing her, and there didn't seem anything for it, except to let his own arms come around her, too. His back was against the wall, and she leaned against him, the two of them falling into the classic pose of smitten teenagers. "No. I didn't know about the eight hundred, either. If I had, it would've made dating a lot easier."

She made a noise. "If you're not picky."

His arms tightened around her. "Yeah, but I was. That's why I didn't know about the other eight hundred. I only had eyes for you."

Her eyes widened and then he lost sight of them as she pressed her cheek against his chest. "That's something the old Jack would say."

He thumb-stroked her spine. "I'm not sure that he exists anymore, Linds. Sometimes I don't know if he ever did."

She pushed away from him, the fierceness of her move belied by her huge grin. "That I can prove beyond a doubt." Naked, she ran to her walk-in closet and with a thump and a crash, hauled out a storage tub. "Come. Look."

He came over as she stripped the lid off. "Can you see? Do you want a light?"

He shook his head in answer to her questions and in disbelief at what he saw. A box filled with him. Letters and postcards from him, framed pictures of them together and a rock the size of a cabbage.

"The atacamite. You kept this?" He crouched down and touched its roughness.

She grinned. "For my fifteenth birthday. You remember?"

"Yeah. I'd found it down in the tunnels. Some hole in a wall. It was shoved way back on this ledge, and I don't even know why I hauled it out. When I did, I realized that it wasn't just any old rock—"

"Oh no," Lindsay said and lifted it out, kneeling to set it on her lap. "Not just any old rock would do for me."

"It wasn't. It had bright green crystals growing on it…that are normally only found in the driest deserts. I remember wondering how it got there. It wasn't all that valuable money-wise, those crystals grow in Arizona—"

"You telling me that I've been packing around a worthless rock?"

"—so why go to all the trouble of storing it away? That was the only thing down there in the hole, I checked all—" Jack stopped. She hadn't forgotten him. Ever. This woman with all her compulsion for things to be neat and complete, had packed away a memory of him, no matter that it was heavy and awkward and probably dirty. "Why would you do this? Why keep all this when you wouldn't even keep in touch with me?"

She rubbed the rock over and over. "After my family passed," she whispered, "it wasn't that I didn't need you. It was that I needed you too much and I'd nothing to give back. That's why I shut myself off."

Oh, Christ. She'd said it. She'd said exactly what was happening to him. He needed her memories, her grip on life, her need for *him*.

He reached for her, his hand fisted into her hair. His touchstone to reality. She would know he wanted her, but not the way she deserved. "Linds, I could do all kinds of things with you, right here, right now. I could mate with you, I could copulate, fornicate, I could…fuck you. That's what they left me. I can't make love to you. Do you understand?"

In answer, she set the rock back into the tub and pressed her mouth to his, stroked his tongue with hers, teased his lips with her teeth. Then she pulled back until their lips barely touched.

"Then fuck me, Jack."

That was enough.

He hauled her up against him, tumbled the both of them

back onto the bed, lifted her so she was fully on the mattress, completely at his disposal. She laid there, lips open, legs parted, her breasts—. He clamped his mouth over a hard nipple and she gasped; he sucked and the gasps deepened to moans.

He cupped his hand between her legs and stroked her wet folds, and her moans deepened into something guttural. He sprung his mouth free to watch her face, her lower lip trembleing, her eyelids squeezed shut from the sensation. Her breathing matched his, ragged and distorted with want. He raised himself to a kneeling position alongside her. Ran his free hand over her breasts, her ribs, her hips, squeezing and kneading her curves with raw abandon, his touch rough and hot and urgent.

Her mouth opened in a pant, and he shifted the hand between her legs upwards, a fingertip finding her clit, stroking it, his heart pounding. She laid before him, eyes still closed, her legs splayed, her hips still rotating in time as his finger played with her sex—primed and ready for fucking as any woman had ever been. His cock stood straight and hard, bumping the curve of her side, and wrapping his hand into her hair he suddenly thrust two fingers deep inside her tight channel. She yelped, her eyes snapped open...and she gave him a wide smile.

He pumped his fingers in and out of her as she arched and thrashed beneath him. Her body rose straight off the bed until only her shoulders and feet were on the sheets, then collapsed back down, her pussy gripping his fingers. He didn't stop, and neither did she, till at last she came, hard and long and loud.

He slid his fingers from her warm cavity and held them before her, glistening fluid trickling down to his palm, then brought them to her mouth. Lindsay sheathed her mouth over his fingers, sucked them strong and deep, flicked her tongue on their undersides with pornographic hunger what his cock ached for. The display was so hot his every muscle screamed for her. Yes it was lust, but it was *his* lust. His choice. He who wanted her.

His balls tight, he straddled her, then leaned forward on one hand until his cock tip touched her navel. The tickle of her sweaty indentation pulsed through his shaft and he had to pause, get control. A soft, laugh-tinged sigh escaped from her mouth past his fingers. He eased forward on his knees, his cock trailing upward along her mid-line until it rested between her breasts.

He watched her mouth, waiting for the moment to replace his fingers with his cock when her hands came down and mashed her soft breasts around him. Fuck, *fuck*. His cock began to ride between the white mounds. He rocked himself and she rolled and massaged, the dark tip of his hardness pushing free of her breasts. He could come like this, spill onto the pale column of her neck. Much more of this and he would. Painful as it was, he lifted away from her, a bead of pre-cum suspended there. Her mouth immediately opened to catch it. He brought his moist tip forward, rested it on her lower lip. Her tongue skimmed the head, and rising above her and changing his angle, he slid further past her lips, into her mouth.

Fingers entwined in her hair, he worked his hardness back and forth along her hot, slippery tongue. His hips thrust, using her mouth. Again, it was getting too much, and he pulled free, his shaft slick with her saliva.

Every muscle in his body corded with need, burning to connect completely with her, and by the look in her eyes there was no doubt she burned for it too. He eased away and aligned himself with her wet pussy. She whimpered and bucked up her hips, her eyes pleading for all of him.

"You still want me to fuck you?"

Her answer was a quick and hard surrender. "Yes!"

He filled her in one smooth thrust and his name ripped from her throat. Jack fucked her with deep, pounding strokes and she paid him back as her nails raked his shoulders, and scored his back. She cried and gasped his name but he couldn't speak, couldn't form a single coherent thought. All he could feel was her, and he drowned himself in the act of simply fucking her, letting that animalistic need tear through as he drove into her as deep and hard and savagely as he could. His muscles and mind ran white hot, and when she yowled in orgasm, felt her sex constrict around him, it threw him over the edge. He roared as he emptied every drop of himself into her core, and his mind went blank for what seemed like forever

# CHAPTER TEN

TASHA.

He had to tell Lindsay about Tasha. It was his first thought upon waking. He laid in her bed, still mostly asleep, his eyes not yet open but the clarity of his resolution was as bright and certain as the noonday sun. Once Lindsay knew about her, she would understand his insanity, he could find a way back to her. And after sex with her, he wanted that more than anything. He had thought he'd be an animal with her. Instead, it had made him feel halfway human again.

They'd slept in the same bed last night. After, she'd flipped out of bed and gone to the bathroom, a feat he'd thought miraculous given that he couldn't move a muscle. When she'd emerged, he expected her to return to the couch. Instead she climbed back into bed and pulled the covers over the both of them. He'd panicked with anticipation and dread that she wanted to cuddle, have pillow talk. All she did was snuggle into the other side of the bed and mumble, "I'm beat. Let's talk in the morning." She was asleep two heartbeats later. And listening to her gentle breathing, he'd followed close behind.

Now, floating in a cloud of sleep, he reached for her. All

he got was a rumpled sheet. He jerked awake. She was gone, and there was too much morning light in her room. He read the clock on her bedside table. Quarter past nine. *Shit.* He couldn't remember the last time he'd slept that long without the aid of a pill.

He cocked his head to listen. Silence.

Jack pulled on his jeans as he took the hallway to the living room. The couch bed was already tucked away. No one except for that damn stuffed lion. Where the hell was she? Had she gone to work? Why, when she herself had said that they'd talk in the morning?

He stood in her empty apartment and in crept a paralyzing fear. She regretted last night. After all, she not tried to touch him afterwards. It was something he might do, not something he pictured Lindsay wanting. Then why had she even slept in the same bed with him? Fuck. He did not need these mind games.

He heard the key in the lock and hit the foyer at the same time the door opened.

"Where the hell were—?" He broke off when he saw who was behind Lindsay. Reggie was holding a cup of takeout coffee in each hand, one of which he shoved at Jack. The big man took in Jack's bare feet and mussed hair, and his face lit up in congratulatory pride.

"Mornin', Jack! Slept well, huh? Had yourself some sweet dreams?"

Lindsay was at the closet, unzipping herself out of a fleece-lined suede jacket, uncovering a breast-molding sweater underneath. He kept his mind focused. "What's Reggie doing here?"

"You know, Jack, you have this very silly habit of referring to people in your presence in the third person," she observed. She shut the closet door and headed to the kitchen with a bakery bag. His stomach squeaked in longing for its contents.

Jack turned to Reggie. "What's with her?"

"See what I mean?" Lindsay called over the clatter of dishes.

This was not what he'd planned. Not that he'd come up with anything solid. He needed to talk to Lindsay about last night. That wasn't going to happen with Reggie here. He scowled at his best friend. "What the hell you doing here?"

Reggie squared himself before Jack. "What, no poor black folk allowed in Chelsea?"

"That's not what I mean and you know it," Jack growled. "I'm asking what you're doing *here*."

Lindsay popped her head around the corner. "I invited him. Come on. Let's have something to eat."

Jack stared at her. "You invited him? For breakfast?"

Reggie kicked off his boots and made for the kitchen, as if breakfast at Lindsay's was an everyday occurrence. "Lindsay told me the Moles took Seline 'cause they're trying to get you back. She told me that you two were coming up with a plan and said I should be part of that."

Jack's coffee rose to the brim as his grip tightened on the cup.

"Nice place, Lindsay," he heard Reggie comment. "You know I have a buddy who can get you some real nice stuff, real cheap...."

Jack simmered in the foyer as the two chatted on about décor, then made to follow them.

That's when he heard a key in the lock and the door open as far as the chain would allow. "Yoo-hoo, Lindsay!"

Lindsay swept by him on her way to the door. "Janice!"

Janice was as he remembered her—a broad-hipped woman who wore color. Her full-length red coat opened onto a dress that looked ready to ignite. And her boots...her and Lindsay shopped the same places. She set down a grocery bag and gathered Lindsay in a hug, and took him in over her shoulder. He became acutely aware he was shirtless and in his bare feet.

"So you're Jack Cole. All grown up."

He stuck out his hand. "Yes, I am, and I remember you," he said, hoping his politeness masked the fact that he looked like a beach bum. "I know I've changed but you haven't aged a day."

Janice made a sound that indicated she wasn't big on flattery. She removed her coat. "Hang that up for me, will you Jack? I thought you two would like a surprise breakfast. That is, if you haven't already eaten."

Picking up the grocery bag, Janice headed for the kitchen, Lindsay trailing after her. While he did coat-check duties, he heard Janice meet Reggie.

"Oh... hello."

"Janice, this is Jack's friend, Reggie."

"Would you look at the size of you? Good thing I got an extra carton of eggs."

Jack cut to the bedroom and came to the kitchen, wearing a shirt and socks. Janice, spatula in hand, had taken note from which room he'd emerged. She tightened her apron strings and turned her back on him to fuss with the grill. Reggie gestured to the bar stool his ass wasn't parked on. "Have a seat, Jack."

He tried to catch Lindsay's eye to get a read on how she was feeling but her attention was on applying cream cheese to toasted bagels. When she did look up, it was to ask, "Anyone for orange juice?"

"Sure," Reggie replied.

"No," Jack said. Beside him, Reggie whacked his knee against his own. "No, thanks," he modified. He didn't need etiquette lessons from a man who used his tongue for a dish-cloth. What he needed to know was that he hadn't messed things up with Lindsay. Even with Reggie and the mother hen here, she could at least look at him, smile, come close, any-thing except ask him if he wanted fucking orange juice. Or that was her answer: carry on as if nothing happened.

So he did. He picked up his bagel. "I'm guessing you and Reggie have discussed something already."

"No details, other than it involves kicking ass," Reggie updated. "Apologies," he added quickly in Janice's direction.

"Heard worse, hon," Janice said, above the sizzle of eggs and bacon. "Sounds like I've arrived right in the middle of something. Are you any closer to finding Seline?"

Jack pulled the bagel back from his mouth, muttering to Reggie. "Perhaps you remember what happened the last time a certain someone antagonized the Moles? We go down there with numbers and it's going to be another massacre."

Janice's eyes darted from one to the other of them, finally settling on him. "What's going on here? Moles? Massacre?"

Jack looked at Lindsay. He didn't know what to say and he didn't think it was his call. Janice followed his direction. "Lindsay? What is he talking about?"

Lindsay turned to face Janice. "Janice, we've found out who's got Seline. Reggie's here to help work out a plan to get her back and—"

"She's been kidnapped?" interrupted Janice, eyes wide. "Well haven't you called the police? For God's sake, Lindsay, why are we standing here if she's being ransomed?"

"She's not being ransomed. It's not that simple. There are

these...things under the city. They're the ones that have her."

Janice clicked off the stove. "Things? Lindsay, listen to yourself. I don't know what these two are trying to pull here, but if you know where she is then you need professionals. Police. Detectives. Not two miscreants looking to profit from Seline's disappearance."

Jack had had enough. Standing he planted his hands on the counter, his golden eyes flashing in anger. "I understand you mean well," he growled. "The fact is you have no idea what you're dealing with or who you're talking to. Captain Monroe gave Lindsay my number because he knew I was the only one who could help, and I happen to have a fucking doctorate from Oxford. So I'm not going to be questioned by some big-mouthed, small-minded woman who thinks she knows everything just because she's figured out how to work a search engine."

Everybody's jaws were practically on the floor. He wasn't done quite yet.

"Now, if you want to help then shut your mouth and open your ears, because you've got a lot to learn before you get to have an opinion. And by the way, yes, Lindsay and I spent last night fucking. She's a grown woman, and that was her choice. You're in no position to judge either of us, got it?"

There was dead silence in the apartment for a moment.

"Okay," replied Janice.

"Good. Now to recap: there are monsters under the city. We've learned that they captured Seline. No one will go down there, except for us. Now let's move on."

It was Reggie's turn to venture speaking. "We can do it. If nobody's got the cajones to stand up to those freaks, then what're they going to do next? The line's got to be drawn, Jack. Lot of people look up to you. If you take on the Moles then they might, too."

"If we go down there to fight, we'll lose."

"And if we don't, Seline is lost," Lindsay countered.

Jack dipped his head. That was the truth of it.

Janice turned the stove back on, busying herself with breakfast.

"We won't lose if we come ready," continued Reggie. "Sumptown's got a whole arsenal Mr. Moore would lend us."

Jack shook his head. "In case you haven't been keeping count there's only three of us, and Lindsay doesn't know the first thing about tunnel fighting. Give her a gun and she'll be more a danger to us than the Moles. Do I really have to tell you what a bad idea all this is?"

He really needed a coffee. He looked past Reggie to the pot and watched Janice drain the last of it into her mug. Figured.

Reggie took a healthy slurp from his steaming cup. "I know what you're saying. Only with Lindsay's dollars we could get ourselves some serious muscle. Killers that know how to fight in the dark."

"Are you out of your mind? Who could we get that would be any good?"

Reggie stuck out his thick jaw. "Najib knows some people. Real hard cases, and tunnel folk, too. They'd go down with us if the money was right, and he told me we could drop his name. Anyway, we'll need someone to help walk Seline out of there. Lindsay's good for that."

Janice divvied up scrambled eggs and bacon onto four plates, one of which got shortchanged by half. Surprise, surprise, that was the one she laid in front of him.

He pushed away his half-portion of breakfast, looking from Lindsay to Reggie and back again. Shit, they were serious. "No way."

Reggie folded his massive arms over his chest. "No choice. We're coming." A glimmer of his golden smile appeared. "Lindsay said you know you can't do it alone."

Jack shot her a look. He'd bared his soul to her, confessed his need, and she'd told Reggie the very next day. What had she told him about last night? Had it all been a bit of fun for her? Who had used who for sex?

Her gaze drifted to him, a small smile on her lips. It dropped away the second she registered his expression. She shrugged and reached for the orange juice, topping up Reggie's glass. Behind her, Janice scowled.

Fucking women and their mind games.

His gut, head and heart all felt as if they'd taken a pounding.

"Fine," he growled. "But if we're doing this then we do it my way. No questions, no complaints. Agreed?"

To his surprise everyone, even Janice, nodded.

———————————

WHEN SELINE FIRST saw the moving shapes in the dark, she had put them down to hallucinations, products of her fear and isolation. Then she noticed that if she held her hand in front of her she could discern outlines. She'd been in the dark so long that her eyes had gradually adjusted, and were now able to perceive the minute amount of phosphorescent light that radiated throughout the chamber.

Since that discovery she'd detected the silent forms slipping past her regularly, though not often. If she could somehow ditch the collar, she might be able to escape during their absence. Only what then? It was insane to think she could ever navigate her way back to the surface in one piece. Even if she evaded her captors, there were the packs of carnivorous rats that prowled the deep tunnels. She wasn't a mile from the surface, and yet it might as well be a hundred for all the good it did her.

She was sitting cross-legged on her sleeping bag when another of the dark shapes came into view. Unlike the others, which had never stopped, this one silently approached her, pausing perhaps a dozen feet away. If her weak perception wasn't deceiving her, it was smaller than the others.

"Hello?" she whispered tentatively.

She thought she heard it sniff.

"My name's Seline. What's your name?"

The shadow paced back and forth like an animal in a cage, then squatted down a few feet away to study her.

Seline wet her lips. "Please talk to me."

A heavy silence hung between them, and Seline had concluded that this captor was as mute as its fellows, it made a sound. It was soft and rhythmic, and perfectly mimicked the drip of water. Astonished, Seline leaned forward, and the sound changed to the distant echo of a subway rumbling through the tunnels.

No wonder she hadn't heard them. They could have a conversation ten feet away from her and she'd never realize it.

"I don't understand what you're saying," she said slowly. "Do you speak any English?"

There was no reply. The small form—it would probably come up to her waist—stayed put.

Could it be… a *child*?

"Don't be afraid," she soothed, trying to keep her voice steady. "I'm not going to hurt you. I'm not here to hurt anybody."

It inched closer.

"Do you live here?" Seline asked. "I'm from the city above. That's where I live."

The small form tilted its head, as if listening.

"I have an aunt up there...more of a sister, and I really miss her. I know she must be very worried about me."

For a moment that seemed to stretch on forever, neither of them moved, then cautiously it extended its hand to her.

Seline sighed with relief. If she could establish a dialogue with one of them, even a child, then they'd see she was no threat. Ultimately these were people she was dealing with, no matter how strange. And all people, especially children, could be reached.

Carefully, so as not to frighten the little shadow, she stretched out her open hand. A universal gesture of peace and friendship anyone could understand....

The thing seized her wrist, embedding black teeth into the soft flesh of her palm. Seline yelped and kicked out, but it was already gone, its skittering footsteps fading into the dark.

"Little bastard!" She clutched her bleeding hand and rocked back and forth, the pain of the bite excruciating. And despite her best efforts to remain brave, she let out a sob of pain, fear and frustration. Then her ears caught the sound of other scuttling footfalls. Many more.

Pressing back against the column she searched the blackness, her pulse racing. From the darting movements there were at least three or four of them now, a couple smaller than the first one.

"Please...leave me alone...."

The sound of dripping water began again, this time from all around her. She scrambled to her feet, swinging her head to locate her tormentors. The water gave way to the rumble of a subway, loud and echoing this time, coming through the darkness at her, about to crush her beneath its wheels.

Then all at once they swarmed her. They harried her, one snapping at her while the others circled around, ripped at her clothes, yanked at her hair, drew blood again and again. She tripped over her chain and they wrestled to the cold floor. Screaming, she kicked one off. Another leapt onto her chest, its weight slamming the air out of her lungs as it sunk its teeth into her shoulder. Slashing with tooth and claw, they tore at her, then suddenly they abandoned the fight, scuttling away fast.

It took a moment for her to realize they were gone, but in that same instant she sensed she still wasn't alone. A burning metallic smell wafted over the stench of blood, and looking up she saw a dark shape loom over her.

"Please...help me..." she begged, sobs wracking her body. "Please let me go."

It seized her by the back of the neck, fingers hard and strong as iron, and dragged her to her feet.

"You tried to escape," came a cold, cracking voice, the first she'd heard since her capture an eternity ago.

"No...I was just talking to them...just talking and they attacked me...."

The thing shoved her face against the column. She didn't dare resist, restricting herself to a gasp of revulsion as it inspected her, its cold hand groping. She stood there, not wanting to think of what was about to happen, then to her amazement, she felt her collar slip from her.

Her keeper didn't let go, however. He spun her around and marched her forward, her neck still in its vice-like hold.

"Where...where are we going?"

No answer.

She was propelled down unseen corridors and crumbling steps, the metallic reek of her guide making her nostrils burn and eyes water. It jerked her to a halt.

"Where are we?"

She heard the flick of a lighter, and behind her a small orange flame lit up the chamber to impossible brightness. Her eyes took in what could only be described as a nursery, and then focused on what the little shadows played with in the dark. Again Seline screamed, and this time she couldn't stop.

---

FRANK MOORE PULLED aside the gray tarp that camouflaged the entrance to a dead-end tunnel, and led Lindsay, Jack and Reggie inside. Both sides of the warren were lined with lockers, boxes and small crates, along with stacks of firewood and oil drums full of kerosene, gasoline and water. So much of it that there was only a narrow fissure down the middle for them to walk single file, and Lindsay worried that if she knocked anything it would trigger a slide that'd bury them alive.

"Been building up this stockpile for almost ten years now," Frank said in a voice loud enough to carry down the line. "Down here we can survive about anything, but it's not only about living. Sumptown's a little seed of civilization buried in the ground. No matter what happens upstairs, we'll be here to start things over again."

"Kind of like an insurance policy for humanity?" Lindsay asked from right behind him, squeezing past what looked like parts of a helicopter.

The miner's headlight on the mayor bobbed. "Yeah, I like the way you put it. That's exactly what we are. I mean, all the presidents and kings and whatnots are going to make it through the collapse thanks to their bunkers and secret moon bases. Down here we have a place where the common man has a chance to ride out the storm."

Moon bases? Frank really was off his rocker. Then again only a week ago, she would never have believed in Sumptown or Mole people or mysterious subterranean cultures. Why *not* moon bases?

Frank stopped at a sturdy steel locker and opened its bulky padlock with a key from his shirt pocket. "The Moles can't stand bright light, and they don't use firearms from my experience, maybe because they're sensitive to sound. That might give you enough of an edge to beat them, especially with these."

Inside was a row of submachine guns, each fitted with a powerful flashlight beneath its barrel. He pulled one out, slapped in a clip of ammunition, and handed it to Lindsay.

"This switch here is the safety," he explained, flicking it on and off. "It's a good idea to keep it on when you're shouldering the gun. Always keep it off when you're in Mole territory—that being the deep tunnels anywhere outside my town."

"Okay," she said, nervous as Frank moved behind her, showing her how to hold the weapon.

"Keep it close to your body so they can't pull it out of your hands, and lean into it when you fire. You don't need to worry too much about aiming, seeing as you'll be fighting in close quarters, but don't pull the trigger unless you know who you're shooting at. This weapon's one hundred percent lethal, so there's not going to be any second chances for a person on the wrong end of it."

"Any other advice?" she asked, trying to hold the gun as

if she did it all the time.

"Ma'am, I'd need two months to make you halfway competent with that weapon. I will tell you this: always remember you're in a three-dimensional environment. You're vulnerable from above, from below and from all around. Whenever you look up, look down. Whenever you check right, check left. Only that kind of three-sixty awareness is going to keep you breathing."

The mayor handed guns to Jack and Reggie, and though Jack handled his like a Ranger, Lindsay saw that Reggie didn't look any more comfortable with a firearm than she did. The big man caught her look and shrugged.

"Never liked guns much."

Jack nodded his thanks to the mayor. "I'll make sure we return them in good condition, Mr. Moore."

"Don't worry about the guns, Mr. Cole. I've got enough for an army down here. I'm thinking it'll be nice seeing 'em used for a good cause."

As the three of them left Sumptown on the bridge, Lindsay looked over her shoulder at Reggie. "So, where do we find these mercenaries Najib told you about?"

"They're called 'The Tecos'. They guard a community beneath Central Park. A place called Seneca."

"Seneca?"

"Back in the 1800's Seneca used to be a village," Jack spoke up. Other than a few terse answers this was the first time he'd volunteered anything to her since they'd left her apartment. He was pissed about something she couldn't begin to fathom. "The place had Manhattan's first significant population of black property owners, which got erased when they built Central Park, and the community we're heading to is located right beneath where it used to be."

"Is it like Sumptown?" Lindsay asked.

"No," Reggie answered this time. "I only been there once. Even then it was a lot bigger and a lot meaner. The people running it got a drug lab. They make meth, ecstasy...that sort of stuff, and I heard they keep slaves, too. Been doing all that for almost twenty years now, since they're too deep in the tunnels for the cops to catch them."

Jack reached the end of the bridge, and this time when he spoke, it was almost to himself. "The trick will be getting the Tecos to go down into The Pits with us. We'll have to offer them a lot of cash to make it worth their while, especially given the money they must be earning with the lab."

Reggie stepped off the bridge behind Lindsay and slung his gun over his back, a thoughtful look on his face. "Maybe not. Najib knew them pretty good. Told me he's owed a favor by a man called Tocat. And that Tocat is a man of honor." He paused. "Considering."

"Considering...?" Lindsay prompted.

Jack looked at her in faint astonishment. "What do you think? Considering they kill people the way you swat flies."

# CHAPTER ELEVEN

THE TUNNELS SEEMED infinite in their reach, and that Jack and Reggie could navigate their way through them with such certainty still impressed Lindsay. A New Yorker all her life, she knew how confusing the surface could be, so mastering its underground was no small feat. This time down, she'd been trying to estimate where under the city they were, and presently had them beneath Park Avenue, somewhere near the reservoir.

Together their small group made their way though mile after mile of concrete corridors, passing through regions of ever-increasing strangeness and desolation. They crossed through a huge pillared chamber whose ceiling was stuccoed with purple crystals, and over a catwalk that spanned a reeking garbage pit. They waded through a narrow drainage tunnel ankle-deep with blood-red water, and climbed though a jagged rock fissure into the crypt of some forgotten blueblood family, their caskets long since broken open and grave-robbed.

The silent march was long and grueling, but at length they came to a stop at a rust-stained metal door, emblazoned with the emblem of the Pennsylvania Railroad Company, along with the year of its placement—1922.

Reggie pulled open the heavy portal, its hinges groaning.

"Now you're going to see something, Lindsay," Reggie whispered, a wide grin on his face. "Welcome to The Gallery."

Following Jack though the doorway, Lindsay entered what appeared to be an abandoned train tunnel, judging by the rubble-littered tracks that ran down its center.

"Turn on your flashlight and look around," Jack said quietly into her ear. There was, in his voice, something she'd not heard since they were kids: excitement. "You can't visit the underground and not see this place."

Intrigued, Lindsay shone her powerful flashlight about, and gasped.

Covering the high wall was a grand mural depicting the expulsion of Adam and Eve from the Garden of Eden. Lindsay recognized it instantly as a detail from Michelangelo's Sistine Chapel. Though the colors were muted from the grime of years, there was a mastery and vision to the work that took Lindsay aback. She drew closer, admiring the artistry and the sheer audacity of the artist to dare imitate one of the masters. Then something caught her eye.

"Adam's black! I mean not because of the dirt—he's black!"

Reggie gave an appreciative whistle. "I was wondering if you'd clue in. Look at him after the angel kicked him and his woman out."

Lindsay peered at the figures on the far right of the 'canvas'. "He's white." She laughed. "I guess I know what the race of the artist was." She frowned. "OK, if black is the superior color, why is Eve white in both cases?"

"Because the woman was trouble right from the start," Jack said, from directly behind her. Reggie rolled out a length of appreciative chuckles.

She ignored both of them. From the corner of her eye she caught another departure from the original. She stepped back to make certain and bumped up against Jack.

She turned to him. "Look, look. The Adam and Eve after the fall, below their feet, they're about to step onto an open manhole. It's not quite the same as the ground. See? Here and here."

Jack's expression changed from lofty amusement to avid interest. His light came up beside hers and followed to where she was pointing. He squatted down to take a closer look. "I'll be damned. I never noticed that before. You, Reggie?"

Reggie shook his head, and Lindsay felt the same pride of a child who'd done what had stumped an adult.

"They're about to go down into the tunnels," Jack said quietly, then added darkly, "Eat an apple, go to hell. Good eye, Lindsay."

He swung his light slowly along the tunnel wall, and Lindsay gave a low sound of surprise. Paintings stretched off into the darkness, all powerful representations of the originals. A light bulb went on in Lindsay's head.

"We're near the Met, aren't we?"

Something like admiration flickered across Jack's face. "You're quick," he said. "We're more or less below the Museum right now. If you listen carefully you can hear the trains pull in every so often. The artist must've known their collections pretty well, maybe even worked there. Take a look at them, Lindsay. You'll like this."

He took hold of her hand and tugged her along, stopping before what seemed like a faithful reproduction of Degas' *Dancers*. Girls in tutus gracefully stretched and unfolded themselves. The wall-length mirror caught their serene reflections, but behind them in the glass were other dancers, ragged

149

figures, their bodies contorted, their hair wild. There moved the tunnel dwellers in dark counterpoint.

Each painting was like that. On the surface easily recognizable, yet undermined by some reference to New York's underground. Rats swam in the calm blue waters in the idyllic *Boating*. The statuesque *Madame X* was inverted by showing an ebony woman wearing a threadbare white dress. The lute player in *The Musicians* was holding a guitar with broken strings. Lindsay felt alternately amused at the ingenious twists of the artist and heartsick at the realities so starkly portrayed.

"Who did this?" she asked, walking down the tunnel, shining her flashlight back and forth at the grand display.

"This place was sealed in the 40s," Jack explained. "Tunnel people found it in the early 70s, and when they did all this was here. Nobody knows who the artist was, or how she found her way down."

"She?"

"They found painting supplies and scaffolding, and amongst it all were some old paint-stained dresses, probably to wear while working. I suppose the artist could have been a cross-dresser. However, the paintings are generally maintained to be by a woman."

As Lindsay listened to the authority and openness in Jack's voice, it struck her that this was where he needed to be. Here in this dark world he came alive. He became an explorer again, seeking to understand what he didn't know, bringing what he had learned to others. Maybe he was a spider, spreading a web not between the lairs of the Moles, but between this world and the one above. He wouldn't want to hear that, though.

Nor would he appreciate hearing that he was holding her hand. She kept the conversation to the art. "They're incredible.

Doesn't anyone on the surface know about them?"

Jack shook his head. "No. Not that I'm aware of. There are other works, not on as large a scale, in the underground, though."

"Why would anyone want to put their paintings where they'd never be seen?"

Jack shrugged. "Maybe these paintings are like Mrs. Moore's jacket."

"Ah. Some things are only beautiful if not brought to the light of day." He frowned and seemed to noticed their joined hands for the first time. He moved to let go. She tightened her hold.

"Hey," she said quietly, "remember the first time we held hands?"

She expected him to jerk free, but maybe because he was in a place where the old Jack had come out, he stayed with her. "You mean when you held my hand. Took years to get the circulation back."

Encouraged by his humor, she said, "This is where you need to be, Jack. Here with these pictures, telling the world about the beauty beneath their feet."

She felt him start to pull away and snared him back. "Jack—"

"You think I can skip on down here anytime I want? Take notes, pictures...maybe, lead a tour? Every step I take risks me being captured again, forced back into chains, of losing my ability to speak, to think, to remember. You have no idea what they did to me, Linds. What they made me do to other people." He flung his arm at the pictures. "You see things of beauty. Turn off your light and you'll see what's really here. Blackness. Fear. A mass grave for New York's forgotten and insane. That's what I see, Lindsay, even when the lights are on."

She didn't believe that, she couldn't. Not after what they shared last night."And what about when you look at me?"

His voice remained hard. "You're beautiful. That's not me saying it, that's a fact. But I look at you and all I see is what I can't have."

"You had me last night."

He gave a derisive snort. "Did I really? Because I'm beginning to doubt anything ever happened. I wake up, you're not there, and when you come back—not alone—you bring bagels."

"I didn't want to come on all hot and heavy with Reggie and Janice there."

"I didn't know eye contact was hot and heavy."Again, he jerked at his hand and again she didn't let go.

"Listen, I didn't want you feeling you had to act differently around me, I wanted to give you space."

"You know, Lindsay, how screwed up I am. The last thing I need is for you to pretend something didn't happen when it did. Not something this fucking important."

Of course. What had she been thinking? "I'm sorry, Jack. I didn't want you believing you needed to feel things for me that you can't. I wanted you to know that I was okay with that. What happened last night might not have been romantic, but it was real…and for me, it felt like a new beginning for us."

It was hardly the time to be talking about the future what with dirt and danger all around. Yet, incredibly, Jack softened. "Listen, Lindsay, before we go on, I need to tell you something. I'd planned to do it this morning. It's about somebody." He winced at the last word and paused, clearly thinking about how to go on. Then suddenly he stiffened. Cocked his head. Looked at his watch.

"You hear that, Reggie?"

Reggie, who'd been giving them some space, responded after a pause, "What did you catch?"

"The clicking of subway wheels…"

Lindsay looked upwards. "We're near a station."

"…at the wrong time."

"Think it's them?" Reggie said.

"I don't know. We can't stay here, even if it's me being paranoid." He turned back to her and lowered his voice, his grip so tight on her hand she got a taste of what it was like for him all those years ago. "Listen, Linds. You need to understand that all the mystery of this place is a trap. Go any deeper and nothing will be the same. The underground will change you, and none of it will be for the good."

"You think I'm not already changed? What do you think happened when my family was wiped out except for Seline?"

"I'm not going to pretend I know what that was like but in the end, it didn't keep you from living your dreams, from being who you are, maybe even something more."

Now, she understood. "Is that what happened to you, Jack? They took part of you?"

"I lost my *soul*, Linds. Anyone who experiences the Moles is damaged. Even if Seline surfaces alive, she won't be the same. In a very real way, no one gets out of here alive. And dammit, I need you alive."

His pain and desperation cut into her, squeezed her heart as hard as his hand on hers. She shook her head in denial of everything he was telling her. She couldn't go back. Seline needed her. They would all make it back. Everything would come right. Then, she looked into Jack's haunted eyes, and didn't know what to think anymore.

Reggie called from across the room. "We got to move. Still another hour before we reach Agharta."

Still holding his gaze, she said the only thing she could. "Coming!"

―――――――――――――――

SO BUSY WAS Lindsay thinking through her conversation with Jack that they were almost at the end of the abandoned train tunnel before she registered Reggie's final words. "Agharta? I thought the place was called Seneca."

"We have to pass though Agharta to reach Seneca, and again on our way to The Pits," Reggie explained. "It's about the size of Sumptown."

"They survivalists, too?"

Reggie hitched up the strap of his gun, his flashlight an ever-moving search beam. "Everybody's a survivalist down here. These people are more like tunnel doctors, and pretty good ones too. One of them especially. She'd kill you if you crossed her, but you'd swear she could raise the dead the way she—" He halted his chatter, then steered it in another direction. "They got all kinds of weird ideas about the tunnels being part of Atlantis or something. Got started in The Burbs, then set up their own place down here after the cops came. Me and Jack know a couple of them, so they'll be cool with us showing up."

Lindsay looked over her shoulder. "Spent much time there, Jack?"

"Yeah." A single edged word. There was more to it than that. There was always more when it came to him.

Reggie stopped, Lindsay almost bumping into him. He was standing at a thick steel door similar to the one that had allowed them into The Gallery, except this one was set within a massive brick wall that sealed the tunnel from the outside world. Yanking the heavy portal open Reggie revealed a damp, crumbling hallway, its walls studded with leprous-looking mushrooms, at the end of which was an old-fashioned service elevator—minus the elevator.

The metal lattice doors of the elevators were eerily intact. Reggie slammed them open with his shoulders, launching a screech that echoed loudly downwards. "Best they know someone's coming," he explained in a full voice. "You don't want to be surprising nobody. Thrill killers pay 'em a visit now and then, so they're quick with their trigger fingers."

Lindsay eyed the empty elevator shaft, a hard lump in her throat. "Thrill killers?"

Jack stepped around her, inspecting the shaft and area with his light. "Psychos. They find each other at fetish clubs, racist cliques, the internet...and come down here hunting tunnel folk. Most call themselves vigilantes, think they're doing the city a favor by exterminating vermin."

Lindsay recoiled. "People actually do that?"

Reggie held his beam back down the way they'd come. "Kill a topsider and you've got the NYPD all over your ass. Down here there ain't no laws, so this is where they come to get their kicks."

"Only sometimes they never make it back," Jack added.

Something in his tone made Lindsay and Reggie stare at him uncertainly.

He didn't seem to notice. "We're wasting time. Let's get going."

Anchored to the lattice panel was a thick nylon rope which extended down into the depths, its length tied into knots every couple of feet or so. Lindsay aimed her light over the edge. It was a long, long way down. Her legs almost buckled, and she backpedaled away—fast.

She couldn't miss the looks of dismay the two men exchanged. Damn. She couldn't let them down. Reggie checked his pack and gun, then said with forced cheer, "I'll call when I reach the bottom."

Taking hold of the rope, Reggie swung out, then began to shimmy down. Lindsay watched the beam from his light ricochet around the shaft for a few seconds, and then it and Reggie were swallowed into the darkness. Jack snapped on the flashlight beneath his gun as the illumination from Reggie faded.

"The rules still apply. Get going, woman."

Lindsay's legs were trembling. "Quit being a jerk and give me a minute."

"Oh, nice one. I'm the jerk," he said quietly, then he slammed his fist against the lattice, rattling the metalwork. "Didn't I tell you I'd do this myself?" he exploded. "But oh no, you think that just because you conquered the world on the surface, you're smart enough to take on the underground. You think you can handle everything, then you come up against the first little challenge and you fall apart—"

"I'm not falling apart! I'm taking a moment to get myself together, all right?"

"No, it's not all right. What are you going to do if we're on the run from the Moles? 'Excuse me, I'm a little nervous around heights. Give me a moment to get myself together and then we'll continue the chase.' If you're in the way, Lindsay, then it could cost lives. Reggie's. Seline's. And most certainly your own precious hide."

Lindsay's patience with him snapped. "What about you, Jack? Aren't I endangering your life, too?"

"I already told you I'll live."

"Oh, yeah, right. You can outrun Moles to the surface and

then you're lost. You'll crawl into a hole, pull the plugs and eat scrambled egg sandwiches for the rest of your life."

"At least I'll be alive. Except then I'll have Reggie's death on my hands. He's down here because he feels guilty, and wants to make things right. You're down here because you think you can make things right, despite what I just got through telling you. He's a good man. You're a fool."

Lindsay flinched, then looked away. She walked stiffly to the edge of the shaft. She stared at the rope as it swayed from Reggie's movements. It gave a wild shake and Reggie's voice echoed from below. "Yo!"

The rope came to a standstill, and Lindsay grabbed for it. Her backpack and the gun unbalanced her, and she swung out into the dark opening, her grip slipping. She cried out and flailed with her legs, failing to wrap them around the rope, she went into an uncontrolled slide.

It all happened in a split second and then the rope steadied. Jack's voice boomed down at her. "Lindsay, feet against the wall! Now!"

Her boots thudded against the concrete surface about six feet below the opening. Her heart hammered loud in her ears.

Jack set his light at the edge of the pit. "I'm going to pull you up. Hold on tight and walk up the wall."

When her head and shoulders appeared above the edge, Jack reached down and hauled her up by her ass. She laid flat on her stomach, her face tucked in the crook of her arm.

Reggie's voice rose hollowly up the shaft. "Everything OK?"

"Yeah," Jack called back to him. That same word, this time weary and resigned. It had Lindsay pushing herself onto all fours. "Listen—" he started in.

"Don't say it, Jack. I know what you're thinking, and I

157

don't need to hear it again."

"I already told you before that you don't know what I'm thinking."

Lindsay stood, swaying only a little. "Fine, Jack. Fine. Except this time whatever it is, I don't want to hear it." She made for the shaft. "Just tell me how to get down this fucking rope, all right?"

He gave a small sigh, which she didn't care to interpret. "First of all," he said, "take off your gun and pack."

Lindsay did so, her body relaxing from the release of the weight.

"Okay, now the bottom of the shaft isn't all that far down," he continued. "I'll steady the rope for you, and all you have to do is take hold of it and step out. You ever play on a tire swing when you were a kid?"

"Yes."

"Well, it's no harder than that. You stand on the knot below you, lower your hands, then your feet, and inchworm your way down. Keep your eyes on the wall, not up or down, and you won't get vertigo. Take it nice and easy, and you'll reach the bottom before you know it, okay?"

"Okay."

He leaned out and snagged the rope, handing it to her. She took it and drew a deep lungful of air.

"Good. Now, hold tight and step off. I'll keep it steady."

Lindsay closed her eyes, took another deep breath, and swung gently out into space, her hands clutching the rope. Her feet instantly found the knot beneath them, and then she bumped against the wall of the pit.

She opened her eyes, and without thinking, looked down. The light from Reggie's flashlight was a glowing pinprick, and she realized that she was hanging a good five stories above him.

*Jack, you lying bastard.* Shutting her eyes, she clamped her body around her lifeline.

"You're okay, Lindsay," came Jack's calm voice. "Just lower your hands to the next knot, and ease your way down."

Stiff with fear, she slowly uncurled one hand from the rope, bringing it down to the next knot, then repeated the process with the other.

"Good work," Jack said. "Now your feet. Hold on and bring them down together."

After several shaky seconds, Lindsay managed to comply.

"Okay," he encouraged her. "You're now two feet lower than you were. All you have to do is repeat that till you get to the bottom. No problem, right?"

"Right," she whispered, keeping her eyes on the pitted concrete wall of the shaft. "No problem."

Her descent was painfully slow, each movement a mental battle between determination and fear, with the former only narrowly winning each round. A time came when there was a draw, and Lindsay hung in the pitch darkness where neither the light from Jack nor Reggie illuminated her. Senselessly she glanced upward to Jack. Not surprisingly, she saw only blackness, and with her head tilted back, her hat dropped off. *Damn, her hat would make it down before she did. If she did.*

"Bastard." Somehow the expletive made her feel better, gifting her momentary release from her fear.

"Bastard," she repeated experimentally and found her hand opened more easily than before. She swore again and her legs slid down the rope. Cursing thusly in self-encouragement, she continued on. Her fear didn't lose its grip on her—sweat slicked her body and her hands were starting to cramp—but she'd found a way to keep going.

Like the proverbial light at the end of the tunnel, she saw the beam of Reggie's flashlight playing bright and bold upon the wall. Sneaking a look down, she saw he stood only ten feet below her, atop the shattered remains of the missing elevator car.

"You go, girl!" he laughed. "You're almost here."

Lindsay slithered the rest of the way in relief. Reggie put one of his huge hands on her shoulder. "You okay?"

"I am now," she smiled, at first weakly, then in broad triumph. She gave Reggie a hard, strangling hug. "God, am I glad to see you."

She shook the rope and shouted up the shaft, "Yo!"

The rope wiggled in response as Jack began his descent.

Reggie climbed off the car, her following. She turned to him and found his face serious, his gaze trailing off along the dark corridor that led from the shaft. He switched his gun light on and tossed his flashlight to Lindsay as he pointed the weapon into the blackness.

"What is it?" she whispered. Reggie didn't answer. Instead he motioned her over to the wall, himself taking cover behind some of the wreckage while he waited for whatever he was sensing to show itself.

For long moment all was quiet save the soft creak of the rope, then from out of the darkness came a man's voice, sharp and rasping.

"You made a wrong turn, asshole. Better go back."

"Neil?" Reggie called back. "That you?"

"Who's that?"

"It's me, Reggie. Remember me from The Burbs? I got a couple of people with me. It cool if we come down?"

From out of the shadows a figure appeared, and Reggie lowered his weapon as it materialized into a ragged-looking middle-aged man. His long black hair, broadly streaked with gray, was tied back severely, and he was bundled into several layers of mismatching clothes, all of which looked like they were garbage fodder. He carried a battered rifle held together by duct tape, probably more of a danger to him than anyone else.

Neil held up a hand to shield his eyes. "Who you got with you?"

"Jack Cole...and his woman."

The man stopped, staring up as Jack appeared on the rope, then glanced at Lindsay, his expression hardening into suspicion and distaste.

Jack touched down and hopped from the wreckage to join them. He shot Lindsay a look as clearly disapproving as Neil's had been, causing her back to straighten. What had she done now? And then he did exactly what Neil had done, turned away and ignored her completely. He even angled himself in front of her, effectively cutting her out of the discussion. Jack was soaking up this submission stuff for all it was worth, and she couldn't do a damn thing about it.

Yet.

Jack smiled urbanely, as if they'd arrived at an upscale dinner party. "Sorry for the intrusion."

Neil nodded in wary acknowledgement. "You're all a long way from Grand Central. What's brought you down to us?"

"Just renewing old acquaintances," Jack said.

---

DEEP BELOW CENTRAL Park ran a subterranean offshoot of the Hudson River, its cold waters cutting though a natural cavern to create an underground canyon. Perched on the edge of this dark gorge sat Agharta, its cinderblock huts huddled close to one another in the deep chill. Unlike Sumptown, however, the tiny community was relatively well lit, illuminated by cheerful lanterns that hung outside the homes and several inviting campfires. People were gathered about the fires, talking and joking, and were it not for the gloomy setting, the tiny village would have looked almost homey.

Approaching the outskirts, Lindsay heard the lilting melody from a flute echoing through the chamber, the muffled cooing of what sounded like pigeons, and the giggling of children. Several youngsters were running about the little village in a game of tag, and spotting Neil, they came scampering toward him, obviously delighted at his return and showing no fear of the visitors he was with—except Lindsay.

"Neil! Neil! Who's them?" A little girl with twin black braids and a pointed chin grabbed his sleeve, and hopped up and down. She was surprisingly clean, her face and hands a pale grey in the light. The other children, too, showed the same shine, a miracle of maternal devotion given the unhygienic conditions.

Neil tugged on a braid. "Reggie and Cole."

And Lindsay, Cole's woman. Remember? What was she, a pariah?

"Put your cap on," Jack ordered over his shoulder.

"I can't. Lost it in the elevator shaft," she hissed.

"Figures. No one will talk to you because of your hair. They think you're a Nazi."

"A Nazi? Because I'm blonde?"

"Later."

A couple of children smiled up at Jack, and he crouched to be eye level with them, shaking several small hands and introducing himself. Their clear favorite, though, was the giant Reggie. From the moment he cracked his wide golden smile, they thronged around him, bombarding him with questions.

"You come to talk to Shamba?"

"Where you from?"

"You bring us presents?"

Prezzies. That was it. Gifts had cemented a bond with Mrs. Moore, and it might help ease the hostility here. She was easing her pack off when her chance was lost. Hoisting the girl with braids onto his shoulders, Neil led them to the largest of the cinderblock huts, its front bragging not one, but two lanterns. The kids gathered about them, their dark eyes shining with excitement, and about the village, people approached, wary looks on their gray faces.

"Shamba. We've got visitors," Neil called. "Reggie from the Burbs, and Jack Cole."

The thick blanket that served as a door lifted away, and an elderly man appeared. Though the years had stooped his shoulders, he was still tall. Like Neil, Shamba was dressed in rags, except over them were displayed a host of necklaces, medals and talismans, and even in his long grey hair were strung beads and ornaments. The entire works clinked together in soft cacophony as he hobbled out of his home, using an old crowbar as a cane. His deeply wrinkled face looked at them, his eyes gentle and benign, an instant balm to Lindsay's shredded nerves.

The old man studied his visitors, then gave a broad, toothless grin. "Welcome back to Agharta. You must be tired and hungry if you came all the way from Grand Central."

Reggie smiled. "You got that right, Shamba. We'd be real grateful if you would let us camp here for the night."

"Our home is your home," the old man replied, before

turning to Jack.

Jack inclined his head respectfully. "Shamba."

"Hello, Jack. It's good to see you again."

"Thank you."

"I see you've gotten yourself a woman," Shamba continued, not so much as glancing in Lindsay's direction.

"I'm a topsider now, Shamba. So is she." There was a stiffness to the words Lindsay didn't understand. Where else would Jack live?

"I see. You know you're always welcome here, Jack, and I'm sure Gali will be very happy to see you, too."

Jack gave a tight smile, and let the elder lead them to the nearest fire. The smell of a barbecue sent Lindsay's mouth salivating. Then she saw what was on the spit. A pair of huge rats, each easily the size of a large cat.

There were vinyl cushions scattered about the fire. Jack tossed one out of the circle, and gestured with his head for her to sit. Like a good little dog, she obeyed as he cozied up to the fire, blocking both the heat and a view.

All the villagers were young and dressed in the same tatty fashion as Neil and Shamba, and to her surprise, almost all of them were women. She smiled at a few, receiving sneers and glares in return. She kept her eyes down and tucked her hair down the back of her jacket. She never thought that she'd regret being blonde, but right here and now she knew for a fact that brunettes would have more fun.

Shamba got the conversational ball rolling. "So, what brings you down to us?"

"We're on our way to Seneca," Reggie answered.

"Very dangerous place. Why are you going there?"

"We're looking for the Tecos."

Lindsay started as someone prodded her on the shoulder,

and looking up saw that Neil was offering her a plate of daintily sliced... Lindsay darted a look at the spits and groaned inwardly to see that they were now empty. She accepted it as graciously as she could, though he didn't seem particularly impressed by her manners. He chin-pointed to Jack.

Happily Lindsay leaned forward and set the steaming plate beside him, hoping that her turn would be overlooked.

"We're looking to get their help with something," Reggie said. "They owe a favor to Najib."

Shamba raised his bushy eyebrows. "Must be serious to call in such a debt."

Jack picked up the plate and passed it to Reggie. "It is."

Neil handed Lindsay another full plate, and she followed the ritual of setting it beside Jack. He took it without a backward glance. Another appeared, with only two thin slices on it. She glanced up at Neil uncertainly, and he chin-pointed at her. She forced out a smile of thanks, before realizing he'd already turned away. Jack was chewing on the meat as contentedly as if it were the Colonel's chicken. Well, the Sumptown oatmeal had proved delicious. She brought the plate up close to her mouth, and gave a nibble. It was...edible. Edible like boiled tree bark.

"Where you get these?" Reggie asked, his mouth full. "They're good."

"We started farming them," Shamba answered proudly. "Pigeons and guinea pigs too, though we still depend on Dyer Pass for the food staples. Their runners bring us that and medicine, and in return we give them medical care, and...."

The elderly leader trailed off as a woman arrived at the fire. She was as young as the others living in Agharta, but held herself in a manner that bespoke of strength and pride. Across her chest was a bandolier of wicked-looking knives, and at her side was holstered a tarnished though clearly operable pistol.

"Hello, Gali," Jack greeted her, his voice level.

The woman switched her dark gaze from Jack to Lindsay, and though her face betrayed only mild disdain, Lindsay could see the woman's eyes flash with fury.

"Hello, Jack," she replied, equally coolly.

Shamba cleared his throat. "I was telling our guests about our trade with Dyer Pass. Why don't you join us, Gali?"

The woman sat down across the fire from Jack, and instantly a heaping plate of rat appeared for her. Gali waved it away like a queen.

"You're looking well, Jack. Much better than when I first saw you."

"For which you'll always have my thanks."

Gali's hand came to rest on the butt of her largest knife. "Funny way of showing it. I guess you got over Tasha, huh?"

Lindsay watched Jack's back stiffen. "I think we ought to change the subject."

"Awful good rat," Reggie spoke up. "Yessir, that's tasty."

Aside from Gali, who looked ready to toss Lindsay into the chasm, and Jack, who seemed studiously neutral, everybody else around the fire looked decidedly uncomfortable, and Lindsay was no exception. Unlike Sumptown, the people of this community hadn't warmed to her in the slightest, and the looks Gali was casting her way could have burned stone. She should have kept her head down. Instead, she squarely returned the woman's gaze.

*Back off. He's with me.*

But what had happened between Jack and Gali? And who the hell was Tasha?

# CHAPTER TWELVE

*JACK TRACKED THE five men by the green glow of their night-vision goggles, their flashlight beams cutting the darkness of the abandoned train station. Their kind was well known under the streets—thrill killers that came deep underground in search of victims to rape, torture, and kill.*

*They imagined themselves the top predators of the underground. They were about to learn that was not the case. Unwittingly they'd just crossed the border into Mole territory.*

*Beside him, Jack heard the faint hiss of a leaking steam pipe, and felt the hard curve of a Mole's claw on his shoulder. Like its shadow, he followed the thing behind a heap of rubble and unsheathed the heavy and razor-sharp butcher knife he'd been given.*

*The gang moved closer, their footfalls echoing on the wet concrete floor, then the sound of dripping water began around them. They remained oblivious as dark forms slid along the catwalks above them, well out of their narrow vision, and even as a rumbling subway sound began to vibrate through the rank air, they didn't realize the peril they were in. Only when a small package fell from the catwalks did they turn their heads.*

*There was a loud crack as the bundle exploded, the force of it harmless, but the brilliance of the burst blinded their low-*

*light goggles—and then the Moles struck.*

*Like spiders they dropped from above, landing on the intruders with grappling claws and biting fangs, wrenching guns from hands and goggles from faces. Two of the psychos got shots off, firing blindly against the suddenly animate darkness. More Moles were flooding in from all sides, and among them was Jack.*

*One of the gangers managed to break free of the pack and was wrestling for his gun when he saw Jack coming. Cursing he let go of the firearm and attacked with a wicked Bowie knife from his belt.*

*Jack ducked and swung his blade, slicing the man's belly open in a single clean stroke. Clutching his gut, the ganger tried to slash back, but Jack's knife arced downwards, cleaving off his opponent's hand. Blood jetted from the stump as the screaming man stumbled back against the wall. Jack turned away as the younger Moles swarmed the man, tearing at the spilled innards, a hot spray of blood splattering his naked body.*

*He was almost one of them now. One of the monsters that guarded the darkest pits of New York. The stuff of nightmares, insanity, and unspeakable urban legend. His body had darkened to a granite gray, his frame grown so lean and wiry that his every muscle rippled under his skin, his eyes faint rings of flashing gold encircling bottomless pools of black. Outwardly he was a part of the pack, another cunning animal as inhuman as the one he'd finished butchering. Everything had been erased from his mind save her, a precious seed buried in the blackness of his psyche, a time capsule containing everything he'd been and loved.*

*They'd brought him along on this hunt as a final test to confirm they'd successfully torn down every remnant of who*

*he'd once been. His only hope to reclaim himself now depend-
ed on convincing them that they'd succeeded. To make them
believe his old self was well and truly dead, and that they
could trust him to do anything without question.*

*The four remaining men were being stripped now, their
gear and equipment torn from them to uncover pale, quivering
flesh. Cables were knotted around their wrists, and howling in
panic they were hauled upwards till all of them hung in a row,
feet dangling. Then the youngest, a long-haired punk covered
in obscene tattoos, had his ankles lashed together with wire so
he couldn't kick.*

*This was it, Jack realized. God help these men. God help
him.*

*He approached the young man silently, bloodied knife in
his hand.*

*"Please..." the man gibbered, twisting against his bonds,
pissing himself in fear. "Oh fuck, please don't kill me...please
...please...please..."*

*Jack grasped his arm, steadying him. Kill? No, he'd do
much worse than that.*

*He began to shave away skin, deafening himself to the
shrieks of pure agony and terror, ignoring the blood that ran
in torrents down his arms. This was the only way back to
Tasha, and he didn't stop cutting until all four of them were
done.*

---

WITH GALI THERE, the conversation around the fire grew
tense and sporadic, and no sooner had Jack and Reggie finished their tunnel cuisine than Shamba suggested they go and
stow their gear. Neil guided them to a pair of cinderblock

guesthouses, and Jack nudged Lindsay inside one of them while Reggie reiterated their thanks for the accommodation.

The hut was completely bare, with the exception of three thick candles, a large fur rug and a small wall-hanging that read 'There's no place like hole.'

"There certainly isn't," Lindsay muttered, dropping her pack in the corner and resting her gun against it. She looked down at the rug. It was stitched together from rat pelts. "There's something you won't see at Macy's."

Jack fished a lighter out of his bag, lighting the candles before pulling closed the curtain door. "Trust me, there're much worse places to be."

"What the hell is with these people?" she whispered. "They've been treating me like a leper since we arrived, and that Gali keeps looking at me like I'm her worst enemy."

Jack was his usual chatty self. "Don't worry about it. We're here to sleep and then we'll leave."

"Look, I've kept my mouth shut and played by your rules. Now that we're tucked out of sight, why can't you tell me what's going on?"

Jack hunkered down in the corner beside the candles. "A long time ago Shamba was a doctor—a very successful surgeon, actually. How he wound up below ground is complicated. Suffice to say, when he got here he began to explore the tunnels, and as time passed, they became a bit of an obsession with him."

"Like it is with you?"

"You want me to tell you about this place or not?"

Lindsay took a small package of crackers from her pack, then dropped them back. It'd make the ideal gift for one of the kiddies. "Okay, okay. Please continue."

"Shamba came to believe that part of the underground is

the remnants of an ancient civilization called Agharta—hence the name of this community. His theory is that tens of thousands of years ago the Aghartans got into a war with another civilization called Lemuria, and that the two annihilated each other. A tiny portion of the Aghartan population survived, and he believes that those survivors developed a subterranean culture that still exists today."

"You mean the Moles?"

"Exactly. Supposedly they've honeycombed the earth with a network of tunnels, some stretching across the oceans. He thinks that UFOs are really Aghartan craft, that the world is hollow, and a load of other bullshit."

"So does everyone here believe this big underground story?"

"More or less." He set his piercing eyes on her. "Whatever you might think of Shamba, he's a gentleman, and he's taken a lot of young women under his wing over the years. He's kept them and their children safe, and they look up to him as a kind of father figure."

Jack seemed to think she scorned these people. And maybe once he'd been right. "I can see that," she said quietly. "Only I don't know why they'd think I'm a Nazi."

"Shamba read some book about how a German Antarctic expedition discovered an entrance to the inner world back in the 1930's, and that they made contact with the Aghartans. According to another source the Nazis kept the entrance a secret, and when the Second World War ended a bunch of their top scientists and military brass fled there."

"They think that because I've got blonde hair I'm some sort of cave Nazi?" Lindsay almost laughed at the sheer absurdity of the notion.

"They think fascist spies are operating in the under-

171

ground, so they're suspicious of anyone with Aryan features."

Okay, she might not feel scorn anymore but…. "In conclusion, they're completely bat-shit crazy."

Jack shrugged. "When it comes to UFOs and Nazi conspiracies I'd say you're right. There might be a grain of truth to the Agharta story. About the global subterranean culture. I told you about the tunnel markings and how many cities they're under. It means something, what I don't know."

"Okay, so what about Gali? What's her problem?"

"Lindsay, we're leaving in a few hours. Does it really matter?"

"Given all the number of sharp things she carries around I'd like to know how upset she is with me and why. Wouldn't you?"

He pressed his lips so hard together they almost disappeared and when he spoke, he kept his eyes on the candles. "Agharta survives as a community by being a kind of underground hospital. They treat tunnel folk who get injured or sick, and they help deliver babies born down here, which is why they have so many young mothers and kids. Shamba's taught everyone here the basics of medicine, and most are as skilled as your average paramedic. When I escaped from the Moles, it was Gali who found me and nursed me back to health."

"And…" Lindsay prompted.

If possible, his attention on the candles became even more focused. "And I guess she got a bit of a crush on me."

"A bit of a crush? She looked ready to crush *me*. I take it you two played 'doctor' before you left?"

He looked up now, his eyes glowing like that of a nocturnal animal. "Don't be coarse, Lindsay. The fact of the matter is that I owe my life to her, and I'm not about to be rude to her because you think she's competition."

Lindsay sputtered, unnerved that Jack had hit home. "Competition? What, for your affections? Give me a break. We left that Cole's woman routine at the door."

"Fuck. Forget it." He got to his feet and made for the entrance.

Was he actually walking out on her after all the shit she'd taken from him and the good people of Agharta? "Who's Tasha?" It burst from her like an insult, a deliberate goad.

"None of your goddamn business."

"Was she the somebody you wanted to talk about in The Gallery?"

"No."

"Liar."

"Least of my faults, Linds. You had your chance to turn back, you didn't, so fuck talking to you about anything. You're finding out yourself how wrong it is for you to be here."

"Wrong because I got a thing with heights? Because my hair's the wrong color? Because I don't like rat?"

"Yes! How many clues do you need? Do you need to be fucking skinned alive first?"

He broke off, pressed the heels of his hands into his temples, as if wracked by a sudden migraine. He fumbled with the curtain and left.

Lindsay stared at the curtain which was still trembling under the force of his departure.

"Jesus, Jack. Jesus." What had those Moles done to him?

She wanted to follow but she didn't think that was wise. She twisted open a bottle of water and chugged it down like an alcoholic with beer. Ten minutes later, she was no closer to knowing what to do and her bladder was ready to burst. Great. She'd no idea when Jack would be back, or where the latrines were. She unwound a yard of toilet paper from a roll in her pack, stuffed it into pocket and, remembering, she took a couple packs of crackers before heading out.

She could make out Jack sitting with Shamba by a fire. No way was she going to try to get his attention, especially given the nature of her request. He would throttle her then and there, with Gali looking gleefully on.

She surveyed the site, then spied the girl with braids skipping rope or, upon closer inspection, knotted rags. Lindsay turned on her brightest smile and called softly out to her.

"Hey there, I've got something for you—"

The little girl's eyes widened as Lindsay reached toward her with the little treat. And then she started screaming. Ear-piercing, terrified shrieks that rebounded around the cavern until it seemed that there were hundreds of them.

Alarmed, Lindsay did the most natural thing possible—and the stupidest. She rushed to the child to calm her. "No, listen, it's okay. I'm not—"

The girl was swept out from her reach, and Lindsay was tackled from all sides.

# CHAPTER
# THiRTEEN

HER FACE AND hands were clawed, her hair yanked back to a neck-snapping angle, and then she was kicked and punched in her stomach, her kidneys, her legs. She kicked and clawed back, finally pinned down as others joined in. Her attackers were all women, and they fought dirty.

All at once, there was a shout and the gang widened their circle. She was roughly hauled to her feet, her back pulled against the solid front of a man. Jack. Panting, she leaned in gratitude against him, her head on his shoulder.

Reggie was beside her, looming large, looking her over with a mix of disapproval and sympathy. Off to the side, Shamba regarded her impassively. The women were gathered in a loose semi-circle, aggression and hatred uniform in their expressions. The little girl, her screams having turned to sobs, was in the arms of one woman with matching features, clearly her mother.

Gali stepped up to Lindsay. "You going to live?"

What the hell do you think? Lindsay felt Jack's arm tighten in warning around her.

"Yes, thank you." She kept her voice low as she wiped blood from her nose.

"What were you doing to the girl?"

"Nothing! I…" She glanced around. The whole village was there, ready to finish her off. "I…I wanted to know where the washrooms were." The truth sounded so lame.

"Why did you ask the girl, then?"

"Because…I…" Lindsay floundered, and Jack cut in.

"It's my fault, Gali. I didn't tell her where she was supposed to go. Let me deal with her."

Gali turned to Shamba. He gave a faint shrug, a clear signal that it was up to Gali how she called it.

She switched back to Lindsay. "I'll turn you over to Jack, for his sake. Don't be mistaken into thinking that you were mistreated today. You're in our world now, topsider. You play by our rules."

Lindsay felt like spitting in her face, but she nodded.

"The latrine's there." Gali waved to a trail that ran alongside the gorge, then strode away.

Jack lowered his mouth to Lindsay's ear. "Go, and then back to the guesthouse." He gave her a push in the right direction.

Humiliation bowed Lindsay's head. She could feel every eye in the village following her. It was bad enough that the people openly despised her; to have Jack play along made it even worse. Then again, considering the way they'd parted, maybe it hadn't been an act.

When she got to end of the trail, she groaned in disbelief. She had reached a point where the gorge narrowed to some twenty feet across. Planks laid on ropes formed a kind of swinging bridge over it, and out in the middle was a small suspended hut that hung over the waters.

The toilet.

She had no idea how far down that gorge went, and she

didn't need to know.

"Bastard. Bastard. *Bastard.*"

---

JACK WAS SITTING on the rat rug, his back against the far wall of the hut when Lindsay returned. At the sight of him she dropped into the opposite corner, drew up her knees and buried her face in her arms.

Shit. He dragged a hand down his face. "Hey, Linds," he said softly. "I'm sorry about what happened out there. I should've explained things a little more clearly to you." He paused. "Are you okay? I can take you to Shamba, if you need help."

No answer.

"That rule about complaining and whining. You can have a break from it for the rest of the day."

In response she turned her head to the side and twisted herself more deeply into the corner. Her exposed cheek was red and swollen, and Jack wondered how many more bruises were slowly mottling her pale skin. He cursed himself for not having gotten to her sooner. Like all of them around the fire, he'd been thrown by how the screams rebounded off the walls. It was the rush of the women toward the guesthouse that had alerted him, and even then he'd approached slowly, thinking it a village matter.

When he'd seen Lindsay twisting helplessly under their blows it was as if he was the one getting it in the gut. And when he'd pulled her against him, it was all he could do not to lift her up and take her away from it all. He knew that he had to abide by Agharta's customs, though, or it would go even harder for her.

"This is the thing," he explained quietly. "These women are down here because if they were upstairs they wouldn't be allowed to keep their children. The law states that if a parent cannot provide a home for their kids, then they're taken away. And for most of these women, that's exactly what the state tried to do. Instead of giving them a place to live, they decided to take the children and abandon the mothers to the street. They're not down here because they think a cave is the best place to raise kids, but because they don't have anywhere else to go. Given their history, they have reason to be protective."

Lindsay stirred and said in a hoarse whisper, "Jack, could you leave me alone for a little while?"

"You...sure?"

She nodded. Hesitantly, he rose. "All right, then. Do you want me to bring you anything?"

She shook her head.

Jack made his way back to the fire, now free of people, and stared into the flames. He'd screwed up. He thought of the previous night when she'd shared her body with him, and now she wouldn't even show him her face.

He heard footsteps and looked up as Reggie took a seat beside him.

"How she doing?" he asked in a low voice.

Jack shrugged. "Fine, I guess. She wanted time to herself."

Reggie pulled back to get a good look at his friend. "That what she told you?"

"Yeah."

"She been jumped by a gang, made to feel lower than dirt, and then had to walk that tightrope out to the can—"

Jack groaned. "I forgot about that."

"—and you believe her when she tells you that she wants

to be alone. Man, you been out of the loop too long."

"Why would she say it if she doesn't mean it?"

Reggie threw up his hands. "How the hell should I know? I learned the hard way that's how women work. If I were you I'd head right on back or you're going to get no peace tonight."

"Why don't you visit her? You two get along well enough."

Reggie stared in disbelief. "Shit, Jack, I already got my own woman to deal with. No man deserves more trouble than that."

---

SHE APPEARED ASLEEP when he pulled back the curtain. From the looks of it, she'd gone through a kind of nighttime routine. Her outer clothes were folded in a pile by her side, a half-empty bottle of water within reach. She was lying on her belly in her sleeping bag, her head turned to the wall. Her face was pale, a red scratch scored across her cheek. Her hair—the root of her troubles and his small, pure joy—was bound back in a tight braid.

She didn't move at all when he entered, a sign that she was faking sleep.

"Feeling better, Linds?" He shed his jacket and sat next to her.

Lindsay turned her head, this cheek sporting a bruise. Her eyes flickered open, then closed again. "No."

"You need to see Shamba or Gali, then. You can't go on injured or it'll get worse." Worry sharpened his voice.

Her eyelids fluttered open. "I told you, I'm fine." She closed her eyes again. "Isn't it time we got some sleep? I'm tired."

She was using his line.

"Right. Sleep." He blew out the candles except for one a little beyond their heads, which he intended for a night light. Taking off his boots, he stretched out on the rat rug beside her.

"Goodnight," he said, but she didn't reply. He laid on his back, closed his eyes, and wondered when—or if—he would fall asleep tonight. It didn't help that Lindsay, as bruised and battered as she was, was lying so close beside him, and that he could detect the scent of her shampoo and hear her light breathing. He concentrated on emptying his mind, tossing out all sorts of mental garbage. In the end, he was left with one thing too heavy to discard. An apology.

He turned on his side and whispered, "Linds. I am sorry for treating you the way I have. I'm sorry you were hurt. I said out there it was my fault and it's the truth. You have to know I'm trying to be like the old Jack. I really am."

He waited for her to say something. She didn't move, her face remained averted. He fell back and shut his eyes. There, at least he'd said it. Now maybe he'd get to lose himself in sleep.

Lindsay shifted beside him, her mouth came against his ear. "I deserved that beating. In fact, I'm grateful for it."

He flinched and without thinking, his arm came hard around her middle. "Lindsay, don't be stupid. How can you say that?"

She didn't resist his hold but she didn't stop either, her soft words brushing against his ear. "I always want to make things right, Jack. I've always liked beautiful, perfect things. I had a beautiful family. A beautiful niece. I made a business of taking old places and making them new again, even married a man because he matched me, like I was pairing up two paint colors or something.

"That storage bin with your things. That's an unfinished project I wanted to complete. And when Seline went missing I wanted her back, all clean and polished exactly like she'd been when she left. Only the world doesn't work that way. There's no making things right."

His arm tightened around her. "She'll be okay, Linds."

She sighed, a long, exasperated sound. "You're not understanding me, Jack. Of course she will, but she'll be a different person after this. Everybody down here is well beyond being 'fixed'. I had this insane idea that I could make the people in this village believe I wasn't evil by giving one of their children a pack of crackers. *Crackers.* Like some stupid little present would make everything good. It took a beating to knock sense into me. "

"You didn't know, Linds."

"I knew their life was hard. I knew they kept their kids clean and healthy as they could. I should've known better then to push myself on them, and now, I do. Seline will never be the same again. Same with you. I know you say you're trying, and I'm saying, there's no point."

No, no, she couldn't have said that.

"You can't be the old Jack," she carried on. "It's impossible. So, I've got a choice. When we get Seline out of here, I can spend the rest of my life trying to make her as she was, or I can accept that she's altered and get on with things. The fact is you don't need fixing, Jack. None of us do."

Jack couldn't believe what he'd heard. She might as well as stabbed him in the heart, for the pain, anger and desolation that seared through him. In one fluid motion he was crouched over her.

"You're wrong, Lindsay." He could hear how cold and sharp he sounded, could see it in the widening of her eyes.

She rose onto her elbows and moved to speak but he wrapped his hand around her neck and her mouth closed. He could feel her Adam's apple as she swallowed, knew the mild asphyxiated sensation she must be having. "This epiphany of yours is a betrayal. Of Seline. Of me. Even of yourself. And before we take one more step on this little adventure, we're going to get something real straight. Got it?"

She nodded.

"When your family was wiped out, and your brother was lying in that hospital bed with the life trickling out of him, did you say 'Oh well, nothing I can do?' Did you look into his eyes and say 'Nothing's wrong. Everything's okay?' Did you?"

Lindsay shook her head. Under his fingers, her pulse pounded.

"Of course you didn't. You stepped up and became the guardian of your niece, and with Janice's help, you rebuilt your life brick by brick. You didn't make some weak compromise, but created something bright and prosperous and beautiful. Didn't you?"

"Yes," she whispered.

"Then get this through your head, Linds, and don't you *dare* ever forget it. I crawled through a world of shit, blood and razors to get back to the surface. I sacrificed parts of me I never thought I could lose and still live. Did terrible things to others to save myself. And right now I am as deeply, majorly broken as your brother was after having his body smashed by that truck."

Her face was pale, her pulse pumping, her eyes dark liquid pools in the candlelight.

"It's never been said, but we've made a pact, you and me. I'm risking everything, more than I pray you're ever able to comprehend, to get back Seline. And when we do, she's going to be a shell of the girl that went down here. She will need someone—I will need someone—who pulls us back into the light. Someone who works to make us whole again, because I can tell you from personal experience, we're not going to be able to get there on our own.

"I was already on the surface, Linds. I already survived. So I'm not gambling everything I am to return to some empty fucking basement. I am coming back for a woman with blue eyes and bright hair, and by God, I expect you to do everything in your power to fix me. To fix her. Because if not, we might as well just leave her down here. It would be kinder than someone she loves looking her in the face and saying '*You don't need fixing*'. You get me?"

Last time his hand was around her neck she'd looked for understanding and he'd not given it to her. Now he was, and she gave it back to him straight. "I get you, Jack."

From Lindsay that was all he needed. A few soft words of knowing, of promise. His anger melted into something else. Sorrow for not being the man she'd remembered. The shame of having had to lay bear the frailty of his mind and spirit to the one person who'd always held a claim on his soul. But amidst it, he realized that something else had taken root. Something planted when he'd woken in her bed this morning.

It was a tiny, shriveled thing, alive by the thinnest of margins. Yet it was there.

Hope.

He released his hold on her, and immediately she sat up and curved her hand by his ear, and made good on her promise. She kissed him.

She took her time on his mouth, playing her lips lightly against his, her tongue skimming his own. And he lost no time in kissing her back. He could've spent the night that way, if he hadn't become distracted by the bruise under her right eye. His lips brushed it and turning to her other cheek, he lined tiny kisses along the scratch there.

"Kissing it better?" Her words were soft and low, carried to him on a wisp of breathlessness.

"Is it working?"

Her answer was throaty murmur. "Yes."

"Would you like me to do all the others the same way?"

And exactly as she had the night before, she laid herself down, spread herself before him in silent invitation. In the glow of the trembling candlelight, he unbuttoned her shirt. Sadness and guilt washed over him at the sight of her cuts and bruises. He shimmied off her jeans, and kissed each mark on her shins and her thighs. He rolled her onto her stomach and kissed her lower back, her ribs, her shoulder blades. He eased her back and continued his tender ritual of healing. And all the while he felt the quiet marvel of once again touching without fear or hurt or loss. He was fixing her. Fixing himself.

The last mark was on her left breast right above the cut of her bra. When he raised his head from it, his fingers took to stroking the black lace. The nipple hardened. He paused. He hadn't intended that. He only wanted to make her feel better, not to turn it into sex.

He looked up to tell her that.

Her expression had softened, taken on that same languidness as when he'd had her on the bed and not this god-awful rat rug. She covered his hand on her breast with her own, guided his thumb back to her nipple. "Aches there, too."

He sucked in his breath, and easily popped open her bra clasp to expose her perfect breasts. He lowered his mouth—

A gunshot rang out. Then several more, followed by the

shrieking of women and children.

"Fuck!" Jack snarled, his voice alive with frustration as much as alarm. Lindsay looked up at him startled and confused, and he gave her a short, hard kiss. "Stay here." He pulled his boots on, seized his gun, and backhanding the curtain open, he left, torn from her again.

# CHAPTER FOURTEEN

LINDSAY GRABBED HER gun, backpedaling to the rear of the cinderblock hut, and trained it on the entrance. Crouched there, she clicked the light on and the safety off, ready for anything.

She strained to hear what was happening, especially anything from Jack or Reggie. A couple of times she picked out Reggie's booming bass, but nothing from Jack.

Long minutes passed, no more shots were heard, and the sounds of Agharta's startled inhabitants settled, too. Lindsay was patting through the gear for her pants when the curtain billowed inwards.

Jack caught her in her underwear and a gun aimed at his heart. He drew a deep breath. "Get dressed, Linds. We've got to get out of here."

"What happened?" she said, securing the safety before turning to her clothes.

"A Mole."

Lindsay's hands stilled on the waistband of her jeans. "What? Here?"

"Neil spotted it on the outskirts and scared it off with a warning shot. It was likely a scout, though they don't usually come up this far. We can't stay here any longer." Jack pulled a face. "Our showing up and its appearance are no coincidence. Dammit, I knew that I'd heard them back in The Gallery. Should've trusted my instincts. Now the entire camp is at risk. They can't defend themselves."

Lindsay thought of the number they'd done on her, and begged to differ. If anyone could stand up against the Moles it would be these women protecting their young. Still, this wasn't their battle to fight, and that was the point. She pulled a t-shirt over her head, and when she could see again, she could tell Jack had been looking at her naked torso.

His eyes met hers. "You need to get yourself checked out before we go."

"Jack, I told you—"

"And I'm telling you, you're getting yourself checked out." He grabbed his stuff and shoved it into his bag. "I'll meet you outside. Hurry up."

"My bruises are not your fault, and neither are the Moles," she said softly.

He was at the door, his hand on the tarp. "You're not the only one who's wanted to make things right." He hitched his gun over his shoulder. "I'll wait for you outside. And kill the candles on your wait out."

The hospital was a hut constructed completely, straight down to the door, in corrugated metal. Jack tapped on the door and pushed it open. "No one's here. Go in and I'll send someone over. I'll be by the fire when you're done. Okay?"

Lindsay slipped inside and sat on a low wooden bench that ran along one wall. The only light from a large kerosene lamp that hung from a hook in the middle of the ceiling was sufficient to make out her surroundings. The place was large compared to its neighbors, roughly the size of an ambulance's interior, and like an ambulance, it was fitted with rows of cupboards stuffed with assorted medical supplies and equipment.

She expected Shamba, but it was not to be. Gali banged open the door and unbuckled her bandolier of knives, draping them over a peg above the bench as if it were an old coat. She stared down at Lindsay, her eyes like the cold gleam of her blades. Instinctively Lindsay squared her shoulders.

The two faced each other in a silent showdown. It was Gali whose gaze shifted away first, though her next words showed that she was only changing tack.

"Strip. I need to see where you're injured."

Lindsay opened her mouth to tell her what to do with that directive, then thought better of it. If Lindsay refused treatment, Gali wouldn't care, and it would appear that she was disobeying Jack. So with as much nonchalance as she could muster, she shed clothes until she was left shivering in her underwear.

Gali inspected the numerous bruises. Lindsay was tempted to say that Jack had kissed them all better. There were a few places where she'd been struck hard enough to draw blood, and these Gali began to clean with a stinging antiseptic, pouring on way more than necessary in Lindsay's opinion. Even the follow-up bandages were pressed forcefully onto her broken flesh. It was as if she was getting a beating all over again. Determined not to show pain, Lindsay focused on the erratic patterns of shadows that the lantern cast on the walls.

Gali was applying a bandage on Lindsay's upper thigh with enough force to embed it there, when she spoke. "You know how long I've lived in these tunnels?"

Lindsay shook her head.

"Fifteen years. Ever since I was thirteen. A friend of mine brought me down here to have my baby."

"Oh...."

"I wasn't a whore, if that's what you're thinking."

"I wasn't thinking that at all."

"Then what were you thinking?"

"That thirteen's very young to be having a baby."

"It is," Gali's voice was clipped. "I guess some men don't care much about that. That's why I came down here. So my baby wouldn't be put through the same shit I was."

"That's brave of you."

Gali finished the bandage with one final tight yank. "Didn't do any good. I lost her at birth. Would have died myself if it wasn't for Shamba."

Lindsay didn't know what to say. This was Gali's tale of brokenness, part of the anthology everyone in the tunnels had contributed to. What else could have brought them to this dark and dangerous world? Seline was constantly telling her about the people who fell through the cracks in the system. Here they were, having literally dropped past sewers, holes, tunnels to land in this pit. And yet they called it home, a place to raise a family.

As sad as Gali's story was, Lindsay knew her sympathy wasn't wanted. She looked the woman in the eye. "Why did you tell me this?"

The answer came quick. "So you know that you're no match for me. Jack needs to be down here. You're just a *topsider*." The last word was spat out like poison.

Lindsay hopped off the table, landing so she was chest to chest, nose to nose with her rival. Because Gali was a rival, intent on stealing Jack away from her and in so doing, dragging him into the underground where he would once again lose himself in this soul-shriveling world.

"It's because I *am* a topsider that Jack needs me. He had a whole year to come back to you, and he didn't. That should tell you something, Gali. He wants to be up in the world, and I give him reason to be there."

Gali's lips curled, and she tapped her head. "In his mind he never left. That's where it counts. He's come back and this time he'll stay. You'll see."

The steely confidence in the woman's voice chilled Lindsay, not because she believed her but because she could see that Gali believed it. And any woman who carried knives as easily as another woman did a purse would likely fight for her convictions.

Lindsay stepped around Gali and began pulling on her clothes. This little doctor's visit was over as far as she was concerned, and from the way the woman was tossing the bandages back into the kit, the feeling was mutual.

Gali was done first and, leaning against the wall, watched Lindsay put on her boots. "The tunnels have a way of keeping people, even if they don't want to be kept."

Lindsay yanked on her laces. "I think Jack's strong enough to make his own choices."

"Then what is he doing back here?" Gali retorted. "Last time he walked out of here I was sure I'd never see him again. Especially considering his wife."

Lindsay felt a sudden buzzing in her ears, as if the breath had been knocked out of her. It was only good luck that she was bent over her boots, otherwise her face would've betrayed her. She licked her lips. "Wife?"

Lindsay had aimed for casualness. It didn't work. Gali gave a laugh of pure pleasure, like a chess player who'd discovered the winning move. "You don't know about her? Well, well. Jack always was good at keeping secrets, though I didn't think he was the cheating type. Not that it would've mattered to me. I'm not so hung up on the marriage thing. You've probably fallen for all that romantic crap. Probably why he kept his mouth shut about it."

Lindsay remembered Jack's version of events. "How do you know that he didn't just say that? Did you consider it was his way of cooling the hots you had for him?"

Gali's eyes flared at Lindsay's goading question, though her smile didn't fade. "If you don't believe me, ask Reggie."

It riled Lindsay that Gali should know more about Jack than herself, and made her sick to know that Jack hadn't shared that intimate detail.

"I guess I will." She sounded like a pathetic little girl trying to stand up to a bully. "I suppose that's the Tasha you mentioned before."

"Sure is."

No wonder Jack hadn't wanted to talk about the mystery woman. Was she involved with a married man? Why then wasn't he living with his wife?

He said he'd only marry for love. He said that if he couldn't be with the woman he loved he wouldn't want to be friends, either. So either she was dead or they were divorced. Either way, she felt heartsick. For him. And for herself.

"Anyway, I'm sure Jack can mind his own *affairs*," Gali said, opening the tin door with a grand sweeping motion.

Lindsay stood with as much dignity as possible. "Thanks for your help," she said with absolutely no sincerity.

Gali smirked. "My pleasure. The pain will stop soon enough, I'm sure."

Lindsay knew the woman wasn't referring to the bruises.

---

ONE LOOK AT Lindsay's grim expression and Jack knew that Gali had got to her. God knows what had been said, but considering that Lindsay was looking at him with all the suspicion of an alley cat, he guessed it was about Tasha. And once again, there was no time to deal with it. Maybe that was a good thing. Better for now to focus on the reason that they were down in these godforsaken tunnels in the first place.

They left Agharta via a crawlway, squeezing down its narrow passage until it opened into a larger tunnel. Reggie led the way with Lindsay steps behind, and him on her ass. She stumbled once, quickly righting herself, though he knew that with her injuries, it was all she could do not to slow them down any more than she was. Still he crowded her every step, silently urging her on.

His eyes were peeled, his ears strained for all sounds. Reggie would be doing the same, but Jack had more experience. The Moles weren't near, but they were coming. The scout would've reached The Pits by now, and his old keeper would be plotting moves on Jack. Perhaps the things were already on their way up. He needed to get Lindsay and Reggie behind the secure walls of Seneca.

The passages were becoming older now, the concrete hallways giving way to moldering brickwork and hewn rock. They wove their way through endless dark corridors, some hot and misty with steam, others cold and slippery with ice, till at last they emerged into a large circular chamber, its walls supported by massive stone arches and lined with countless dust-covered bottles. The air stunk of acid, and he saw Lindsay wrinkle her nose.

"What's this?" she whispered, following Reggie's beam of light over the ceiling-high racks easily containing a thousand bottles. She answered her own question. "A wine cellar."

Reggie pulled out a bottle at random and held it up for her to read the label.

"Oh my God, that's a 1905 Latour...do you know what that bottle is worth?"

Jack could've spent a day here with Lindsay, showing her the links between the bottles and New York's history but, as usual, there was no time. "Probably not much," he cut in. "All of this is vinegar by now, otherwise someone would have looted it. Let's keep moving. We're almost there. This cellar is on the outskirts of Seneca."

They worked their way through a maze of ancient tunnels until they came to a featureless metal door set at the end of one of the passages. A small electric light and security camera were set above it, as well as an intercom installed to one side.

"This is new," Reggie said. "Looks like hiring the Tecos isn't the only thing they've done to upgrade security."

Jack glanced over his shoulder. The feeling from The Gallery had returned, and this time he wasn't going to ignore it. They were being watched, and by more than the camera.

"Time to say hello." He stepped to the door and pressed the intercom button.

There was a long silence. C'mon, c'mon. He was about to try again when a gravelly Hispanic voice came over the speaker. "Who are you?"

Jack looked up at the camera. "My name is Jack Cole, and I'm here with my woman and Reggie from Grand Central. We've come to speak with the Tecoacualli. Najib sent us."

Another drawn-out silence before the voice returned. "Place your weapons and shit by the door and get up against the wall."

Jack nodded, then turned to Reggie and muttered, "I sure hope Najib knows what he's talking about."

They did as instructed while the security camera swiveled back and forth to verify their compliance. Only then did the heavy door unlock, and from out of the brilliant light beyond came a group of five men, all armed with heavy automatics and clad in black army-style clothing.

They fanned out—two watched the tunnel, one snagged the sub-machine guns and packs, and two frisked their visitors, running a small metal detector over them for good measure. Inspection complete, the contingent escorted them inside.

Jack squinted under the glare of harsh fluorescent lighting, his eyes watering as they were led down a short corridor and through a barred security door. It opened into a large bunker-like chamber decorated with a collage of psychedelic posters and hardcore pornography, furnished with ratty furniture and reeking of what smelt like ammonia. A small boom box in the corner played Spanish rap music, and the room featured a grimy kitchenette, a bathroom and a row of monitors displaying Seneca's primitive laboratories. None of it would have looked at all impressive to an average New Yorker, but the very fact that Seneca enjoyed water, sewage and electricity testified to the prosperity of this outlaw community.

One of the men, the left side of his face disfigured by burns, disappeared down an adjoining hall, while another sat Jack and Reggie, Lindsay between them, down on an old couch to wait. Lindsay shook free her hair and unzipped her jacket. The eyes of the three guards were immediately riveted to her. Sexual interest animated their deadpan expressions. Apparently Nazi conspiracy theories didn't reach this far.

"Najib told us that there's a man here named Tocat," Reggie said. "He around?"

One grizzled fighter dragged his eyes sideways to

Reggie."He'll be here soon, man. Relax."

After a quarter of an hour passed, the guards took up the surrounding chairs, keeping their pistols in hand. By now Lindsay had completely undone her jacket and she was about to wiggle out of it when he tugged it back over her shoulders and shook his head. She shrugged and complied. She'd be glad of a jacket if, as he was beginning to worry, they had to make a run for it.

The guards all looked to be in their mid-thirties, though rough living had left the lot of them scarred, calloused and tougher than old boards. All of them were sporting a variety of gang tattoos, including an Aztec-styled one of a snake that ran around each man's left wrist. Their clothing looked as dark and dirty as the tunnels; their guns were all clean and polished. Without a doubt these were the Tecos—brutal renegades of New York's most feared Hispanic gangs. Marked men from topsider gangs like El Esquadron, La Raza and the Mexican Mafia. They were all outcasts to begin with, when they formed their own gang in the Burbs. The lot of them had relocated to Seneca shortly before the cops came, otherwise the carnage would have been even worse.

The military marching of heavy boots came down the hallway, and into the room arrived a short and extremely muscular man with the same uniform and wrist tattoo as his companions. Unlike his dead-eyed men, however, his gaze shone with a fierce intelligence, and by his confident stride, he was the undisputed leader of the group.

He waved his hand and a seat was vacated. He sat and leaned forward to rest his elbows on his knees, as if about to engage in a friendly chat.

"So, Najib sent you, huh? Been a long time since I heard his name."

As in the old days, Jack let Reggie do the talking. The big black man had developed his own effective brand of people skills. "Najib said you owed him a favor or two. Told me I could call them in."

The man leaned back in his chair, easing into a near-smile. "Najib's a smart man. Now you'll owe him. What do you want?"

"There's a topsider that got taken by the Moles. We need help going down to The Pits to rescue her."

The hardened men exchanged nervous glances, and even Tocat's composed expression tightened. "That's some favor."

"We can pay," Reggie continued. "I'm talking five grand for the each of you. Najib told me you Tecos are the most dangerous men in the underground, so that's why we've come here. We need the best."

Tocat gave a slow, calculating nod. Greed versus fear, Jack supposed. Which would win out? "It's a big job, man, going after the Moles where they live. Five grand isn't going to—"

His words were cut off by the slam of a door down the hallway, followed by a string of harsh obscenities. Jack and Reggie exchanged looks and, as one, turned to Lindsay between them. She seemed more pissed than scared. "Just when we were getting somewhere," she said through thinned lips.

Heavy footfalls bore down on them, and there emerged a huge, fat, greasy man, all of his chins quivering with rage. He gestured to the couch and snarled, "What the fuck is this shit? When did I say you motherfuckers could let anyone in?"

Tocat didn't even glance up. "Chill out, King. They're here to see me."

"Oh, that's nice. So who the fuck are they? Fucking cops?"

"Cops never come this deep."

"They will if we open the fucking doors for them. I pay you motherfuckers to guard this place, not have your fucking friends over for some pizza fucking party. You think I'm going to let anyone wander the fuck through Seneca on your say-so?"

Tocat rose, his controlled stance hardening into hostility. Jack double-checked the exit, scrambled to think of a deal to make. The Teco leader strolled over until the fat man, who was a good half-foot taller, had to sink his chins into his chest.

"So what you want us to do?" asked Tocat, his tone calm, dangerous.

King didn't budge an inch. "For starters I want to be told when people show up, but seeing as how you've already rolled out the red fucking carpet for them I'd like to know a few other things. Like who the fuck they are, why they're fucking here and why I shouldn't cap the fucking lot of them in the head."

Tocat jerked a thumb at Jack. "That man's name is Jack Cole. You heard of him?"

King turned piggy eyes to Jack, then fixed them back on Tocat, raising a pudgy finger to the Teco leader's face.

"I want them frisked, cuffed and brought to my fucking office. And don't you *ever* let anyone through that fucking door without my permission again, or—" King stopped.

"Or what?" Tocat's voice was a chilling taunt.

King's already red face turned almost purple with anger. "Just bring them to my fucking office." He stalked out of the room. From down the hallway came a loud "Fuck!"

Jack knew now who their real enemy was. He took a risk. "Who the fuck does that fat fuck think he fucking is?"

It worked. Tocat broke into a broad grin. "Fuck man, he's the fucking mayor of fucking Seneca."

# CHAPTER FIFTEEN

SENECA WASN'T PLEASANT, but it was large. With several poorly ventilated labs, a small warehouse for chemical and drug storage, and long rows of bunk beds for its workers, the place was a full-fledged narcotics factory. This Lindsay learned as she was led handcuffed along with Jack and Reggie through the corridors, past room after room where empty-eyed, emaciated people ate, slept and slaved under the watchful eye of Teco guards.

"Place is a lot bigger than when I was last here," Reggie said, out of the side of his mouth.

"Profits must be up," Jack noted. "Let's hope they're not recruiting."

King's office was at the far end of the complex, a grubby room filled with cheap furniture where the smell of cigarette smoke barely overlaid the more noxious fumes of the labs. He sat behind his desk like a poisonous toad, his pale skin a sickly green hue in the fluorescent lighting. He had them cuffed to three weighty metal chairs, then dismissed the Teco guards.

The sentries exchanged looks, hesitating, slowly complying after King yelled at them to get the fuck out. The fat man turned to his guests, his lips still curled into a feral snarl. "Did you see that? Only orders those fucking bastards take is to go on a fucking coffee break. Which," he added, as if it needed clarifying, "I don't fucking give."

He looked at each of them in turn, his eyes settling on Lindsay for a long full draw of his cigarette. His free hand disappeared under the desk, and adjusted his crotch area, and then stayed down there. Lindsay balled her hands into fists and glancing to the side, saw that both Jack and Reggie had done the same, their knuckles white.

King's gaze drifted to Jack. "So, I hear you're one serious badass. A fucking Mole-killer. That right?"

Only Jack's mouth moved. "I did escape them. That much is true."

King rubbed his chins. "So you want to rescue some poor bastard from those freaks, huh?"

Jack nodded. "That's right."

"Who?"

"A topsider."

"Why?"

"Friend of a friend."

"Must be quite the fucking friend," King said. "I wouldn't go down there to save my own mother."

"I believe you."

The greaseball gave a genuine laugh. "I'd be thrilled to help the esteemed Jack-fucking-Cole, only I got fucking headaches of my own right now. Built this place up with my own two hands, and now those Aztec motherfuckers think they're my fucking partners."

"Um…Mr. King," Reggie said. "We only came by to see if we could hire some backup here. We don't want to be getting in your way or nothing."

King trained his beady eyes on Reggie. "And who exactly

the fuck are you?"

"Name's Reggie Watkins. I got the gate at Grand Central."

"Right. I remember you. I paid you protection way back, didn't I? How the mighty have fucking fallen."

Lindsay saw the muscles in Reggie's face convulse, even as he gave an indifferent shrug.

"So who's she?" King continued, addressing his question to Jack. Lindsay hardly blinked at the chauvinism. On King's long list of character flaws, being a sexist pig was probably the least serious.

"Lindsay," Jack replied.

King stared, obviously expecting more. Jack looked impassively back.

The man dropped his cigarette butt into his cup of coffee where it hissed and died, and took in Lindsay again. More adjustments were made under the desk. "She yours?"

Jack's expression was closed, unreadable. "Yes."

"Well then, I think we can come to a fucking arrangement."

Jack remained silent so long that King was forced to carry on unprompted. "I'll send Tocat and a few of his men down to The Pits with you, while your woman stays here as my guest. Wouldn't want her getting hurt down there, would you?"

Lindsay shot Jack her "Don't-you-even-think-about-it" glare. He didn't look at her. "What do you want in return?"

"It's not what I want, Cole. It's what I don't want. And what I don't fucking want is the people I give you making it back alive."

"You're asking us to kill your own men?" Reggie's voice was hard with disbelief.

"I don't care if it's you or the fucking Moles. I don't want to see them again."

Lindsay watched Jack's white-knuckled fists convulse. "How do you propose we do that? There'll only be two of us against at least five or six of them. And their guns look well cared for."

King shook his head, his loose jowls flapping like a bloodhound. "Well, looks like you got yourself a fucking challenge there, Cole. I'm sure if you outran them Moles, you'll think of something."

"I was thinking we could leave and not trouble you any further."

King grinned. "Yeah? Then maybe you should think again. I mean, this can be a fucking win-win situation for us. You get the men you need for the rescue, and I get rid of the little steroid pumping fuck who's trying to muscle in on my operation. Or—"

Again Jack waited him out.

"—or the alternative is a lose-lose proposition. My fucking problem doesn't get solved, you two get shot and your woman winds up with a lifetime contract here in Seneca."

Both men jerked simultaneously against their handcuffs. Lindsay wished she could tell them that it was okay. Assure them that she'd tear King's balls off before she became a Seneca slave.

She stretched her hands toward Jack and he glanced down at them. He drew a long, steadying breath. "And what if we tell Tocat and his crew about your little plan?"

"Go right fucking ahead. You think that fuck doesn't already know I'm planning to off him? You tell him, he'll thank you, then put a fucking bullet through your face. No sense in him waiting around for you to do the same. He'd kill me in a fucking heartbeat if he didn't need me to run this fucking show. Seeing as he does there's not much for me to lose in trying, hmm?"

King pressed a button on his desk. "Why don't you take some time to think about it? I'm guessing you'll come around."

The doors of the office opened, and the Teco escorts stepped inside.

"Take these two fucks to a guest room. Feed them, but I don't want them going anywhere or talking to fucking anyone. Get it?"

"What about her?" one of the men asked.

"Leave her," King replied. "I'll look after her myself."

Jack's amber eyes burned as the guards uncuffed him from the chair. "Lay a finger on her and there'll be hell to pay."

Seneca's mayor chuckled. "In case you haven't noticed, Cole, we're already in fucking hell. Now it's a question of who gets to be the devil."

---

LINDSAY WATCHED AS Jack and Reggie were led to the office door, trying her best to disguise her fear at being left behind. Jack didn't take his eyes off her, and in them she read worry and—something more.

She lifted her chin. "I'll be okay, Jack." She hoped her voice didn't sound as shaky as she felt. He gave one short nod, as he was dragged out. The guards shut the thick office door behind them, and turning back, Lindsay found King was settling his bulky backside on the corner of his desk. His pants zipper was half-open.

"Alone at last." His gaze dropped to her chest. She wish she'd left her jacket zipped.

"Mr. King, I'm sure you're right about Jack coming around to your way of thinking," she lied. "But you heard what would happen if I'm harmed."

The man touched her bruised cheek. "Looks to me like he's gone lax on that. Fucking shame, too, with what a beautiful woman he's got. Looking at you is a nice fucking change from the burnt-out whores and tunnel scum I got working for me. A really nice change." He smacked his flabby lips, and Lindsay's stomach lurched.

One touch from him and she'd vomit. Best keep him talking. "I'm sure a man with your wealth could have any girl he wanted."

He fished a pack of cigarettes and a lighter from his shirt pocket. "There was a time when you'd have been right. I used to fuck a woman as pretty as you every night, and some nights two or three. It took a lot of fucking planning and elbow grease to set this operation up. Once it was, this place made me so much money I was living in a fucking Manhattan penthouse with a first-class city view. I was a V.I.P. at the hottest clubs, drove a Rolls-Royce and had enough cash to pay off any cop that got near me. Fuck, I had more money than I could spend, and believe me I could burn through it."

"So what happened?" she asked.

He lit up his cigarette and took a long draw. "The cops turned out to be fucking smarter than I thought. Their homicide team, anyhow. I wound up with three warrants for my arrest and a case against me so strong even Johnnie-fucking-Cochrane couldn't have got me off. I'm facing at least one life sentence if they find me, and all because some stupid whore had to go and steal from me. Yet another fucking waste."

"So you hid out down here," Lindsay finished.

"That's right, sweetheart. Stuck down here with all these

sub-human fucks, breathing carcinogenic air and forgetting what the sun looks like. Fucking ironic, isn't it?"

There was justice in the world.

Then he turned philosopher-King. "Funny thing is that everybody here is in the same boat. If Tocat or his buddies showed up on the surface they'd be in even worse trouble. All of them fucked with their gangs in one way or another, and upstairs that's at least a fucking death sentence. So we're all prisoners down here. Even the guards and warden. What do you think of that?"

"I think that's very sad." She was going to have to do a lot of lying with the man.

King took another drag on his cigarette, then reached for her cheek. She flinched involuntarily, and his hand stilled.

"You're worried about what I'm going to do to you, aren't you, sweetie?" He blew a jet of smoke in her direction like some blubbery dragon.

She managed to keep her voice even. "Should I be?"

He withdrew his hand, cupped his crotch and gave it a suggestive hitch. "I've learned that what I want and what I get aren't the same fucking things."

Lindsay sucked in her breath. That's what she'd been thinking about Jack. "You're a fighter, got pride, even if Cole knocks you around a little. You're tough, and quite frankly I don't have the fucking energy to beat you down."

"I suppose I should take that as a compliment."

"Take it any way you like. But the Tecos…those assholes are a whole other fucking story," he continued. "There's a dozen of them in all, and I think they're the kind of men who might like a woman like you. Someone who'd put up a bit of a struggle, you know? It's a power thing with them. A challenge."

Lindsay forced herself to look him in the eye. "Why are you telling me all this?"

He leaned in, his stale breath almost gagging her. "I'm telling you because I'm going to send you back to your boyfriend now, and I want you to convince him to cooperate. If you don't then you're going to wind up getting fucked by the men that he refused to kill, and then you'll be living as pathetic a fucking existence as I am, won't you?"

Lindsay's lips tightened. King could be very convincing. "I'll talk to him."

"Good girl." He gave a painful pat to her cheek. "I always knew you blondes were just playing dumb."

---

SENECA'S 'GUEST' ROOM featured electric lighting, two bunk beds and even a small bathroom. They were granted a meal of topside food: microwave dinners of pasta and three cans of cola. From Lindsay's experiences so far, this would be the underground's version of the Ritz, if it weren't for the fact that the door locked from the outside.

When she'd been escorted there after her chat with King, Jack had reached for her but she'd stiffened at the thought of what she was expected to make him and Reggie do. Jack must've connected her discomfort with him, and had stepped back. She was certain that he knew she had learned about Tasha from Gali, and figured she was angry with him, and without a doubt she was. That didn't stop her from needing him. She found herself sitting down beside him on the lower bunk, seeking his presence. Even if he was a dirty, rotten, lying bastard.

"It could be worse," Lindsay suggested, referring mostly

to the situation with King.

"If death is worse," Jack said to the floor.

"Don't think we got too much in the way of choices," Reggie said, from the upper bunk. "Guy's holding all the cards."

Jack set his elbows on his knees. "I should never have let you two come down here with me. Stupidest thing I ever did."

"Don't think that was an option," Reggie reminded him.

"We'll get out of this mess," Lindsay said.

Jack turned to her, his expression bleak. "And how do you know that?"

She didn't know. "I just do."

The bunks shook as Reggie made himself comfortable. "I'd say King's right when he said to think on it," he contributed. "What with all the excitement at Agharta we haven't got any shuteye since we left Grand Central."

"I suppose so," Jack agreed, not making any move to lie down. Was he wondering like her where they'd sleep? If things were different between them, the single bed would be the clear winner. But then she never did know where she stood with him, did she?

Lindsay shed her boots and jacket, and flipped off the light switch. Aside from the narrow strip of illumination from beneath the door, all was dark, and fumbling, she slipped behind Jack to stretch out on the narrow mattress.

Jack stayed hunched. It wasn't his fault that they'd wound up in the mess they were in, though by the looks of him he was taking it onto his shoulders. Nothing down in the tunnels made sense, and nothing reflected that maddening confusion more than her feelings for him. Despite how close they seemed to have become so soon, and the undeniable warmth that flowed through her every time she was with him, he was still a mystery to her.

Why hadn't he told her about his wife? Was it that he had intended to hide that fact from her, or was there some more understandable reason for his secrecy? It could be anything at all because in the end *he hadn't shared with her.*

And yet it was clear that he wanted to open up. He'd made her vow that she would fix him, would knock down the cold, hard barrier between them. So dammit, she'd keep battering away.

Reggie had begun to snore—a surprisingly gentle sound considering the man's size, and still Jack sat there.

"Jack?" she whispered.

"Yeah?"

"None of this is your fault."

"Who's to blame if not me, Linds?"

"King. The Tecos were hearing us out, so it certainly wasn't Najib or Reggie that led us down the wrong path. Tocat might have agreed to let us hire them. It was King that decided to play this game."

"I suppose he's got to keep himself amused somehow," Jack said humorlessly.

"You should get some sleep now, Jack. You're not going to do us any good if you're exhausted."

"Don't worry about me. Get some rest yourself."

"I will when you do."

He sighed. "You never let up, do you?"

The way he said it, all soft and resigned, made her smile. "Remember? We have a pact."

She saw him hunch over, then heard the subtle rasp of boots being unlaced. Had he decided where he was sleeping? "Jack…" she began, then paused.

"Yes?"

"You know Gali told me about your wife, right?"

She sensed more than saw Jack lower his head to his hands. "Yes." The single word was muffled.

He was in pain and she wanted to take it away. If only he would trust her enough. "I won't push it. However,"—this was outright blackmail she was pulling here—"I never said anything about Reggie. Maybe he and I could have a conversation when he wakes up."

It was a safe threat. She wanted to hear the story from Jack and Jack alone, and she knew Reggie would never betray his friend's confidence. It was a way of showing, once again, that she wasn't giving up on him.

Jack pulled off one of his boots. "The man would have to be asleep first." He heaved his size eleven to the upper bunk.

It tumbled back as Reggie knocked it aside. "Shit," he said, obviously embarrassed at having been caught out. "How'd you know?"

"You've slept in the same room as me before. I know— hell, the neighborhood knows—what you snore like. You're going to have to crank the volume if you're going to fool anyone. Now goodnight, you two."

"Goodnight," Reggie grumbled.

Jack yanked off his other boot and made to move away. Not thinking, Lindsay hooked a finger in his belt loop and tugged. That was all it took. He stretched out beside her, his arm coming around her to tuck her back tight against his front. Every single bone and muscle in her body softened and sank into him.

His mouth came to her ear. "I'll tell you, okay?"

"Okay," she whispered back.

She felt him bury his face in her hair, felt him breathe deeply. And hearing him, she breathed too, deep and long, and it felt like her first real breath since leaving topside. She didn't remember drawing a second one before she fell asleep.

# CHAPTER
## SiXTEEN

*JACK GAVE THE rubber ball a gentle push, its dim shape rolling across the floor to the little Mole. It seized the toy, claws clenching around it, worried it like a cat with a mouse, then slowly rolled it back.*

*From the corner of his eye, Jack watched as two other youngsters dangled a pigeon leg in front of their pet, a boy given by their elders to keep them entertained. He was probably about fourteen years old, and after thirty sleeps in his new home, was already quite mad. He snatched at the meat through the bars, whining like a whipped dog when his masters pulled it a little beyond reach.*

*Jack caught the ball and sent it back, continuing the game. The Moles were slowly starving the boy to death, curious about how long he could survive on how little. Though Jack had snuck some of his own food between the bars, the boy wouldn't last much longer. Thin when he'd arrived, he was now a living skeleton.*

*This time when the ball reached the young Mole, it hurled the toy at Jack. Lightning fast, Jack caught it and fired it back, bouncing it off the thing's head. With a hiss of annoyance, the creature scuttled off to retrieve it.*

*Jack had taught this nasty version of 'catch' to the young Moles here in the nursery, a simple game culled from the fragments of his memory. Bit by bit, his keeper was giving him back his past, telling him who he was and what he'd done. Though he knew they had been warped, the stories rung of too much truth for him not to claim them. He remembered now his passion for the underground and his exciting exploration of its reaches. How he and Lindsay...no, Tasha, had journeyed to labyrinths all over the globe, and how much she had loved him for all the adventures he had given her.*

*His mind had a memory for when the nameless people of the city above had taken her away from him and exiled him down to the darkness, a pariah left to wander alone. It was the Moles that had saved him, who had recognized him as a brother and taken him in. He knew that wasn't quite what had happened.*

*He knew for sure that Tasha wasn't with him anymore.*

*He knew that because he had no memory of her death, she might still be alive.*

*He knew that he needed to get back to her. To find her. To find himself.*

*The good thing was the Moles thought of him as a junior member now, no longer bothering to chain or cage him. The bad thing was that they never traveled alone. Communal by nature, some of them were always with him, having no concept of privacy or solitude. He was waiting for the right opportunity, when only two or three of them would be present, to make his move and flee. That in itself presented problems.*

*The moldering passage of Devil's Crawl was the only way into The Pits, and the Moles had posted sentries. To pass that way alone was sure to draw sharp suspicion, and he couldn't think of an excuse that they might believe. Not that he could leave without the boy, anyway. He'd held in his mind a single pure fragment of Tasha, the real Tasha, a talisman that kept the last shreds of his humanity from slipping away. And it was that humanity that wouldn't let him abandon the kid to his fate.*

*His Mole playmate tossed aside the ball. "I tire of this," it said in its own language, a hissing, crackling sound like water spilled on a hotplate.*

*Jack gritted his teeth, replying in the same tongue. "What game do you want?"*

*"Rat bones."*

*That game involved knives and tweezers, and consisted of seeing how many bones could be removed from a living rodent before it died. Jack shook his head. "We have no rat."*

*"We catch one. In the river."*

*Jack made sure he didn't sound too curious. "River?"*

*The little Mole rose on its haunches. "Follow."*

*As they moved to leave the room the other Moles instinctively loped after them, and together the four of them wound through the halls of the Moles' lair, eventually turning down a passage Jack hadn't visited before.*

*The phosphorescent light of the Moles' tunnels faded to nothing, and Jack fell back on his finely attuned hearing to make his way. The dim luminescence returned as they emerged into a natural cavern, through which ran a river. The chamber was cold, and patches of icy filth floated on the sluggish flow.*

*Jack felt a clutch of excitement. This river had to empty somewhere. "Where does this go?" he asked, praying the younger Moles didn't sense the emotion beating inside him.*

*One of the pair that had been tormenting the boy pointed a crooked claw downstream. "Hudson. Passage is underwater." It swung its arm in the opposite direction. "Agharta."*

212

*Jack was tempted to ask how far it was to the tunnel dwellers' community, but didn't dare. If he waited till summer he could slip away upstream in relative safety. Trying to make it now in the frigid waters was way more dangerous. Too easy to be caught in the undertow and swept away.*

*Except the boy wouldn't last that long.*

*Like everything else with the Moles, they slept in groups, and when the juveniles grew tired, Jack curled up amongst them and waited for them to sleep. Only then did he slowly lean over the eldest of them. With infinite care he undid the clasp that held the key there. Sweat trickled down his brow at the thought of what would happen if caught.*

*A moment later the key was his.*

*As silently as a shadow, he slid away from them and over to the cage. "Are you awake?" Jack whispered to the still form inside, his words thick and slurred, his tongue no longer used to English.*

*The boy twitched, whimpered.*

*"We're getting out of here, but you have to be quiet. Okay?"*

*There was no reply. Jack unlocked the door, wincing at the low creak it made.*

*One of the Moles stirred, and gripping the bars of the cage door, Jack froze. It shuffled over, and snuggled closer to its fellows, then lay still again.*

*He exhaled his held breath. Suddenly the boy seized him by the arm and began screaming. "He let me out! He did! He should be in the cage! Not me!"*

*No saving the boy now, and bolting from the room, Jack abandoned the shrieking prisoner. He'd learned to move fast in the tunnels, navigating them in near blackness as fast as a normal man in daylight. His only hope now was getting to the river, and God help him were he to run into any of the Moles on the way.*

*His heart pounded as he sprinted down the corridors. His mind was running too, charting the quickest route to the water, while avoiding the passages the alerted Moles would be taking to the nursery. Luck was with him, and skidding around a final side passage, he flew down the last stretch.*

*The icy burn of the water was worse than he could've imagined, and still he waded out into it, driving himself mercilessly in the direction of Agharta. How long could he go before the cold killed him? He had no idea. But better to drown in the fouled waters than lose his one chance to reach Tasha.*

---

JACK JERKED AWAKE as the door flew open, Tocat shining an industrial flashlight in their faces. "Get up! Now!"

The lights in the hall were off. Seneca had been plunged into darkness. "When did the lights go?" Jack asked, uncurling himself from around Lindsay and pulling on his boots before her or Reggie were even fully conscious.

"Twenty minutes ago." Tocat's voice was sharp. "Thought it might be a blackout, until we realized we're still getting juice to the labs. Someone's cut the lines for the lights. I want to know who."

"Who the hell do you think?" Jack snapped as he stood. Lindsay was bent over her boots, her fingers trembling on the laces. Fuck. He wished he'd told her what he'd done down in the tunnels. What he'd do again in order to protect her. Even if she thought him a monster, she'd know she was safe.

"Why?" Tocat demanded from behind Jack. "What do

those things want?"

Jack gave a mirthless smile. "Unless you secure this place fast you'll get your answer. And they're not big on conversation. Let's move it."

In the hallway they were joined by three more men, each armed with a submachine gun that looked decidedly familiar. They were keeping their cool; by the panicked sounds echoing through Seneca, the other residents weren't.

"Only two ways in are the tunnel door and an emergency elevator to the surface," Tocat said as they hustled down the hallway. "All the vents are too small for a person to get through."

Jack dug his hand into Tocat's shoulder, pulled him up short. "I'll say this once. We're not dealing with people. We're dealing with *monsters*. Remember that and you might live to see tomorrow."

The gang leader opened his mouth, shut it and nodded. They carried on, faster than before. King and three of his finest were waiting for them in his office. A couple of floodlights and strategically placed flashlights made everyone visible.

"He says it's Moles," Tocat said, gesturing with his head to Jack. "We have to be ready for a fight."

King waved a hand like Tocat's words were so many annoying flies. "They can't get inside, but we're going to need to go to the tunnels to reconnect the fucking power."

"Can't we run it from the labs?" Tocat asked.

"Not without a week of rewiring, and there's nothing stopping them from cutting that line, too. Fucking bastards must understand the electrical grid."

"They also understand the phone lines, sewers, water mains, fiber optics and everything else down here," Jack said through clenched teeth. King's attitude was going to get them all killed.

"Regular fucking scientists, aren't they?"

"The underground is their environment. They know it like a cabbie knows the city, or an Amazon native knows the jungle. This is their home."

"Fine. They want to fuck with Seneca, well, they just made a big fucking mistake. Tocat, take Cole and Reggie into the tunnels. Juan, too. Fix the fucking cable and then get back here."

Tocat's grip on his weapon tightened. "They'll cut it again."

King looked down at the leader of the Tecos, curling his baboon-like upper lip. "So what are you saying, Tocat? That we sit here in the dark for the rest of our fucking lives?"

"I'm saying we send these three back where they came from. They're the ones that brought the Moles here."

"Yeah, well, I'm the one who runs this fucking place and I'm telling you to go fix the fucking cable. What, you too fucking pussy to go out there? Is that it?"

"I'm not afraid of anything," Tocat growled.

"Then prove it."

The two men glared at each other, then Tocat snapped at the man beside him. "Let's go."

King grinned at Jack and Reggie. "Don't fucking disappoint me, guys. And, as per our fucking agreement, your woman stays with me."

Jack walked up to King's desk, his words as slow and precise as his steps. "The Moles won't harm me, because they think I belong to them. What belongs to me also belongs to them, and Lindsay is one of those things. If anything happens to her, you will be the next person I skin alive. Is that clear, you fat fuck?"

Jack didn't wait for an answer and he didn't look at Lindsay. He left, leading the others. King leaned back in his chair as the door clicked shut. With three bodyguards in a locked room there was a sneer of confidence on his face, yet the fingers that lifted his cigarette to his mouth trembled.

And Lindsay knew she was safe, at least from him.

---

THE TUNNEL DOOR closed behind Tocat, the only illumination coming from the lights on the sub-machine guns he and Juan held.

Jack looked pointedly at the guns. "Care to share?"

"Get going," Tocat said, aiming at a cable that ran along the tunnel ceiling. "The sooner we find where this thing was cut, the sooner we get back."

Jack and Reggie exchanged beleaguered looks, then set off down the tunnel, the two Tecos trailing their footsteps. The light from behind cast Jack's and Reggie's shadows a long way ahead of them, the silhouette of their forms gliding over the crumbling brickwork like living things. The two peered into the darkness, both straining for any sound that might betray an ambush, but all was deathly quiet.

The electrical line led them on a zigzag path through the underground, till after a few minutes, it came to a large chamber ankle-deep in icy, brackish water. There the cable neatly severed, with the live end lying on the far end of the room by the water's edge, barely visible in the shadows.

Jack shot out a hand to halt Reggie, and pointed. "Over there."

Tocat peered through the darkness. "I'll go make sure the tunnel is clear. Juan, you stay here and watch my back."

"I wouldn't do that," Jack said before the man could move.

"Why not?"

"Because as soon as you're halfway through the room the Moles are going to kick that cable into the water and electrocute you."

Juan looked at his boss, his eyes wide. "We should go back," he whispered.

Tocat's mouth thinned. "No, we're getting this done. We'll go around through the wine cellar. There's another way through from there."

It was a trap. Had to be. Jack gave Reggie a hard look and his friend nodded in understanding. The four retraced their steps back to the main passage, heading along it toward the cellar. Halfway there Jack stopped them, closing his eyes and cocking his head to one side. Reggie did the same. "Yeah, Jack, I hear it, too."

"Hear what?" Tocat said from behind.

Jack opened his eyes. "Dripping water."

"So?"

"So it stopped. They're up ahead, and more are circling around behind."

Juan spun around, casting his light back down the long empty corridor. Tocat made a disgusted noise. "So what? They don't have guns, do they?"

Jack shook his head.

"So we have the edge."

"They don't have guns because they don't need them," Reggie said. "We need more guys to do this."

Tocat looked up at Reggie, pipsqueak to giant. "Those freaks show their faces they're going to get them blown off. Now quit with all the ghost stories and get moving."

At the entrance to the wine cellar, Tocat and Juan hung back, letting Jack and Reggie cross the room in case any traps had been laid.

"Fuck," Reggie grumbled. "The least they could have done is arm us."

But Jack wasn't thinking about his own safety, or even that of his friend. They were both veterans of the underground, and whatever happened, they had a fighting chance. His worries were for Lindsay, and what would befall her should they not return.

At best she would end up as one of the nameless slaves in King's community, set to work in those toxic labs amidst the unstable addicts the criminal had collected. At worst...well, that was a fate he couldn't bear to think of.

"We'll make it back," Jack muttered.

"Shut up and keep moving," Tocat ordered, he and Juan now following them into the chamber. "We're almost there."

Jack was crossing the far doorway, with Juan and Tocat halfway across the room, when a fearsome groan sounded from behind them. Before he could spin around, Reggie was tackling him, the two of them sprawling out of harm's way as one of the massive wine racks came crashing down. Juan yelped, his cry cut off by a deafening collapse of metal, wood and glass. The reek of spoiled wine blew over Jack on a blast of air, and his eyes watered from the intense acrid fumes. Struggling up, Jack and Reggie looked back. The mass of heavy timbers and shattered glass had landed squarely on Juan, and on the far side of the chamber, Tocat was against the wall, his left leg pinned beneath the wreckage.

He cursed wildly, and aiming his weapon high, let off a long burst of gunfire. With the noise of the shelving still echoing through the chamber, the noise was almost unbearable, and with his hands over his ears, Jack looked up to where Tocat was firing. The bullets were tearing up the entrance of a small shaft, barely wide enough for a child. Even through the dust, Jack could see that whatever had been there was already gone.

"Stop firing!" he yelled at Tocat, who surprisingly did as he was told.

Gagging on the wine fumes, Reggie staggered across the room, searching for Juan under the jagged debris.

"Forget it, Reggie. He'd dead," Jack said, making for Tocat. "Come over here and help me."

Together, the two of them shifted heavy timber from off the Teco leader. The man's kneecap had been broken by the weight of it, yet he didn't cry out despite his agony. He clutched his ruined leg. "We have to get back."

Reggie heaved the gang leader over his massive shoulders. "No kidding."

Jack grabbed the half-empty gun, and pointed its light in the direction they'd come. Nothing. "Let's go. They'll be on us any second."

Jack and Reggie ran the corridor, the light from Jack's weapon skittering over the walls as they retreated back to the doorway. To his surprise they made it, and Jack hit the intercom.

"It's us! Let us in!" he yelled.

He could hear the low crackle of static that proved the device was working, but there was no reply.

Reggie angled Tocat to the intercom. "Tell them to let us in!"

"¡Abra la puerta!" Tocat shouted. "Open the fucking door!"

The intercom was quiet. Down the hall came the echo of what sounded like a rumbling subway.

"Fuck," Jack said. He leveled his gun at the lock and fired. Amid the rattling burst of gunfire, the edge of the door disintegrated.

One hard kick forced it open, then Jack beamed his light back down the tunnel to blind their pursuers as Reggie and Tocat stumbled inside. He was at their heels, and slamming the door shut, braced his shoulder against it.

An instant later, he was almost thrown off his feet as the Moles thudded against it. Reggie dumped Tocat to the floor and jumped to Jack's side, pressing the heavy door back against the fierce ramming from the Moles. Again and again, the door jerked violently inward, Jack and Reggie fighting to hold it back, then as suddenly as it had started, the battering ceased.

The two of them looked at each other in the blackness, then cautiously Jack kneeled down, squinting through the jagged hole where the lock had been.

"They're gone," he whispered. "For now."

They moved to Tocat's side. Despite being tough as nails, the man was obviously suffering, his pant leg dark with blood. "Where the hell is everybody?" he said through gritted teeth.

Jack was wondering that himself. Motioning for Reggie to stay where he was, he rushed to the end of the short hallway, shining his light through the open door into the darkness beyond. All was silent and empty, then on the floor he saw something that clutched at his heart.

Bodies. Blood.

*Lindsay.*

# CHAPTER
# SEVENTEEN

LINDSAY SAT IN the heavy metal chair as the mayor of Seneca fiddled with his flashlight, playing its beam around the darkened room and over her chest. The man with his perpetual sneer was insufferable. Especially when she knew that it was all show. His fingers trembled every time he took a cigarette, and the ashtray was overflowing. The three Tecoacualli members in the room looked bored, though from the tight grip on their weapons Lindsay could see they, too, were nervous as hell.

"Well, I think that's enough fucking time," King said more loudly than necessary, turning his light on one of his men. "Jorge, go make sure all the workers are secure, then bring everybody here. Seems we're going to need a bigger team to go fix that fucking cable."

Jorge didn't move. "What about Tocat? Shouldn't we wait for him?

King shone his flashlight right into Jorge's eyes, purposely blinding him. "If he's still alive, he obviously needs some fucking help. Stop with the questions and get the fuck moving."

Jorge flicked on his flashlight and pushed open the office

door. Lindsay listened to him march down the hallway, hard and fast. A man contemplating violence. Rico, another guard, closed the door behind him.

King chuckled, and set his flashlight on his desk, the beam pointing upwards. Lacing his fingers together over his bovine belly he smiled. "How you doing, Lindsay?" he asked in mock concern. "You're not scared, are you?"

"Just waiting." Not that a man like King could ever comprehend what she meant by that. He'd sent her friends on a suicide mission, not only to face the Moles but to somehow kill Tocat as well. The fact wrenched at her gut, and as each minute crept past, the torture of her fears for Jack and Reggie had grown till she thought she would scream.

King rubbed his belly, the folds of fat rolling up in a wave. "I bet you are."

Through the thick office door came the muffled blast of an automatic weapon, almost instantly cut short.

All was quiet.

"Rico," King said, his voice stripped of joviality, "go see what that was."

The Teco edged to the door, cracking it open enough to insert his flashlight, his pistol at the ready. "I don't see anything."

"Then go take a fucking look, you moron!" King bellowed.

The man drew breath, then disappeared through the door.

"Tito, lock the fucking door."

The remaining guard jumped to his duty, sliding a heavy bolt into place.

"Probably some idiot shooting at fucking shadows," King said, not very confidently.

Lindsay eyed the narrow vent above King's desk. Exactly

how big were the Moles, anyway? "Are you sure there's no way for them to get in?"

"Not unless the fuckers can walk through walls."

"Or in them. Like rats." Lindsay's suggestion was more whimsical than serious. King didn't take it that way. The tip of his cigarette bobbed in the dim light like a firefly. Lindsay shifted in her seat uneasily. They waited in silence for Rico's return, King's apprehension deteriorating into brooding fear. Suddenly he turned to Lindsay.

"Is this some fucking trick of Cole's?"

"Jack's not stupid." This wasn't some action movie where he and Reggie could overcome a complex full of armed guards with their bare hands. Had there been an exchange of gunfire or sounds of pitched battle she may have believed that it was a rescue attempt, but whatever fate had befallen Jorge and Rico, she was sure Jack hadn't been the one to deal it.

"You had fucking others with you, didn't you? People waiting outside in case you three got trapped in here. Who is it? Those crazy fucks from Sumptown? Reggie's crew from Grand Central?"

Lindsay didn't care to answer, her eyes riveted to the door.

King jerked open one of his desk drawers and took out a huge revolver. Getting up he seized Lindsay by her hair and yanked her painfully to her feet.

"Tito! Open the fucking door!" he demanded, jamming the cold point of the revolver against the small of her back.

The man shook his head. "I don't think that's a good idea, boss."

"Do what I fucking tell you! I give the fucking orders here!"

Tito stayed put. "Those are Moles out there. They got

Tocat and Jorge and Rico! They're not human!"

"It's only Cole, you fucking retard! The Moles are just a bunch of psycho crack-heads, not fucking monsters! It's all a bunch of fucking bullshit! The fucker must have had people waiting for him outside, and now they're trying to rescue his woman. Fuck that. We're going to use her as a fucking hostage. Now do as I fucking say or we're going to lose this whole fucking place."

Tito cringed under the verbal onslaught, his fear of King and fear of the Moles crushing him like a vice.

"Open the fucking door!"

"No!"

Twisting her neck, Lindsay saw King's face was purple with rage and fear, sweat dripping down his brow despite the coolness.

"Fuck you, Tito!" he snarled, and shoved Lindsay toward the frightened guard. Lindsay fell to the ground at his feet, while King snatched the flashlight from his desk and turned it to the door.

"Keep your fucking gun on her!" King growled, and drew back the heavy bolt.

For a moment there was silence, and all Lindsay could see was King's massive silhouette before the blank metal of the door, gun in one hand, flashlight in the other. Then he slipped the gun into the waistband of his pants and slowly, very slowly, turned the doorknob. It opened with a creak, and the room dimmed as King focused his light into the hallway.

In an instant, the light was gone.

There was a sudden squeal from King, and Lindsay felt the vibration of his huge body crashing to the office floor, struggling with something at his throat. "Aggh! Fucking kill it!" he shrieked, his voice high with terror, and the room lit up with the flash of Tito's pistol.

That brief instant of light caught an image that burned into Lindsay's mind. Some shapeless ragged thing at King's bloodied throat, its jaws locked on his jugular. Another crouched before Tito, ready to spring like some nightmare carnivore.

Too terrified to scream, she scrambled away, her shoulder banging painfully against the desk as she rolled under it, clutching her ears as King's frantic screams and Tito's gunfire filled the room. There was a horrible wet chopping sound, a heavy thud against the floor, and a long, gurgling moan from King. All was silent again.

Lindsay huddled in the pitch blackness, her knees curled to her chin, arms over her head, heart pounding. Her thoughts skittered to Jack. *Don't let them get you, Jack. Don't let them get you....*

A strange crackling noise flittered through the room and then another. A metallic smell drifted to her and away, the sounds dropped off, and she felt that whatever horrors had come to Seneca had withdrawn. Still, long minutes passed before she gathered the courage to crawl out from under King's desk.

Blindly, she crept in the direction of the exit, running her hand along the edge of the desk to guide her, her foot catching on King's motionless form. Biting her lip, she inched past him, to the wide open door. Carefully she got down on her knees, groping for the flashlight, only to discover it was useless—the Moles had smashed it.

"Shit," she muttered. She saw a flicker of light ahead, the beam of a flashlight from an adjoining corridor. It had to be one of the guards.

Scuttling back, her ankle bumped against something

heavy. It was King's revolver, and taking it, she flattened herself against the wall beside the doorframe. The beam of light shone through the open door, and looking down, Lindsay almost retched from what it illuminated.

King's throat had been torn out as if he'd been attacked by some huge dog, and Tito's limp form, lying in the far corner amidst spent bullet cartridges, had so much blood over it she couldn't even tell how much of the man was really left. The room looked more like an abattoir than an office.

The light intensified as it approached, her grip tightened on the massive revolver and she tried to control her panicked breaths. Quietly she rose to her feet. She didn't want to kill anyone, but she would sooner that than let the Tecos get hold of her.

The person with the light paused on the threshold of the office, no doubt taking in the scene of carnage, then entered.

"Freeze!" Lindsay cried, pressing the gun against the back of his head. "One move and I'll—"

"Thank God," Jack exhaled, turning to face her.

Sobbing with relief she dropped the pistol and fell into his arms. He hugged her hard.

"You okay?" he whispered.

"Oh Jack...I saw them...."

"It's okay." She could feel his heart pound against her. "Are you hurt?"

"No...they burst into the room and killed King and... and...."

"Linds, we have to get out of here. They're not gone."

Her breath caught in her throat as she looked into Jack's amber eyes, their piercing brightness almost luminescent in the dark.

Picking up King's pistol, he led her back through the door

to where Reggie and Tocat were waiting, the former keeping his sub-machine gun trained down the hallway. Tocat was hobbling along with Reggie's aid, his face pale and slick with sweat.

"King's dead," Jack whispered. "Where's that elevator, Tocat?"

"Down there." He pointed to a nearby juncture.

Reggie led the way forward, Lindsay now becoming Tocat's crutch, Jack walking backwards behind the group, his heavy revolver at the ready. They made several turns, stepped over the bloody bodies of a couple more guards, their corpses as mutilated as the ones in King's office and past rooms where people were crying with fear.

"Shouldn't we help them?" Lindsay wondered, her baser instincts not lending to charity but unable to ignore them, either.

"The Moles want me," Jack said. "We clear the area, things'll settle and they'll find their way out."

Good enough. The four reached a small warehouse space, stacked with assorted crates and boxes, and at its rear was an elevator not much larger than a dumbwaiter. Reggie slung his gun over his shoulder and pressed the button alongside it. Everyone blew out their breath when the machine hummed to life, the doors sliding open to reveal barely enough space for two people.

"It can only be controlled from here," Tocat gritted out. "Once it goes up it has to be brought back down."

"Lindsay, you and Tocat get in," Jack ordered. "We'll follow."

With Reggie's help, Lindsay maneuvered Tocat inside, then wedged herself beside the man. Jack hit a button and the doors closed, the machinery rumbling as it began its ascent.

"That's one lucky woman," Reggie whispered. "Why didn't the Moles kill her?"

Jack watched the elevator rise towards safety. "I wasn't bullshitting King. The Moles thinks she belongs to me. Besides, she's not much of a threat."

Reggie shook his head. "I get the feeling we ain't much of one, either. How did they get in?"

"They probably sent their young to squeeze through the ventilation ducts. The ones in the labs would have been big enough."

"They sent their kids?" Reggie asked incredulously.

"They're not your typical kids. Either that or there's some other way in that King didn't know about. Could be some forgotten crawlspace, or maybe a sewer line. Who knows?"

Beyond the storeroom's doorway came the sound of several gunshots.

"Oh shit," Reggie whispered, glancing at the elevator display. The thing hadn't reached the surface yet, and still had to return.

"This is taking too long," Jack muttered. "We can't let them corner us here."

"Then to hell with waiting," Reggie said. Turning around he grasped the elevator doors, using his might to wrench them open. There was a service ladder mounted to the far side of the shaft.

"Let's go, Jack. You first."

"How are we going to get out when we reach the top? The elevator car will be in the way."

"Trust me," Reggie said.

Jack did, and began climbing as fast as he could. Reggie squeezed himself into the small shaft right behind him, pushing the doors shut before following.

They climbed through the blackness, the air chilling as they went. "You okay, Reggie?"

"Yeah, everything's cool as long as—"

Below them they heard the doors to the elevator being wrenched open.

"Shit," they both cursed, then Jack banged his head on the bottom of the elevator car.

"Agh!"

"Jack?" It was Lindsay's muffled voice.

"Yeah, it's us!" he yelled to her, looked down at Reggie. "So, what now?"

"We climb up behind the car and cut the cables," he replied. "It'll fall out of our way."

Jack reached up and felt the space between the ladder and the elevator. A tight squeeze—the gap was about a foot wide. "Dammit, Reggie."

There was enough space to lever himself upward. How Reggie was going to do it he had no idea. He jerked his way up, then with a sudden whine of gears the machine began to descend, threatening to scrape him off the ladder.

Releasing all the air from his lungs Jack flattened himself against the wall as the car slid past. The elevator doors on the opposite side of the shaft were open, framing Lindsay. Behind her he could make out the interior of a wooden shed, sunlight blazing through its open door.

Eyes watering, he rolled onto the roof of the elevator as it leveled with the floor, then pulled the pistol from his waistband and blew a huge hole in its motor. With metallic groaning the elevator shuddered to a stop.

He moved to the edge. "Reggie?"

He heard scrambling from below. "I'm trying."

"Take my hand. I'll pull you through."

From out of the darkness Reggie's hand gripped Jack's. Grunting, Reggie fought to push himself up through the gap, but his girth was simply too large.

"Don't give up," Jack ordered, hauling on his friend's arm with all his might. "You can make it."

"... It's no good, Jack..." Reggie choked. "...I fucked up."

Lindsay climbed in beside Jack and seized Reggie by his jacket. They could see the whites of Reggie's eyes in the darkness as he strained upward, then suddenly his body was jerked back. He let out a howl of pain."They've got my leg!"

Reggie's fierce struggles rocked the elevator, and Jack wrenched on his friend's arm with all his might. His muscles trembling from the effort he dragged on Reggie, Lindsay bracing her foot against the wall and adding every ounce of her strength as well.

A ragged arm, inhumanly long and wiry, seized Jack by the ankle at the same instant Reggie burst through the narrow space, the momentum breaking Jack free from the Mole's grip. The three of them tumbled into the sunlit shack, landing beside Tocat in a heap. Jack and Lindsay scrambled to their feet, ready to fight. All that came from the elevator shaft was a screech like ripping metal.

# CHAPTER EIGHTEEN

LINDSAY SWALLOWED HARD as she watched Jack cleanse and wrap Tocat's smashed knee. The criminal was wanted both by the police and his old gangland associates, so taking him to a hospital would have been akin to a death sentence. Instead they had transported him in the back of Lindsay's car to Jack's place, and made him as comfortable as they could on the bed. Jack had loaded him up on over-the-counter painkillers, but they did little to ease his suffering, and leaving Tocat to rest, Lindsay followed Jack out of the bedroom.

Reggie glanced up anxiously from his place in the armchair, his own leg wrapped in a thick layer of bandages and propped up on the other chair.

"If he just had a break I could do a splint," Jack said, going to the kitchen sink. "Only his knee is crushed bad. He needs some real care or he'll lose his leg."

Lindsay leaned against the counter beside Jack as he washed his hands, the water running red. Thank God it wasn't his blood. "Agharta?"

"There's no way I can carry him all the way down there myself, and Reggie isn't in any condition to help. Besides, it's a long trip, and if the rats smell blood they'll swarm us—assuming the Moles don't get us first."

"Then we'll need to get Shamba to come here." She grimaced. "Or Gali."

"Shamba's too old," Reggie said. "It'll take him too long. It'll have to be Gali."

Jack nodded, drying his hands with a paper towel. "I could climb down the elevator shaft back to Seneca. That would make the trip a lot faster."

Lindsay stared. "What about the Moles?"

"They've got no reason to stay there. They only attacked in the hopes of getting me, and I don't think Seneca's survivors will have much interest in hanging around there either. Odds are they've already fled into the tunnels. Or up the shaft."

Lindsay pushed off from the counter. "All right then. Let's go."

Jack shook his head. "No, Lindsay. You're staying here."

When she moved to protest, he held up his hand, cutting her off.

"I'll move faster and quieter on my own, Linds. I know you can handle yourself, but coming with me isn't going to be any help. Besides, you're bruised and exhausted. Out of the three of us I'm the only one who's uninjured. I'm as fresh as this little crew gets."

He was right. In this case he would be better off on his own, as much as she hated to admit it. She tossed her car keys to him.

Catching them, Jack pulled on his thick winter jacket and gloves, then turned to Reggie. "You going to be okay?"

Reggie shrugged. "Lindsay's here. You be careful, man."

Jack gave one last look at Lindsay, then turned for the stairs.

To hell with that. She hooked his upper arm. Her lips

crashed against his in a hard, full kiss. She pulled back, her hands cupping his face. "Remember to come back."

He touched his forehead to hers. "No hope of forgetting."

"Bring some eggs," Reggie called from the chair. "Milk, too."

Lindsay listened as he climbed the stairs, and winced at the sound of the apartment door opening, then quietly closing.

"You got it bad for him, don't you?" Reggie asked.

She dodged the question. "You seem remarkably cheerful."

"I'm alive, ain't I? That's something to be thankful for after what we've been through."

"I suppose so."

"You ain't answered me. You can't resist his charms, can you?"

Lindsay smiled, despite the man's intrusiveness. "Don't see how that's any business of yours, Reggie."

"Maybe not. Still, I think you'd do him a world of good. He doesn't belong in this neighborhood. Man like him is made for better things. He needs to forget what happened to him down in the tunnels, and get on with this life. Needs new, better memories."

Even if it were her exact thoughts, it meant tons coming from Reggie. It felt like a blessing. Lindsay slid onto the kitchen table which creaked but held. "You two are good friends."

Reggie laughed. "Jack and me, we're like brothers. Nothing I wouldn't do for him, and it's the same back."

"How did that happen?"

"Long story."

"We've got time."

Reggie shifted into a more comfortable position. "Well, used to be a time I thought I could be king of the underground.

Me and my crew took over a lot of it, and made our money taxing tunnel-folk. For a while nobody set foot down there without my say-so. Even Seneca was paying me dues to leave 'em in peace."

Reggie's voice dropped. "The only thing people down there feared more than me was the Moles, and I got it into my head that that had to stop.

"Me and my crew, we went down thinking the Moles were nothing but a bunch of crazies running 'round in The Pits. Figured we'd kick their ass and show all New York who was really in control. You can guess what happened."

Reggie bowed his head, and Lindsay gave him a moment of silence before softly prompting, "Did anyone make it out aside from you?"

"No." His own voice was little more than a whisper. "Nobody. Lost my whole crew, and I would have been dead, too, by rights. The Moles let me go as a warning. Let me go so New York could see what happened to men who thought they could be king of the underground. After that I held Grand Central on my own and lived quiet in the Burbs for a while. Only I wanted payback, Lindsay. I was full of hate."

"How does Jack fit into the picture?"

"A few years passed. The Burbs got busted by the cops, and I was slowly putting together another crew when Jack showed up. People told him about me and my fight with the Moles, so he found me and asked a lot of questions.

"I liked Jack. Liked him right away. So I cut a deal with him. He'd pay me enough to arm my new gang, and I'd show him the underground, including The Pits.

"As I was getting my plans made, I had to do a lot of recon, and I took Jack with me. He could keep up, no problem, and we became friends. Never thought I would have some

Oxford professor as a brother.

"Anyhow, the day came that I was ready, and down I went with my new crew, and they was real bad men. Toughest, meanest motherfuckers I could find. And then we had us a war in The Pits. War like you wouldn't believe."

Reggie's eyes became distant and sad, and his great body deflated. This time, Lindsay didn't interrupt the silence but waited it out with him.

"Was my pride that did that, Lindsay. We killed some Moles, except they killed more of us. Next thing I knew I was out of bullets, out of crew, and out of luck. They swarmed me like rats, and when I woke up I was chained to a pillar in some cave. Why they didn't kill me I don't know—guess they wanted me to suffer. And suffer I sure as hell did."

"How did you get out?" Lindsay asked.

"Jack came and got me," Reggie answered. "When I didn't come back he went down there himself and busted my ass out. Took them all on by himself. I never would've believed it if I hadn't been there."

"He got captured?"

Reggie sighed. "Jack led them off my trail—only reason I made it out. And yeah, they got him. I crawled to Grand Central, and it was Najib that looked after me. I went back to holding my gate, and never thought of being king down there again. There's something you got to understand, Lindsay, I thought he was dead after what I saw them do to my guys. If I thought they was holding him I wouldn't have sat on my ass."

Reggie's face was haunted. He would never forgive himself, Lindsay realized, even though Jack already had. Oh yeah, they were brothers. Although they might not share a drop of blood, they'd lost plenty for each other. "So two years later he escaped?"

"Yeah. Second I got wind he'd made it to Agharta I was down there in a flash. Got him to the surface as quick as I could, and into a proper hospital. It was the happiest day of my life, Lindsay. But then…."

Lindsay waited. Reggie smiled.

"But the rest is for Jack to tell, isn't it?"

---

REGGIE SOON FELL asleep in the armchair, head bent to chest, and despite his injuries—or perhaps because of them— Tocat did, too. Lindsay continued to sit on the kitchen table, unable to even think of sleep while Jack was away.

She understood now why her childhood friend had changed so much, and the answer lay ironically in how much he had remained the same. More than anyone she had ever met, he was genuine. Though his suffering had dampened his spirit, his loyalties ran right to his core, and his courage was unshakable. Once again he'd returned to that nightmare land beneath the city, and why? To save the life of a criminal he barely knew, and could have called an enemy.

More than anything she wished for his return, to hold him and be held. Jack and Seline. Both in the underground, both out of her reach. The first might return. The second—. She pressed her knuckles to her lips. How could they ever hope to reach her now?

Eventually Lindsay stretched out on the kitchen table and continued her vigil. For Jack. And Seline. If her eyes closed on their own, fear shot adrenaline through her and she become alert again. She played Tetris on her phone, answered emails from work, surfed the web for articles on post-traumatic stress disorder. Finally when her screen displayed 5:00, Janice's regular wake-up time, she called her.

"Lindsay? That you? You okay? Did you find Seline?"

"Yes, I'm fine," she whispered. "No, no Seline." And no closer to getting to her, either. She couldn't tell Janice that. Saying it made it real somehow. "I'm at Jack's place. We're okay. A man from below got injured so Jack's getting help. He'll be back soon."

"What? Take him to the hospital."

"Can't, Janice. It's complicated. Jack knows a doctor. He'll be back with her soon."

Janice paused. "That's the second time you said that. One more time and you'll have cast a magic spell."

It was what her subconscious had been chanting the second he left. "Yeah. I-I'm worried for him. I know you don't like him much—"

"I said no such nothing."

"Janice! You didn't even try to be nice to him."

"Just because I wasn't nice to him doesn't mean I don't like him."

Lindsay worked through all the negative phrasing to conclude, "You like him."

"He stood up for you. Which is more than I can say about your ex."

"That's because you didn't say anything insulting in front of Dan. He didn't need to defend me."

"I was too bored, that's why. Your Jack gets people fired up."

"I don't know that he's my Jack."

"Who else's would he be?"

Tasha's.

"How about," Janice said, "we all have dinner sometime? After Seline's home? I promise to be sweet as sugar to your honey. Okay?"

Lindsay smiled at the ludicrousness of that ever happening. "Sure. Soon."

And then she caught the sound of footfalls above her. "He's back!" she said and ended the call without waiting for a reply. Rushing to the staircase, she arrived in time to see Gali step over the threshold. The woman was huddled in Jack's coat, her grayish skin making her look like an animated statue, her eyes hidden by a pair of extra dark aviator sunglasses. Gali shed the jacket as she descended the stairs, and beneath it, Lindsay saw that she was still armed with her tarnished pistol and bandolier of knives.

"Where is he?" she said, brushing past Lindsay.

"There," Lindsay pointed to the bedroom, her eyes still focused on the top of the stairwell. Jack stepped onto the landing, a heavy pack strapped to his back.

Lindsay took the steps three at a time, and threw her arms around him, nearly tumbling them both down the stairs.

His arms wrapped around her, as much to regain their balance as anything else. "Whoa, Lindsay. What's going on?"

She smiled at his bewildered expression. "I'm glad you're back, that's all."

Jack squeezed her, a smile softening his haggard face. "Glad to be back," he whispered, then added quickly, "I'm sorry it took so long. Getting up the elevator shaft with this pack was like pushing a truck through a rat hole."

"You didn't run into any trouble, did you?" she asked.

"No," he replied. "But Seneca's gone. Looks like King's slaves managed to free themselves and get back into the tunnels. Helped themselves to the drugs before they left—that and anything else that wasn't nailed down. Everything here been okay?"

"Yeah. Reggie and Tocat slept most of the time. I've been waiting for you."

Jack touched his thumb under her eye, his palm against her cheek. "All night?" His voice was gentle, even humble. Lindsay folded her hand over his. She opened her mouth, but was cut off by Gali's harsh call.

"Hey! Can I get some supplies over here?"

Jack dropped his hand and clumped down the stairs, shucking his pack as he went. It was as if the woman timed it, Lindsay grumped.

Still there was no doubt that Gali needed help. She'd injected Tocat with her strongest painkiller. It would not be enough. She slipped a tightly wound rag between the gangster's teeth, and after having Jack sterilize a number of cruel-looking surgical tools, went to work on his knee.

They had to call on Reggie to hold the man's legs down, and Jack helped by handing Gali the implements she needed. Lindsay sat behind Tocat and mopped his fevered brow with a cool cloth. The bloody business took a solid hour, and all of them were exhausted by the end.

Gali pulled off crimson-stained latex gloves and wiped her forehead with the back of her hand. She bent over to look Tocat in the eye. "Your knee cap got broken into five pieces," she summarized. "I've removed the three smallest ones and wired the other two together. You're going to have to stay in bed for at least a week, and then you're going to have to begin rehab if you ever want to walk without crutches. I'm leaving you some heavy antibiotics for infection, and you've got to keep taking them for three weeks without fail."

Tocat nodded, though his face was deathly pale. "Thanks," he croaked.

Gali paused. "You're a pretty tough guy. I've never met a

man who could take that much pain without screaming and all that bullshit."

Lindsay stared in disbelief at Gali. "The guy had his knee shattered. You make it sound as if feeling pain somehow makes him weak."

Gali turned on her. They were less than arm's length from each other, and her voice dripped venom. "Where I come from weakness means death. Up here, it's an act princesses like you put on to get a man to help you—even if it means he could get himself killed."

Lindsay gasped. "I don't take Jack for granted."

"The hell you don't. You got your hooks into both him and Reggie, and they're too blind to see you for the conniving little bitch you are."

"Gali! That's enough," Jack interrupted.

She never took her eyes from Lindsay, anger tingeing her gray skin to a faint pink. "Don't fret, Jack. I'm leaving. Not before I make a prediction. You'll regret this woman ever walked into your life. And when you do," she turned to Jack, "come to me. I'll be waiting."

"Gali." Jack's voice was soft, but unyielding. "I'm never going to live in the tunnels again. You get that, right?"

Gali's jaw clenched, then she snapped her attention back to Tocat. "I'll be back in a few days to check on you. We'll move you down to Agharta when you're well enough. In the meanwhile, lie low and keep out of"—she sneered at Lindsay —"trouble."

She scooped up her bloodied instruments and headed for the bedroom door. "I'll clean these up in the kitchen before I go, and I'm leaving most of the supplies here so I don't have to lug them up again. And don't worry. I'll see myself out."

Jack closed the bedroom door behind Gali, and Lindsay,

angry as hell, focused on Tocat, handing him a tall glass of water. He gulped it down before turning to Jack.

"I don't know why you helped me, man. I owe you. I owe you my life."

Jack gave a faint smile. "Don't worry about it. You focus on getting better."

Tocat persisted. "You still want to rescue that topsider from the Moles?"

Jack gave a wary nod.

"Good, because I know how to do it."

Lindsay felt a burst of excitement. Jack's brow furrowed. "How?"

"You know the way to The Pits?"

"Through Devil's Crawl. That's the only way to reach them except for Schenley's Chasm, and that's impassable."

Tocat shook his head. "No, it's not. We used the elevator at Seneca to get drugs to our distributor, but sometimes the park got too hot and we used a smuggler to get them out though The Chasm."

Jack's frown deepened. "How? The opening to the Hudson is underwater."

"There's a storm drain that reaches it. Our man brought a boat down in pieces and put it back together underground, so now he can carry stuff from Hell's Kitchen all the way to Dyer's Pass."

"So he could take us right into The Pits," Jack said, understanding. "Who's this guy?"

"His name's Crabbe. Isaac Crabbe."

Jack grabbed pen and paper from the bedside table, noting down the phone number that Tocat gave.

"Drop my name. Give him a couple grand for the job, and he'll do it. He knows this city's guts as good as anyone. "

Jack shoved the paper into his pants pocket. "Thank you, Tocat. That's our way in."

"Just pay those freaks back for taking out my gang." Tocat said. "Tecocualli means 'snakebite'. They may have killed the snake, but that won't save them from our poison."

They left Tocat in peace and gathered in the living room, where Reggie hobbled over to the armchair and eased himself back down into it. Lindsay took cokes from the fridge and passed them out. Above the crack and hiss of cans opening, Reggie said, "So you're going to go in the way you came out, huh? The Moles won't be expecting that."

Lindsay looked at Jack, puzzled. "You escaped through an underground river?"

"Yeah," he answered. "The Chasm runs from the Hudson, past The Pits and Agharta, all the way to another community called Dyer's Pass. I figured I could let its current carry me to the Pass. I didn't count on how cold or sluggish it would be. It was sheer luck that I made it."

Lindsay tried to keep the snark from her voice. "Gali pulled you out, right?"

"She heard me splashing around down there," he confirmed. "Neil lowered her down on a rope and they managed to drag me up. Without them I would have drowned. It was two weeks before I was well enough to take two steps without help."

Reggie smiled at the memory. "Even then you looked like shit. Almost as bad as I did when I made it back to Grand Central."

Jack set sharp eyes on Reggie. "You're not doing so well now, either. You'll have to rest yourself."

Reggie took on a stubborn look. "What about the Moles?"

"Look at your leg. You're not going to be any good in a

fight for at least a couple of weeks. You're in good enough shape to take care of Tocat, and you can help Gali get him back underground when the time's right."

"You can't do it alone, Jack. No way you can carry Seline out of The Pits *and* hold off the Moles."

Lindsay's chin came up. "That's why he's got me."

Jack sighed. "Linds, how many times do we have to go over this?"

She reached for her jacket and her pack. "I don't know, Jack. How about we tally it up at my place?" She handed him his parka. "Reggie and Tocat could do with some rest, and so could you."

She half-expected him to dig in his heels, but he took it from her without hesitating. "I'll see you later then, Reggie."

"Sure. You guys get to bed, okay?" Reggie flashed them a golden grin. "Maybe even sleep."

# CHAPTER NINETEEN

The second Lindsay and Jack got inside her apartment, she headed for the shower, stripping off clothes as she went. Boots, jacket, gloves and socks he expected, then she brazenly peeled off her shirt and was unhooking her bra as she heeled the door closed behind her.

Despite how tired he was, Jack had a mind to follow her in, shed his clothes and make wild love to her as the warm water sluiced away the blood and grime of the underground. What was she doing getting undressed in front of him anyway, unless she wanted him to follow?

Outside the door he could hear the patter and slap of the water as it hit her body, and thought of his own hands entering that stream. His jeans grew very tight.

He turned the doorknob. It was locked.

Guess not.

Jack sought refuge in the kitchen, and, going on her previous invitation to make himself at home, he opened the fridge door. Lettuce, yellow pepper, carrots in the crisper, chicken and fish in the freezer and lots of condiments. The buns, at least, were instantly consumable, and there was always cereal. Just like home.

He concentrated hard on not thinking of Lindsay's naked

body locked away from him at the other end of the apartment, and after what seemed like an eternity he heard her step out.

"It's all yours," she called out, her voice followed by the click of the bedroom door. It'd be a cold day in hell before he made a fool of himself and tried the knob on that one.

He cleaned himself off quickly, then twisted off the faucet and stepped out of the shower, wrapping a towel around his waist. He looked in resignation at his filthy clothing. Nothing wearable. Still, he'd be damned if he was going to put on those—

There was a knock on the bathroom door.

"I'm not putting on that gay underwear again!"

A pause. "Who said anything about wearing anything?" It was said very softly and with great…intent. Jack stared at the door handle. No, he wasn't. It was a trick. He watched the handle turn.

She stood there before him, naked as sin, and stepping forward, snapped the towel away from him.

For the first time in a year, Jack *really* smiled. His arms came around her, his hands skimming the satin smoothness of her back, her buttocks, coming around to cup the soft mounds of her breasts. Her pink nipples perked at his light touch, her instant response sending a jolt of heat through him. He pulled her against him, and twining his fingers through her hair, tilted her face up to his. Her blue eyes were shining, her cheeks glowing, and her dark pink mouth was parted and waiting.

He lowered his mouth, grazing his lips over hers. "You do seduction very well, Linds."

"I've never tried to seduce anyone."

He pulled back slightly. "How's that?"

His mouth out of reach, she moved to his neck, biting hard enough to drive a small groan from him. She smiled in triumph. "I don't consider it trying if there's no doubt of success."

He pressed his full hardness against her lower belly, and she pressed back, her hand sneaking between them to rub her thumb over his engorged tip. He took her wrist, but he didn't stop her, couldn't stop her. "Jesus, Linds, you're going to have to slow down, or it's going to be game over for me."

"Okay," she agreed, and her thumb fell away. Jack risked drawing breath again, to have it cut off when she gripped his length, giving him a long, slow stroke. This time he did pull her hand away and tossed her up onto the bathroom counter.

He bound her wrists behind her back with one hand, then pulled her up solidly against him with the other. His erection slid up along her inner thigh, stopping shy of her opening. "You," he said, "are not playing fair."

She slung her legs around him and dug her heels into the back of his thighs. "I know. But you and I have some unfinished business from Agharta, don't we?" She worked her tongue and teeth on his neck, until twisting, he crushed his mouth against hers.

"My turn first," he murmured.

He ran his tongue over her lips, parting them and slipping in, playing his tongue over hers, pulling out to lick and pluck at her lips and then plunge back inside. Not stopping with his mouth, keeping her arms behind her back with the one hand, Jack let his other one drift to her breasts, at first rolling them sensually beneath his palm, then unexpectedly switching to sharp tugs that sucked the breath from Lindsay, and she could only resume air flow in short, hard pants.

And still he tantalized her mouth, gentle play there counterpoint to the harder workings of his hand. Wetness seeped between her legs. She arched her back, her lower torso rotating, tilting towards him to bring his erection against her softness, seeking connection.

He shifted in another direction.

"Please, Jack. Let me have you."

His kiss deepened and hardened again, except now his mouth moved, sliding over her cheeks and down her neck, and his hand dropped away from her breast, crept over her lower belly and then a finger ran slowly, lightly up her wet crease.

Her entire body jumped, then settled into excited quivers. His finger stroked again and again, tickling her clit, teasing her opening. Her fingers wrapped around the edges of the countertop, her toes curled, her muscles tightened. Her quivers revved into shudders, and in moments she was only aware of the strong band of Jack's arm around her middle and the orgasm growing within her.

Then her body broke loose, arching against his caress and sending bottles, brushes and scented candles crashing down from the countertop. Lindsay writhed against Jack, her climax running through her like a live wire, her body at once trying to ease away from his relentless manipulations while opening for more. Hoarse cries broke from her, siphoning off some of the unbearable tension that wracked her body. And still it coursed within her.

His eyes blazing, he shoved a finger inside her. Her muscles clamped around it and her cries broke into a long scream of release.

She sank against him, her forehead on his shoulder. "I've never orgasmed like that before. Well, except for the last time with you. Didn't even know I was built for this."

He didn't answer. She twisted her head, to face the column of his neck. She could see his pulse beat like it was about to burst out of him. She glided her hand to the left side of his chest. She pulled away to look him in the eye."Why is your heart beating so fast? I'm the one that just went and lost it."

Jack stared at her bright eyes and kiss-swollen mouth. "Don't you know how incredibly sexy it is to see you lose it? To be the one to do it?"

She frowned. He spun her around so that her feet were pressed up against the steamed mirror. He pulled her knees apart, exposing her pink, swollen sex.

"Then, find out for yourself."

And he did it to her all over again. And before he stopped, she had left footprints all over the mirror and her screams were ringing in both of their ears.

This time when she slumped against Jack, she murmured, "Jack, I don't think I can move."

He settled her back against his chest, and crossing his arms in front of her, firmly cupped her breasts. "That's too bad, Lindsay," he said, his amber eyes glinting as she sprawled in front of the mirror. "because, as you said, you and I still have unfinished business." To conclude his point, he pressed his erection against her buttocks.

She smiled weakly, thoughtfully and then fully.

"My turn."

With a kick and spread of her long legs, she turned to face him, and lifting her hips, she melded her wetness tight against the hard head of his penis. Every cell in his body throbbed to enter, yet he held back.

He shakily brought his hands to her face. "Lindsay, I need...I want..."

"I know." She rested his penis in her hand. "Watch." She pressed her labia against his head until it crossed the muscled rim of her opening. He felt those muscles squeeze around his head. She relaxed and flexed again. He gripped her hips. She slid down another wet inch and his cock twitched. She paused and he waited, his eyes locked to where they connected. Then in a long slow glide he saw his penis disappear inside of her, and what he could no longer see he felt—the warm, moist, giving wrap of Linds. His Linds.

Their turn.

His grip on her hips tightened. He wouldn't last long, no more than a few strokes. He lifted his gaze to her hair and eyes, and began to move inside her. He'd never done this before with her but he had a memory for it. Down in the hellhole he'd created a memory of this and now, now, it was real.

He was right. He didn't last long and as he broke inside her, he realized it had finally happened. Something he dreamed of doing since he was a kid in an elevator. He'd made love to Linds.

---

THEY SLUMPED TO the floor, their bodies lying tangled on the cool bathroom tile. Jack had slipped from her onto his side, his arm slung across her breasts and over her waist. The two of them were wedged in the doorframe, and given any other circumstance, Lindsay would have felt uncomfortable.

Except she wasn't. She'd had great sex with the man she loved. And yes, she loved Jack. She'd admitted that to herself in front of her bedroom mirror, readying herself with perfume and lotions while Jack was in the shower. Fixing him meant loving him. The thought scared her more than dangling five stories in the air ever could. But, like the time in the tunnels, she committed to it.

He shifted beside her and propped himself up to look at her face, his hand skimming along her sides and over her hair. His touch was so tender and intimate and—reverential, a teary lump caught in her throat. Keep it light, Lindsay ordered herself.

"I think I've got bruises on my butt." She smiled. "Not that I'm complaining, mind you."

"And I'm thinking that my jaw might never be right from where you head-butted me."

She twisted to face him. "Head-butted? How could I have—?" She thought back to her wildness in front of the mirror. "Oh. Sorry."

He gave her a swift, hard kiss. "I'm not complaining, either." He slanted her a look, "Though I wouldn't mind if you threw a few scraps of food my way."

"Right. What was I thinking of? I got the order mixed up. Dinner, then sex."

She sat upright, and Jack, still on his side, snagged his arm around her waist. Hauling her close, he gave her belly a series of nibbles that made her feel absolutely delicious. "No. You got the order right. Sex, then dinner," His amber eyes, warm and alive, connected with hers. "Then sex for dessert." He went back to sampling tummy appetizers.

"Okay, okay." Lindsay laughed. "Stop before I lose track." She ruffled his hair, then sobered. She wanted to say so much, ask so much, that she had to actually bite her tongue to hold it all back. "Do you still like Chinese?"

He grinned. "Sure. So long as I still get your share of the ginger beef in exchange for the spring rolls."

*He'd remembered.* "You're on."

As if by mutual consent, they both kept the mood playful as they dressed (Jack in a beach towel) and ate takeout together on the couch. They couldn't seem to resist touching each other, their hands sneaking underneath each other's clothing or gliding along exposed skin. There came a point when Jack was tweaking Lindsay's various body parts with chopsticks and Leo proved to be a poor defense. They fell together on the couch with Jack on top. His grin faded, his hands went slow through her hair and he gazed down at her.

"Something I got to tell you, Linds."

This was it. She wished she'd never pushed the whole Tasha business. She had him right here, right now. She didn't want his wife or lover or whoever she was destroying the fragile thing between her and Jack.

He lifted himself off her and sat up, setting her legs across his lap. There was an edge of need, of resolve in him that had her sitting up herself, shifting so she rested sideways against the back cushions.

He lifted himself off her and sat up, setting her legs across his lap. There was an edge of need, of resolve in him that had her sitting up herself, shifting so she rested sideways against the back cushions. "I wanted to tell you about Tasha the morning after—well, the morning after. I knew you'd find out about Tasha in Agharta and I wanted you to hear it from me first. But you brought Reggie, and then Janice showed up. I don't want to lose my chance again.

His hand hooked around her upper leg in casual intimacy, and it felt as nice as when he'd done it by the fire in Sumptown.

"I've already told you how once the Moles caught me, I was tortured, drugged, dehumanized till they cut me off from everything that I knew. The goal was to break my mind, Linds, then to put it back together the way they wanted it, except I found a way to beat them. And that's where Tasha comes in.

"I couldn't hold onto everything they were stripping away from me. It was impossible. So I held fast to Tasha. I figured if I could just remember her and our times together, if I could focus on what our future would be like when I got out, then I could preserve the most important part of myself. So that's what I did. I kept her alive in my mind. I held her face, her hair, her body in my thoughts. I concentrated on trying to remember her voice and her laugh. I concentrated so hard that at times I swear I could hear her. I really believed—as naive as it sounds—that so long as I got out of those damn tunnels everything would be all right."

His hand tightened on the flesh above her knee.

"So what happened?"

"When I found my way back to her, I—I didn't recognize her. She knew who I was, but I couldn't believe it was her. She had to show me pictures of us together before I could accept it. The thing is, she had dark hair and these big brown eyes. She was beautiful in her own way, but she hadn't been what had kept me sane."

He gave her an almost desperate look, his grip on her leg now hard. "My mind got twisted up with the time we were in the tunnels together, with how we'd been friends so many years before. The name, Tasha, stuck with me, but the woman I made it out for had blue eyes and blonde hair, loved Chinese takeout and was scared of heights."

His eyes stayed locked on hers, and she could see he was trying to gauge her reaction. She didn't know what to think or how to feel. She felt happy, vindicated, frustrated, confused. All churned in a volatile brew out of which she extracted one question. "This real Tasha, were you were married to her?"

He bowed his head and seemed to notice for the first time what he was doing to her leg. He let go, his fingers smoothing the redness there. "Yes. When I went down after Reggie we'd been married three months. When I made it back two years later, she was with another man. In fairness to her, she'd thought I was dead, though I wasn't even out of hospital before she was handing me divorce papers."

Lindsay's heart constricted. Hadn't he told her he would only marry for love?

"She felt bad. By then, it didn't matter. She'd moved on. We'd both moved on. Both in love with different people, only mine was imaginary."

"I wasn't imaginary, Jack," she said softly.

"*You* weren't. But the woman in my mind wasn't you, Linds. She was a mix of memories and fantasies of which you were only a part. The Tasha I'd created was my soul mate, and as crazy as it sounds, I loved her with everything that I had. We'd explored the undergrounds of countless cities together. Shared every interest. Every desire. She was the best of you and my wife and maybe a dozen other people, all wrapped up into an ideal."

He was telling her the truth, opening up as she'd wanted him to. Talking was good for Jack. Tension was evaporating from him, his speech was less wooden and harsh with each word as he remembered Tasha. The memory of her was healing him, fixing him.

And killing her. How could she compete with perfection? She lifted her legs off his lap, curled them underneath her. It was too much to know that it wasn't really her he was thinking about when he touched her. He watched her withdrawal and he bent forward into the space she'd occupied, his elbows on his knees, his hands hanging empty.

"I have a confession, Linds."

*Stop, Jack. Please.*

"I once loved you."

*Once.*

Jack gave her an apologetic smile. "When I first came back to New York five years ago, I looked you up. I was still in love with you. I figured if I saw you, maybe it wouldn't be too late for us to have something together. I phoned your place, but you weren't home. I talked to Seline. She told me you were away on your honeymoon. That kind of ended that."

Yes, it had.

"I met Tasha a few months later. She was pretty. A Russian girl with the cutest accent. And she'd been down in the Moscow underground. Organized raves in abandoned catacombs and the like. I figured since you were taken, I wasn't going to find anyone better, so I let myself fall in love.

"It was never the same as what I once felt for you, Linds. Never as strong. Not until the woman in my mind did I ever love anyone as much as I'd loved you.

He paused, waiting for her to speak. He wanted her to accept what he'd said. To understand that with her, he was reliving the Tasha of his imagination. She, the warm, living person, was a substitute for an imaginary savior.

"I know this isn't fair," he said quietly.

No, it wasn't. And even more unfair was that he still expected her to fix him. To be that angel which had lent him the strength to struggle free of the abyss. But how could she be someone that had never existed in the first place? How could he ever love her back when she was a shadow of the mythical Tasha? He wanted forgiveness, understanding, acceptance. And after all he'd risked for her, she knew she needed to give it to him.

"Do you hate me?" he asked.

She bit her lip, hard. "How could I?"

"Because I told you the truth. An ugly one. An unjust one. You deserve better."

"I don't hate you, Jack."

"You want me to leave?" He pressed his fists into the cushions, ready to push off.

"You can't go. Your clothes are still in the wash."

He halted. "That the only thing keeping me here, Linds? Wet clothes?"

She looked away. "I don't hate you, Jack."

"So you said."

"I don't. I…."

"It's okay, Linds. I dumped a whole lot on you. Things I've been holding onto for a year. I don't expect you to have an answer right now."

"An answer? To what?"

He stared at her. "What do you mean? My whole story was one big question."

"I don't understand."

He swept his arm about her place. "Linds, you've got everything, and I can't bring anything to it. I don't have a job, I'm broke, my place is a dump, I'm half-crazy, I've got more connections below ground than above…the only thing I can give you is the hope of finding Seline."

Hope. He had no idea. No idea how that hope had taken away her fear and desperation, had created new hopes. He had no idea what a gift that was. Yet, for him, hope had turned traitor. Had raised him to the surface and then deserted him. And given him nothing else. Denied, he still sought to give it to others.

He kept on. "And there's still hope, Linds. If we can get Tocat's smuggler on side with us, we can get back to the place where I escaped, and I know The Pits better than any person alive. The Moles are dangerous as hell, but they're not omniscient. We could pull this off. We really could, Linds."

She had to stop him. "I know that, Jack. What I don't know is your question."

Sunlight broke through the windows onto Jack's muscled back, pale and hunched. He flinched and darted a look behind him.

"Still not used to the light?" she said softly.

"Sometimes it still takes me by surprise."

"Because you expected it to be one thing and it's another."

He turned to her and the sun glowed warm on his face. "Because," he corrected quietly. "Because she burns so bright. Better than anything I could ever imagine."

Lindsay felt herself dissolving, melting under the power of his words. He took her hand in his, held it as if he were about to propose. His eyes searched hers. "It's the same question I wanted to ask five years ago. Do we have a chance, Linds?"

She didn't think about it. She wrapped herself around him and he lost no time in doing the same with her. In the certainty of the sun and their bodies, she told him, "Yes, Jack. Together we can have something real."

# CHAPTER TWENTY

AS A TRAIN rattled by the window of his dilapidated apartment, Isaac Crabbe ran his hand through his straggly red hair and took a long, nervous drag on his last cigarette. Tocat's pals were due any moment, and as far as he was concerned they couldn't arrive soon enough. His apartment had been without heat for the past week, a result of his failure to pay his bills, as all the cash from welfare and panhandling had gone to smokes, food, and his phone.

A nice, simple smuggling job was just the thing he needed. A day's work, and he'd be back in the black—or at least get his place warmer than a meat locker.

He took another puff, and looked at his watch. It had stopped. "Shit," he mumbled. He struck it against the table and the second hand continued its circular march. There was a time he'd been a professional, master of New York's secret ports, tunnels and byways, ferrying contraband into and around the city like a shadow. But his reputation alerted the police, and the day had come when they'd caught him making a twenty-pound delivery of cocaine. Twelve years of prison later, he had lost his contacts and the city had changed, leaving him to play gopher to small-timers, burnouts and renegades.

Those were the breaks.

He rolled his shoulders under his thick parka, and stubbed his cigarette out in the overflowing ashtray, the centerpiece on his kitchen table. They'd better get here soon. Ever since power was cut off last week, his only light source was from the sun, and here in the late afternoon, it was almost setting.

Despite expecting visitors, he still jumped when there was a knock at the door. Crabbe headed over to the triple-bolted entrance, squinted through the peephole, then opened up.

Jack looked down at the man who answered, and knew that beside him, Lindsay was surprised, too, at seeing the dwarf. Standing a few inches under five feet tall with a rotund physique, Crabbe looked more like a scruffy garden gnome than a smuggler.

"Isaac Crabbe?" Jack asked, uncertain if they'd found the right apartment in the crumbling tenement.

"That's me." He used his foot to hook aside a step-stool from behind the door and swung it wide open. "Come on in. It's colder than a witch's tit in here. Still, we can talk with nobody bothering us."

Jack stepped inside first, scanning the tiny, dingy apartment that made his own spartan home seem like the governor's mansion. Wallpaper the color of a rusted bucket was stained and peeling, and the green carpet was so dirt-matted it looked like turf after a game in the rain. Weighing down a tray table in the living area was a rabbit-eared television, a white-lace doily draped over it like a wig. Behind him, Lindsay emitted a descending scale of groans.

Crabbe led them over to a folding table wedged into the back of his galley kitchen, and, still bundled in outside gear, they squeezed around it. Seeing as how there were only two chairs, their host stood, which meant that they were all pretty much level with each other.

He rubbed his small square hands together. Apparently for warmth as much as anticipation. "So, not many people know about Schenley's Chasm. I'm guessing you two have been dealing with Seneca?"

"We're not drug dealers, if that's what you're asking," Jack said flatly. "We're looking to get a person out of the tunnels. The Pits, to be specific."

Crabbe's cherubic face paled, and his rubbing hands stopped in a prayer-like pose. "Oh. Well, I can get you to the edge of them, but don't ask me to take you in. Them things that live down there—"

"We know," Lindsay interrupted. "We're looking for someone to get us through the Chasm and back again. That's all."

Crabbe ran smoke-yellowed fingers over his bristly chin. "How long you going to want me to wait?"

"Two hours should do it," Jack said. "If we're not back by then it's a safe bet we won't be coming."

"Ten grand, all in advance," the dwarf announced, then flinched at Jack's expression.

"That seems a little steep," Lindsay said.

"I'd be risking my life there, lady. Two hours is a long time to be waiting around The Pits, especially if you're going to be stirring them things up like hornets. I need some kind of hazard pay."

Jack's eyes narrowed. It was a safe bet the man would flee if he thought the Moles had any chance of snatching him. Better to simply pay him for the use of his boat and go it alone. Before he could argue, Lindsay spoke up.

"Fine. Ten grand, only one in advance. The other nine when we're out of the tunnels."

Crabbe's eyes widened as much as Jack's, and he licked his lips. "What if you two don't make it back? And even if you do, what's to say you'll pay me?"

That was it. Enough crap from Crabbe. Jack leaned forward. "You calling us liars?"

"No, no sir," the dwarf stammered. "It's...well...I don't know you two, and you know how these deals can go sideways, sometimes."

Jack felt Lindsay's hand on his thigh. "Look," she said, "we're all going to be taking risks. I think the offer is more than fair, Mr. Crabbe, so let's quit haggling."

The man looked from Lindsay to Jack and back again, then his nervous smile returned, and he bobbed his head. "Okay, okay. When you want to go?"

"When's the soonest you can take us?" Lindsay asked.

"Tomorrow. Tomorrow morning. You two know your way around Riverside Park at all?"

Lindsay nodded.

"Down around 93$^{rd}$ street there's a big statue of a lady on a horse. Meet me there and we'll go down. Let's make it, say, eight in the morning. And don't forget the money, okay?"

Jack remained silent until they were in her car. "Are you nuts? Ten grand?"

Lindsay turned the heaters on full blast. "I want him to have a strong incentive to wait for us, Jack. The only thing that can trump fear is hope, and hope for Crabbe is the color of money."

———————

SELINE SAT AGAINST the concrete pillar, her knees tucked up to her chin and her arms wrapped around them, eyes straight ahead. The chain had been taken away.

She hardly ate anymore, spending all her time either sleeping or staring into the darkness. How long had she been here? Days? Weeks? Months? She had no way of knowing, her perception of time completely lost, and just as frightening was the realization that she didn't care anymore.

All she felt like doing was dreaming. Dreaming of her life above, and all the simple pleasures that ordinary human beings took for granted. The brightness of light and color. The sting of the harsh winter wind on her face, the kiss of raindrops. The tight wrap of Aunt Lindsay's arms around her shoulders. Janice's pat on her cheek. The ordinary act of speaking to them, to someone—anyone.

How had Jack Cole survived for two years? She recalled the strange light in his eyes that burned, she now knew, from his sojourn in Hell. Would she become like him? No, how could she? He, at least, had the willpower to escape.

Had Auntie given up on her? Taken down the Christmas tree alone? Gotten on with living the way the two of them had done after their family died?

A noise shocked her from her spiraling contemplations, and her head jerked up. It took a second for her rattled psyche to register she was hearing words.

"Hello? Anyone home?" The voice was female, with a weird sing-song lilt to it.

Seline unfolded her body and got to her feet, staring about her. "Yes! I can hear you!" Her voice raw, tinged with hysteria.

"Of course you can. I'm over here."

Seline swung her head in the direction of her visitor, and made out the dim outline of a thin female standing on the far side of the room. The mere sight of a human brought tears to

Seline's eyes. "Please help me," she said, her voice trembling.

"You know," the woman replied, "I would, but I'm already helping someone else. How do you think you got here?"

Seline cringed at the silky menace behind the words. "What do you mean?"

The question was ignored; instead, one was posed. "Have you ever wondered what happens to your garbage?"

"What?"

"You know, your garbage. The stuff you throw away. Do you ever wonder what becomes of it?"

"I…I guess it gets burned…or buried."

"That's right. And the same goes for people. Those that aren't wanted anymore must be vanished, so they're either killed or buried. Buried in prisons or asylums or ghettos. And sometimes, just sometimes, they get literally buried. Down beneath your quaint little cities, where everyone can forget they ever existed."

"I came down here so people wouldn't be forgotten," Seline said. "I wanted to help make a place for them up in the city."

"How very nice of you," the voice mocked. "I'm afraid, however, our friends down here have other plans."

"Plans? Who *are* you?"

The shadowy figure cocked her head to one side, and though she couldn't see it, Seline could sense the woman's unwholesome smile.

"Although people like you may have forgotten about us, we've never forgotten about you. No, while you've been busy going about your sane little lives we've been helping our associates down here tap into everything from your water to your phones to your bank accounts. This city is on the cusp of a great transformation, a revelation more wondrous than any-thing that has come before. Never fear, we're not going to pull the trigger—not until it's time. Which, by the way, is why you're here."

Seline shook her head. "I'm not going to help you."

"Not to burst your bubble, dearest, but you already have. You see, our friends have been somewhat scattered, and they're very difficult to find. Only one man has the knowledge of where to look for them, and he'll be making a rescue attempt on you any time now."

"Who?"

"Why, Jack Cole, you silly thing." The woman laughed. "We had tea together the other day. Your auntie, bless her, has persuaded him to retrieve you, and he wasn't having much luck until recently. You see, everyone thinks that there's only one way into The Pits, but I get the sneaking suspicion that Jack knows of another. I haven't told your hosts about it. Imagine how grateful they'll be when I present him all trussed up like a Thanksgiving turkey."

The madwoman's voice rose and verged on the oracular.

*"He will be our devoted spider,*
*And weave our web ever wider,*
*Unfurl our net across the world you're in—*
*Paris, Rome, Moscow, London, and Berlin.*
*And when we're posed to have our way,*
*It'll be over in just one day."*

Seline recoiled at the venomous poetry, the lilting voice like sugar-laced poison.

"You're insane."

"That's what they tell me, dearest. Then again, they don't know the half of it, do they?"

# CHAPTER
## TWENTY ONE

LINDSAY STUDIED RIVERSIDE Park's statue of Joan of Arc, the young saint set upon her steed, sword raised high in a gesture of fierce determination. Today she'd need to share the woman's courage and faith—though not her fate.

Najib had agreed to visit Sumptown the night before on their behalf, and early that morning, had returned with ammunition and a pair of sub-machine guns. However much the weight of the weapon in her backpack was reassuring, she knew from the massacre at Seneca that a successful rescue wouldn't hinge on firepower. The guns were tools of last resort; stealth and knowledge were the only real keys into— and out of—The Pits.

Beside her Jack wore sunglasses against the glare of the sun on the skin of snow, and that, along with the loaded bag at his feet, made him look like an itinerant mercenary. Lindsay checked the time on her phone. Quarter to eight. Fifteen minutes before the descent. By noon she could have Seline back. Or they could all be dead. She scrolled to Janice's name with its thumbnail picture of her broad, smiling face. When Lindsay wanted to call her, Jack had nixed the idea, concerned that her old friend would become a target for the APs, if she wasn't already. So Lindsay now experienced the same regret as when her family had died. Of being robbed of the chance to say goodbye.

His focus straight ahead, Jack spoke quietly, his tone lecture-smooth. "The point where The Pits meet Schenley's Chasm shouldn't be guarded. The Moles don't really use the river for anything, except their young sometimes hunt rats there in the summer."

"How did you learn about it?"

"One of their young told me."

Lindsay frowned. "They speak English?"

"Some can. Usually they talk in their own language." By way of example, Jack gritted his teeth and let out a series of whispery sizzling noises, similar to those she'd heard in King's office. It was eerie to have these sounds of horror come from her lover.

"How much do you know?"

"A fair bit, but it's difficult to master. It's got a very unusual syntax. You know how in French everything has a gender—you refer to a pencil as *un crayon*, an eraser as *une gomme*?"

Lindsay nodded.

"In the Mole language everything is either 'up' or 'down'. Everything belongs to either the tunnels, or the surface world. Water below ground is *sssik*. Water above ground is *ssseh*. There are other sounds that hold more complex meanings.

"For example, *khksssik* is a threat. It means that I won't give you any water until you suffer from thirst. *Khksssiks* means I won't give you any water till you die, and *khksssikk* means I'm going to kill you using water, as in drowning you."

Lindsay flinched. Jack caught her reaction and quieted, looking instead to the park entrance. "I'm not a linguist, though I picked up enough of it. Suffice to say, it's not a pretty language."

He seemed embarrassed to have this knowledge, as if admitting to a dirty past. In her mind, it made him unique and important. Of the few that knew the Moles existed, he was likely the most sane and educated. Aside from the APs, chances were he was the only human who had any understanding of the monsters or their dark culture.

"Don't they ever have anything nice to say? Like 'I'm happy.' or 'Have a nice day?'"

A beat or two passed as he considered her question. "*Thmmussik*. It means 'You are mine.' Depending on who in the hierarchy says it, it's an expression of regard. Their leader said it to me once. After that, none of them touched me. Resources are so scarce that to possess anything earns you respect.

"And nobody ever gives away what they claim. It wants me back because I'm a possession. Whatever its plans with Mad MacMurphy, that's the root of it. Ownership. Domination."

Bitter anger cracked through each word, and Lindsay did the only thing she knew to do. She pressed her body to his, wrapped her arms around his hard middle. "Should I show you once more how wrong they are?"

It was a request to kiss him. Instead he took her, his mouth opening over hers, and they melted against each other. It would likely be the last of the several thousand they'd shared during the past day and night. They'd ate, slept, and made love again and again with a passion sprung from the acceptance of what this day would bring.

Lindsay was gripping Jack's coat for support when she felt him stiffen. His lips rubbed against her cheek. "Here comes our guide for the day."

Twisting around, she spotted Crabbe bustling toward them, his body bundled in a ratty mustard-colored parka, a furry Russian-style hat perched over his long red hair.

"You bring the money?" he asked the moment he was within speaking distance.

Lindsay handed over a roll of hundred-dollar bills. Crabbe tucked the cash inside his moth-eaten parka as quick as a pickpocket. "Okay. Follow me."

He led Lindsay and Jack to the waterfront, leaving behind the towering skyscrapers of Manhattan. They made their way across the frozen park, passed beneath an elevated highway, until at last they came to the bleak, rocky shore of the Hudson River.

Sliding a pry bar from beneath his jacket, Crabbe kicked aside snow to reveal a manhole, then looked at them uncertainly.

"Under our feet is a tunnel. It's on the small side, and it's going to be slippery from the ice, but it'll take us to a cave. The cave's got a drop-off down into the Chasm where I got my boat. Let me tell you, the climb's tricky. I'm warning you two now so you won't be blaming me if one of you falls or gets hurt. This time of year ain't the best for tunnel crawlin'."

Lindsay could feel Jack's worried eyes on her. "If I can pee from a plank hanging higher than a kite, I can handle this." She turned to Crabbe. "Fine. We're ready."

After a furtive scan of the deserted shore, Crabbe pried open the cover, then clambered down the rusted iron rungs. To Lindsay's relief the tunnel lay only a dozen feet below, though Crabbe hadn't been kidding when he said it was small. Even with his undersized physique his chin was pressed into his chest.

Jack stood on the other side of the hole from Lindsay. He'd taken off his sunglasses and his amber eyes held hers with tenderness.

She held that look and said, "Tonight, I'm inviting Janice over for a family dinner. The four of us. Afterwards, we'll take down the Christmas tree together."

The look in his eyes deepened. "I'd like that, Linds."

Their crawl through the drainage tunnel wasn't as bad as Lindsay had expected, the cold having congealed the filth and litter into inoffensive clumps. Still, the pressing confines of the icy pipe meant that she had to push her backpack along ahead of her, and even with the reassuring illumination of her flashlight she was relieved to see the cave appear in her beam.

Crabbe took her hand and popped her into the small chamber, flashing his own light about nervously. Lindsay registered the steep fissure a few feet away but her attention was drawn to the stack of dozens of small crates, all heavily rotted from the damp. One of the boxes perched high up was a little more intact than the others, and Lindsay trained her light on some still legible words.

"Schenley's Whiskey," she read.

Crabbe was unwinding rope. "Yeah, my grandfather used to smuggle in booze from Kingston. Back in the 20's Schenley's was the best you could get."

"So smuggling runs in your family, does it?" Jack asked, pushing out of the passage behind Lindsay.

Their guide turned up his gloved hands. "How else you think I'd know about the Chasm? Hell, it was my grandfather that named it."

The rocky crevice that led down to the underground river was as dirty and cold as the pipe they'd come through, and it was only with rope that a reasonably safe descent was possible. Crabbe went first, surprising Lindsay with his agility.

"It's only about thirty feet down," Crabbe called from below.

Lindsay peered down. "Don't you find it ironic that the underground has so many high places?"

Jack set another knot in the rope. "This whole adventure reeks of irony."

The descent was treacherous, the fissure studded with rocks and long blackened icicles, but she reached its bottom barely shaking. She now stood on the narrow shore of a Stygian waterway, its surface covered in an oily slush. Bobbing in the water was a small metal skiff, large enough for four people, and on its rust-flecked prow was its ominous name.

*The Charon.*

Jack touched down beside her. Crabbe held the boat steady and gestured with his head for Jack and Lindsay to board. The moment they did that, he hopped in and they were away. "This'll go faster if you hold the light while I pole us down the river," he said to Jack. "It should only take us about a half-hour to reach the place, and then the clock starts ticking, okay?"

Jack clicked on his flashlight, shining it on the inky water. "We'll be back." He slanted Lindsay a look. "There's a dinner party I have to attend."

Schenley's Chasm wasn't a neat channel by any stretch of the imagination. Eons ago, water had cut its way through the rock following the path of least resistance, resulting in a narrow subterranean canal that twisted as wildly as an angry serpent. In places the ceiling was high, stretching upward into blackness beyond the reach of their lights, while in others it forced them to duck their heads. The tunnel grew warmer as they progressed, the water melting from an ice-choked mire into a greasy, sulfurous stream.

"You swam in this?" Lindsay whispered to Jack as some unidentifiable piece of carrion floated past them.

He gave a grim nod. "Parts of it are shallow. I walked some of the way."

She looked dubiously at the muck-thickened water. "I can't imagine how. You were brave, Jack."

"No, just desperate. Between the cold and toxins I was lucky to make it to Agharta. If Gali hadn't managed to rappel down and rescue me, I'd have been rat food for sure."

Of course, Jack would downplay his escape but there was one thing he needed to know. "This water brought you out Jack, and it's taking us to Seline. It's going down in my books as the most wonderful waterway this side of Venice."

Jack gave a slow grin. "You know, Venice has a really interesting underside. I'll take you there, sometime. The two of us and some scuba gear."

Lindsay clung to the moment of lightness, to the expectation of a future together. "You're such a romantic."

At length Crabbe brought them to a sizable cavern, its pitted ceiling sharp with glistening stalactites that glowed orange under their flashlights. There was a small graveled shoreline, its black pebbles mixed with the shattered bones of vermin, and beyond it lay a winding passage into the rock. Markings like those Lindsay had seen in the upper tunnels were scratched low upon the walls, the largest of which was the spider Jack bore upon his shoulder.

This was it. They had reached the no-man's land between the world of humankind and that of dark legend. From here, they'd rescue Seline, the niece she had raised and loved as a daughter, or they'd fall into the clutches of the Moles.

She'd presumed that at this moment she would only feel

terror, and while adrenaline pumped through her, she also experienced a strange kind of stillness. Was this what courage felt like? She watched Jack crouched over, double-checking the equipment, and she knew her calmness stemmed partly from his steady presence.

Jack straightened and leaned into Crabbe's face. "Wait here," he growled.

"Two hours." The smuggler tapped his watch. "Starting now."

Lindsay stepped out of the boat and pulled her gun from her pack.

There, in the near dark, Jack's eyes steadied on hers. "Ready?"

She met his gaze. "Ready."

As one, they drew breath and on his signal, she followed him into The Pits.

---

THE NATURAL PASSAGE that led from Schenley's Chasm was less than a hundred feet in length, and opened into a bizarre circular tunnel supported by a seemingly endless row of hewn columns. Set within the walls were numerous small niches and alcoves, each containing horrific little fetish dolls constructed from the bones and pelts of vermin, each a nightmare in miniature. Around the evil shrines were more of the Moles' disconcerting symbols, painted in a dim phosphorescent pigment.

Jack looked both ways down the silent passage, then stepped back to where Lindsay waited. He inhaled deeply through his nose, and she quickly realized why. The unmistakable scent of cold metal hung in the otherwise musty air.

Her lips grazed his ear. "What is this place?"

"One of the tunnels they've dug," he answered. "They extend from a central chamber like a web, and right now we're on the very edge of it. We're deep inside their territory, so we have to keep things as dark and quiet as possible from here on in. Turn off your light, and don't switch it back on unless you absolutely need to, okay?"

"Okay."

"And don't even *touch* any of those rat figures. You don't want to know what's inside of them."

Lindsay swallowed hard and nodded.

"Okay then. Follow close, and stay sharp. If they detect us we won't get two seconds warning before they attack."

They entered the dark tunnel, their senses strained for any hint of danger. Their progress went unimpeded, Jack leading her on a zigzag course through the tunnels toward the heart of the Moles' domain, Lindsay noting each twist and turn. At length they came to a notably different intersection, the bisecting concrete tunnel clearly of human construction.

Jack edged to the corner for a quick look, then guided Lindsay down the stark corridor. "Deep earth bomb shelter from the fifties," Jack whispered. "Phone lines are wired into it."

So much for national security.

The floor of this new tunnel was tiled, and in the grime Lindsay could make out innumerable footprints tracking in both directions. They weren't large, in fact most were smaller than her own. Bare feet whose splay-toed shapes weren't quite right, and whose uneven pattern didn't suggest a human stride.

Even now, after her experiences in Seneca and surrounded by the ghastly evidence of their existence, it was difficult to accept that such things as the Moles existed. No wonder Jack had never presented his findings to the academic community, nor sought police protection after making it back. The very notion of monsters dwelling beneath the city was preposterous, especially when viewed by the scholars and bureaucrats who ran the world from the comfort and safety of their offices.

Jack stopped in his tracks and killed the light, his arm swinging out to flatten her and himself against the wall. Nothing met Lindsay's ears save for her own breathing, but then from down the corridor, she picked up the crackly hiss of the Moles' language. Panic shot through her, until she realized by the echoes that they were still distant.

In the dark, Jack's hand found hers, his strong fingers entwining with her own and tugging her forward. With infinite slowness, he led her toward the sound, then guided her silently around another corner and away. His pace quickened, and the inhuman conversation faded from earshot.

His light came on, and Lindsay found herself in another concrete passage, its walls pitted with bullet holes and stained with the gore of a battle fought years ago.

"This is as far as anyone's ever made it by force," Jack murmured. "We're almost at the phone room. From there we can take a shortcut to where they keep prisoners."

Lindsay's eyes darted about, absorbing the remnants of pitched battle. "This was where Reggie fought them?"

"He and his little army, about forty in all."

"What happened to the bodies?"

He grimaced. "Let's just say the Moles have a lot more of those rat figures now."

Another minute brought them to a heavy metal door, which Jack listened at intently before opening. The chamber beyond was packed with rows of outdated telephones and bulky junction boxes, along with a bank of old-fashioned tape recorders. Everywhere were stacks of New York phone books and boxes of audio tapes, and scrawled on the walls were scrolls of phone numbers. Lindsay's skin crawled as she picked out that of her apartment.

"They monitor the world from here," Jack spoke into her ear. "Even though they don't really understand us in any true sense, they're good at gathering information."

"Who do they listen in on?" Lindsay asked.

"Police, the transit authority—anyone who deals with the underground. That's why people like my father rarely see them. The Moles keep themselves off the radar."

They exited the silent room, emerging into yet another corridor in the Moles' labyrinth. Jack took one turn, then another, guiding her through musty halls, and Lindsay was hard-pressed to keep track of their route.

At last, they came to a door—an unmarked and unremarkable steel door, its surface a cracked mosaic of flaking white paint. The chill metallic scent had sharpened as they had ventured deeper into the Moles' lair, and Lindsay knew in her core that they were now at its very heart.

Cautiously Jack placed his ear to the door, and Lindsay held her breath as the seconds ticked by. He straightened, looked at her for one long immeasurable moment, then gestured to the gun in her hands. She flicked on the light and readied her weapon.

In one quick motion, Jack pushed open the door and the two of them strode in, their beams bathing the chamber in light. A hoarse cry shattered the silence, and Lindsay staggered at what she saw.

The filthy, tiled room was large and bare, a thick concrete pillar rising from the center of its floor to support the ceiling, and huddled behind it was Seline, half-naked, clutching her eyes in agony against the blazing light. Her clothes were shredded, bloodied rags. Her skin was raked with swollen scratches and streaked with tunnel grime.

Lindsay rushed to her side, hugging her tightly. "It's Auntie Lindsay, Seline," she whispered. "Keep your eyes shut and stay quiet. We're going to get you out of here."

Seline was hysterical. "There're things down here... monsters...and this woman...she said you were coming...."

"Shhh, Seline. It's okay," Lindsay said, willing her voice into calmness, despite the growing dread that they'd probably walked into a trap. "Jack Cole's with me, and he's going to lead us out right now, but you have to stay quiet, okay?"

"I can't, Auntie. I can't." She cried softly, her fists balled over her eyes.

"Sure you can. Take my arm, and—"

"No," Seline whimpered. "You don't know what they'll do to me if I try and leave. What they'll make me into. Oh God...just run...."

Jack seized Seline by the wrists, and brought his face within an inch of hers. "And that's what they'll do to Lindsay unless you get off your ass right now. Move it."

Seline hesitated, locked between two terrifying possibilities. Then, she rose to her feet, her expression an alloy of panic and determination.

Lindsay steadied her, Jack took the lead, and together they slipped out, closing the door behind them. Seline had to shade her eyes, her weakness making her slump against Lindsay.

Navigating the dark corridors quickly and quietly, they made it back to the Mole-dug tunnel that led to Schenley's Chasm. They were practically running now, desperate to reach the waterway before Seline was missed, and it was their haste that cost them.

From behind a pillar a huge shape loomed and a massive fist backhanded Jack across the face, the force of it sending him head over heels, his gun clattering across the floor. Before Lindsay could react, another shadow leapt at her from behind, throwing piano wire around her neck. Reflexively, she inserted her gloved hands between the garrote and her throat as her attacker yanked back, and she lost hold of both Seline and her weapon as her knuckles were pulled tight against her windpipe.

Scrambling to his feet, Jack faced Hugo, Randa Mac-Murphy's towering bodyguard, who regarded him with Buddha-like contentment.

"Welcome home, Cole!" MacMurphy let out a gibbering laugh, jerking Lindsay with the wire. "Won't the Moles be happy when they see what we've brought them?"

# CHAPTER
## TWENTY TWO

WHEN JACK LUNGED for Lindsay, Hugo seized him by the scruff of his jacket and pulled him back as easily as a mother with a recalcitrant child. Smiling serenely, the giant moved to take him in a headlock, but Jack spun and threw every ounce of his power into a punch right to the solar plexus.

It was like hitting a stone wall.

Jack staggered backwards, pain shooting up his arm. Hugo's smile widened in amusement, and again he reached for Jack.

MacMurphy planted a foot against the small of Lindsay's back, and yanked viciously in an effort to finish her with the garrote. Lindsay gasped as the wire cut through the leather of her gloves and into her fingers, and she pitched herself backwards, sending them both to the stone floor, fighting to keep back the wire. MacMurphy's grip tightened.

"It's for the best," the madwoman crooned. "Life is full of pain—better to get it over with, right?"

"I'll show you pain," Lindsay gritted out. She wiggled one hand free from the wire and grabbed for her gun.

Jack leaped back and forth before Hugo, barely evading the man's attempts to catch him. He feinted to the right and dove for the sub-machine gun. Hugo stomped his massive boot down on the weapon, narrowly missing Jack's hand. Jack's eyes widened at the crushed gun. Its light flickered, and then fizzled out.

On sheer instinct, Jack launched another fierce punch at a more vulnerable point on the bodyguard. Struck between the legs, Hugo staggered back, his pale green eyes fixing on his opponent, his smile fading. Jack wasn't waiting around for the man to recover.

He scrambled for Lindsay's gun, only to have her unintentionally snatch it from his outstretched fingers.

"Fuck."

Then Hugo grabbed his ankle and dragged him back into the darkness.

Seeing the gun in Lindsay's grasp, MacMurphy twisted as hard as she could on the wire, driving Lindsay's protecting hand into her chin. Pointing the gun blindly over her shoulder, Lindsay tilted her head and pulled the trigger. The force of the recoil loosened her hold on the weapon's grip, and the volume of the blast so close to her ear filled her head with a shrill ringing. The tension on the wire vanished, yet even as Lindsay tossed aside the garrote, the bloodied MacMurphy clamped down on the gun.

Jack was lifted into the air by his ankle, Hugo swinging him and letting go, sailing him straight into a thick stone pillar. There was a sickening crack of bone when Jack made impact, but he struggled through the pain and rolled to his feet.

Hugo was on him again in an instant, this time elevating him in a deadly bear hug. Kicking frantically, Jack felt the steel-hard arms act like a python as they tightened around him until his vertebrae popped. He flailed his fists at the man's thick face, but it was like punching a concrete block. He had to fight as vermin did—vicious and dirty.

The light from Lindsay's gun played wildly about the tunnel as she struggled with MacMurphy. Despite her rail-thin physique and part of her face blown off, the woman fought with the strength of insanity, and to Lindsay's horror, the lunatic was winning. Slowly but surely the gun was slipping from her hands, and in moments, MacMurphy would have the weapon.

Then, with a shrill cry, Seline was there. She grabbed MacMurphy by the hair and drove her fist into the woman's mouth, shattering teeth with a single rage-powered blow. Lindsay jerked the gun away from the AP, and shone its light down the tunnel toward Jack.

Snarling, Jack dug his fingers into Hugo's scalp and chomped down on the soft cartilage of the giant's nose. Roaring in agony, the bodyguard tried to peel Jack off. With the savageness of a rabid rat he held on, and sank his teeth deeper and deeper, blood filling his mouth.

With a deafening shriek, Hugo threw Jack aside, clutching his ruined face. An instant later, a volley of bullets tore through his gigantic frame. He fell against the wall of the passage, then slid down its curved surface with a final rattling gasp.

Lindsay stood wide-eyed in shock, holding her smoking gun. It took a moment to gather her senses, and, aiming her light on Jack's crumpled form, she saw him spit a bloody hunk of flesh onto the ground.

"That," he said hoarsely, "is tunnel-fighting."

———————————

AS THE FAINT echoes of gunfire died away, Crabbe looked

at his watch. It had been a little more than an hour since he'd dropped off his passengers, and if not for the promise of nine grand, he would have hightailed it home the second they were out of sight. He had a grand in his pocket—enough for heat and smokes for weeks. Why press his luck?

There was the roar of some deranged animal and another burst of weapon fire. Whatever his passengers were mixed up in, it wasn't good, and the last thing he wanted was to end his days in his grandfather's chasm, another floater for the cops to fish out of the Hudson.

Then again, a man could do a whole lot of living on ten grand. Hell, he could get a new television, get his cable reconnected with porn channels and everything. There was also the matter of Tocat, who might not take it so well if he came back without Cole and the woman. The Teco might not be as dangerous as the things that crawled the sewers, but he could still snuff out Crabbe like a damp cigarette.

Either way there were risks, and either way there were rewards, and only God knew which path was the best to take. In times like this a smuggler had only one friend, though it'd been a while since they'd last talked.

Pinning the flashlight between his knees, Crabbe reached into his coat pocket and dug out a tarnished quarter—his entire life's savings until he'd been handed the roll of bills up at the park. Balancing it on his dirty thumbnail, he closed his eyes and whispered into the darkness, "Please, Saint Dismas, I'll try and be a better guy, and, however it lands, I'll drop a twe—a ten—in the collection plate next time I get the chance. Help me pick the way to go."

Crossing himself, he flicked up the coin, caught it and slapped it down onto the back of his hand.

"Heads, I wait for 'em," he mumbled. "Tails, they're on

their own."

He slowly lifted his hand from the coin and squinted down at the result.

---

LINDSAY HURRIED TO help Jack to his feet. He tried to stand, every breath like a fresh blow. For sure, he had cracked ribs and a dislocated shoulder, and there was something the hell wrong with his leg, too. "The Moles are going to be here any minute," he wheezed. "You remember the way back?"

Through the ringing in her ears, Lindsay nodded. "Then take Seline and run. I'll catch up." His bout with MacMurphy's thug had left him severely injured, and there was no way he'd make it to the Chasm before the Moles reached them. Not on his own steam, anyway.

Lindsay shook her head. "No way. We're all going, Jack. Now."

He gritted his teeth in pain and frustration. "Linds, I'll make it. Now go."

Lindsay hauled on him. "You sure will. Now *move*, god-damn you."

All Jack needed to do was to drop down; she wasn't strong enough to carry him. The Moles would come and take him, and that would be that. Except Lindsay would fight them, and there would be no way she could fend them all off. She would die horribly. Seline, too. He moaned and pushed to stand.

Lindsay hung on. She shifted so that her arm came around his waist, and slung her gun over her back.

"Seline," she called. "Get on his other side. We're leaving."

---

BEHIND THEM MACMURPHY weakly raised her head and ran her tongue over the jagged remains of her front teeth as she watched the light from the gun disappear down a side passage. Hugo had been a useful follower, and his sacrifice had served its purpose. The Moles were on their way, and Cole was too injured to outrun them. Soon he'd be back where he belonged, and this time his conversion to the underground would be completed. The Moles were very effective at breaking people, but she had a few tricks to add to their psychological arsenal. A cocktail of pentazocine, sertraline and a few other psychotropic drugs would do wonders for his attitude, and with his cooperation, their plans could begin in earnest.

One day soon, New York would be plunged into darkness, their communications severed and their water poisoned. The same fate would befall all the major cities of the world, and in the ensuing chaos, the APs would torch it all. It wouldn't be an act of war, nor one of terrorism, for they had no demands to make of humanity. It would be an act of glorious revenge, and the dawn of a new dark age in which monsters, both human and not, would again stalk the night.

She smiled. Then began to laugh. A high-pitched cackle of unbounded hatred that heightened as a pack of inhuman forms rushed past her into the blackness, hell-bent for Schenley's Chasm.

---

LINDSAY KNEW JACK was fighting to remain conscious. His each gasping breath was pained, each step a visible effort. She and Seline were moving as fast as possible, their breathing labored as they dragged him through the columned halls. In the shifting light all the passages looked the same, the fetish dolls mocking her from their niches upon the hewn walls. She worried that in their haste she had made a wrong turn. The Pits were a labyrinth of tunnels and side passages, no doubt designed to confuse intruders and lure them to dead ends.

Jack rasped out, "You sure you know—?"

Had he sensed her doubt? "Jack, the only thing blonde about me is my hair. We're almost there."

Seline whimpered. "Hurry, I can hear them! They're catching up!"

Lindsay shook her head, trying to get rid of the high-pitched whine that still sounded in her ear. Between it and the thumping of her adrenaline-fueled heart, she could barely hear a thing, but she believed Seline. She had witnessed firsthand the deadly alacrity of the Moles. Their only hope was the Chasm, where the chill, toxic waters might halt the creatures' pursuit.

Then, as if in answer to her prayers, she spotted the natural side passage that led to the underground river. With renewed vigor, she pulled Jack and Seline into the tunnel.

"Only fifty feet more," she whispered, as much in encouragement to herself as them. "Thirty. Twenty. Ten."

They burst into the cavern, with such momentum that Lindsay had to plant her feet to stop them all from going head-long into the filthy water. Desperately she looked about, for a moment incredulous, before rage and panic filled her heart.

The boat was gone.

"Damn you, Isaac Crabbe!" she screamed.

Then, from out of the darkness the man appeared, poling his boat towards them. "I'm here! I'm here! Keep your panties on!"

"Lindsay!" Jack yelled, and with a fierce shove sent her and Seline sprawling into the frigid water. From behind leapt a trio of nightmares, their black jaws snapping where Lindsay had just been. Jack gave a brutal kick at the one closest to him, propelling it into its companions so all three went head over heels.

Lindsay and Seline emerged chest-high in the water, its cold gunk strong enough to burn. She put the gun to her shoulder and pulled the trigger. The small cavern instantly filled with the blaze and thunder of gunfire. Jack hit the floor as gore splashed over the symbols scrawled on the cave walls, two of the Moles going down in the hail of bullets. The third dodged aside, and like a great jungle cat, leaped over the arc of Lindsay's gunfire toward her.

There was a loud crack as Crabbe's pole connected with its head, spinning it into the water. When the monster surfaced, thrashing and sputtering, the smuggler whacked it again with his improvised weapon, dispatching it beneath the churning water.

Lindsay hauled her niece onboard, tipping the boat dangerously. Jack had slid into the water as well, and she struggled to get him into it. His weight was too much for her.

"Help me, Jack!" she yelled. "Get up there! Get on the fucking boat!"

His hand clutching the edge of the skiff, Jack let out a soundless scream as he pulled himself over his damaged shoulder. She shoved him hard and his face thumped onto the rough boards on the bottom of the wildly rocking craft.

Lindsay threw her gun aboard and scrambled to follow as Crabbe madly poled towards the shelter of the deep chasm. She had lifted her torso free of the reeking effluent as the Mole surfaced directly behind her.

Its clawed hands seized her hair, pulling her back with a screech of rage, and from the corner of her eye, Lindsay caught the shadows of a dozen more of the creatures as they charged through the cavern entrance and plunged into the waters in a rabid effort to reclaim their lost prize.

Crabbe saw them too, and poled even more furiously even as the beast tugged at Lindsay. She kicked and struggled, muscles straining, until suddenly the light from the gun shone directly in her eyes. There was a deafening crack of gunfire as Jack put the last bullet squarely into the Mole's forehead. It let go, and with the sudden release of its weight, Lindsay rolled on board to land directly on top of Jack. He gave a tortured groan but held her still.

Despite his compact body, Crabbe's strength was super-human as he pushed the boat to the narrow side passage. The Moles proved weak swimmers, and were left behind, splashing uselessly in the chill waters. Lindsay heard their inhuman howls of frustration, and, righting herself, caught one last glimpse of their ragged forms paddling the water like huge sewer rats.

"They haven't given up," Jack wheezed, lowering the gun as the hellish cavern disappeared into the gloom. "Those things will never give up."

Lindsay turned to him, almost throwing herself into his arms before remembering his injuries. She was freezing, filthy, beaten and half-scared to death, yet more elated than she'd ever been in her life. She took Seline's hand and gripped it hard.

"Neither will we, Jack."

---

LINDSAY WAS ENDLESSLY grateful to her own foresight in having left a backpack of clean, dry clothes in the boat. All three of them were soaked through and didn't worry overmuch about modesty as they struggled into their change of clothes. They couldn't do much about their wet jackets though and Seline didn't have one, so they all huddled under Crabbe's ratty winter coat as he struggled to return them to Riverside Park.

In the uncertain light Crabbe's face gleamed with sweat, and his breath sounded like an asthmatic in a marathon. "Just a few more minutes. We're almost there. Up the rope. Hop and a skip along the drain. And up to the top. A trip to the hospital. Then my nine grand, right?"

Lindsay smiled through her chattering teeth. "That and a bonus."

Turning to Jack, Lindsay found him frighteningly pale, but his amber eyes shone with concentration.

She set her hand on his thigh. "Jack?"

"I'm trying to figure out how MacMurphy knew we'd be coming this way. Even we didn't know about this passage till a couple of days ago."

Lindsay shook her head. "She couldn't have. Otherwise the Moles would have ambushed us as soon as we were inside."

"Then, how was it they were waiting for us as we left? They weren't guarding that passage for fun. They deliberately let us in."

"She said she wanted to bag you herself," Seline piped up through chattering teeth. "Said you were going to help them find other colonies. She knew that you were coming to rescue me."

"How?" Jack asked.

"She didn't say."

"It doesn't matter now, anyway," Lindsay said. "Once we're up, we'll be free of them. We'll tell the authorities about what's going on, and we'll get the Moles chased out of this city forever."

Jack grimaced. "Who's going to believe us, Lindsay?"

She didn't know who. She didn't even know where to begin. "Hey, we survived a Mole attack. New York bureaucracy can't be much worse."

Crabbe reached his makeshift dock, stepped onto the bank of the underground river and secured the boat in place. "I'll go first," he said, eyeing Jack. "As soon as I'm there, I'll pull you up, okay?"

He turned to the rough, icy wall and swore. The rope they'd come down on was gone. Crabbe trailed the beam of his flashlight upward until it focused on an athletic female at the top, an aged revolver in her hand.

"I'm surprised you made it back, Jack," Gali said, the corner of her mouth tugged upward in an ironic smile. "Well, actually, not *that* surprised. That's why I decided to wait and make sure of things."

Of course, Lindsay realized, her gut tightening. Gali hadn't been washing her surgical tools. She'd eavesdropped on the conversation with Tocat.

Jack's eyes narrowed on her. "Why, Gali?"

"Because I love you," she replied, her hard voice cracking with emotion. "I've loved you ever since I first saw you, when you came down to Agharta with Reggie's gang. That's why I saved you. That's why I took care of you."

"So you thought telling the APs about our rescue would put you in my good books?" His voice was weak but hard.

Something in his quiet, intractable tone floated up to Gali.

Her brittle calm broke. "I'll never be in your good books, Jack. To you I'll always be garbage—not even fit to walk on the same ground as your fucking topsiders! Didn't you know I would have done anything for you? I would have given my life for yours. Wasn't that enough? Instead you take up with a Nazi bitch who'll never understand you!"

"What do you want, Gali?" Jack asked. "You want me to die?"

Gali set her jaw. "I'm a healer, Jack. I won't hurt anyone unless they force my hand, but I'm not going to lose you. Not like this. Not to someone like her."

"So what do you want?" he repeated, anger strengthening his pain-slurred voice.

"I want you to go back where you belong, Jack." She wiped at her eyes. "Go back to the Moles."

"They'll kill me, Gali."

"No, they won't." Hysteria wobbled her voice. "Mac-Murphy promised me they wouldn't. She said I could have you once you'd helped them, and don't you see how perfect that'll be? You and me, Jack, we'll be together, safe in Agharta while the world burns. You'll finally be where you belong, and I'll love you more than anyone else ever could. More than my own life."

Jack stared up at her. "Swear to me you'll let everyone else go."

"No, Jack!" Lindsay cried. He didn't spare her a glance.

"I swear I will as long as they don't try anything," Gali said. "And you have to go back with me. We'll go in the boat to The Pits and I'll take care of you till you're well again. Just like before."

"Then, throw down the rope, Gali."

Lindsay turned Jack's face to her. "No, Jack! No way.

You can't go back with her. It's insane!"

Jack smiled slightly, his face so pale as to be ghostlike.

"I love you, Linds," he said quietly.

Lindsay stared into his eyes, unable to say a word. Behind her, the rope uncoiled to the ground, and Gali slid down it to join them on the bank.

"You go first," she ordered Crabbe. "Don't go anywhere. We need you to pull up these two topsiders."

Crabbe nodded, not wasting a second before scrambling up the rope like a monkey. As soon as he reached the top, Gali gestured with her pistol at Seline.

When Seline hesitated, Lindsay waved her on. "Go. Go now."

Shivering, Seline clung to the rope, and Crabbe heaved her up to the ledge.

"You're next, bitch." Gali leveled her pistol at Lindsay. "You got your girl back, so you should be happy. That's all you were fucking him for anyway, wasn't it?"

Lindsay fixed the woman with an icy stare, even though she couldn't be sure that from that distance Gali could see her. "You don't know anything about me, Gali, and you don't know a damn thing about love, either."

Though it was reckless, Lindsay turned away from Gali and pressed her lips to Jack's, molding her body to his. "I love you, too, Jack," she said. "But you're not getting away with this."

"Get away from him!" Gali screamed, her gun trained squarely at Lindsay's back, then she was knocked off her feet by an avalanche of Schenley's whiskey crates thrown from above. Lindsay didn't miss her chance. She jumped Gali, wrestling for the gun in a full-blown cat-fight. Though Gali was strong, Lindsay had the twin edges of desperation and surprise. Beating the woman down with all her might, she wrenched away the gun and tossed it into the oily waters.

Hauling Gali to her feet, Lindsay slammed her hard against the icy wall. "You bitch!" she hissed. "I'm going to do worse than kill you. I'm going to leave you down here in the dark. Down in these sewers like the fucking rat you are." She felt Jack's shaky hand on her shoulder, and slowly she released Gali, allowing him to face the woman.

Through dark eyes, Gali looked up at him, lips trembling. "Please Jack...you're one of us...can't you see that? Up there, you're nothing. Down here, you'll have everything...I need you...."

Jack regarded her, his face softening from grim anger to simple pity. "Go home, Gali."

Lindsay watched Gali slump against the cavern wall. She would be forever grateful to the healer for saving Jack's life, for her part in restoring him to a life of light and connection, to her. Yet the same woman had sought to pull him back down into her own dark and tortured world.

Jack took Lindsay's hand, even as she reached for it with her own. They turned and walked away.

The last thing they heard as they were lifted away, back into the noise and light, into a place of hope and warmth, were the sobs of a lost soul.

# EPILoGUE

*Three months later*

ANOTHER FLUORESCENT LIGHT was on the blink in Captain Monroe's cramped office, and Lindsay was giving it the evil eye when Agent Jill Lever finally arrived. Jack and the captain straightened in their chairs, and even Lindsay caught herself striking an alert pose.

"Sorry I'm late," the plain-suited woman said in a tone that showed her apology was only a formality, and shut the door behind her. "The meeting at the mayor's office went late, resulting in decisions being made."

Nobody replied. This was their third meeting with the CIA agent, and they'd gotten used to her telling them purely what she'd been authorized to share. Asking additional questions was always fruitless.

Not bothering to sit, she turned her martial expression to Captain Monroe. "The military have verified that the Manhattan deep-earth nuclear shelter was indeed breached, and have also confirmed some of Dr. Cole's extraordinary reports regarding the…individuals responsible. Tunnels in the area are being sealed to prevent further trespassing.

"Both the Agency and the mayor's office request that everyone involved in Seline Sterling's rescue keep the matter

292

from the press until further notice. The last thing we want is to provoke a panic, or encourage curiosity-seekers to enter the tunnels. I trust we'll have your full cooperation."

"Your trust is well-placed," Jack said dryly.

Lever kept her hard gray eyes on Monroe. "You, Captain, will receive a substantial increase to your budget in the face of this new danger to the public, but none of your officers are to be briefed on the specific nature of the threat until we've had an opportunity to study it further."

Jack sat back in his chair, folding his arms over his chest. "And who's going to conduct this 'study' of yours?" Lindsay expected him to get the cold shoulder. That didn't happen.

"We were hoping you would, Dr. Cole. We're interested in hiring you as a consultant, and I've been authorized to negotiate the terms."

Lindsay suppressed a gasp of pleasure; Jack looked unimpressed. "I'll think about it and let you know."

Lever nodded quickly as if his answer was par for her course, and placed a business card on the corner of Monroe's desk. "You'd be a tremendous asset to our investigation, Dr. Cole, though you should know that there'll be a great deal of travel involved. Your study will not be limited to New York."

Jack frowned. "What do you mean?"

"I'm afraid I'll only be able to discuss those details if you come on board." She gave a tight smile to Lindsay and Monroe, and without so much as a goodbye, left the office.

Lindsay waited discreetly for a few seconds after the door shut, then turned to Jack. "Not much on charm, is she?"

Between Lindsay and Janice, they had made it their personal mission to bring the matter to the attention of the authorities, namely the FBI. As Jack had expected, the Bureau had balked at the idea of monsters running around beneath

New York. Not a day later, however, the case was taken over by the CIA. To Lever's credit, she had not only heard them out, but conducted a complete investigation, which made him believe that this wasn't the first time or place the Agency had come across the Moles.

Reggie, Crabbe and Seline had all been thoroughly questioned and asked to sign secrecy agreements, and at their second meeting, Lever had requested that Jack put together a complete report on the Moles, including everything from his initial suspicions of their existence eighteen years ago to Seline's rescue. The fact that they now wanted to hire Jack meant they were taking the matter seriously, though she knew from his worry lines, it was little comfort that his enemies still roamed the blackness beneath New York, and probably numerous other cities as well.

Lindsay placed her hand on his. "It'll be okay."

He smiled at her. Lately when she said things like that, he seemed to believe her. He flipped his hand over and gave hers a hard squeeze. She caught a flick of white from the corner of her eye. Monroe was offering Lever's card to Jack. "So what are you doing now, Cole?"

Jack took the card. "I'm teaching a couple of freshman courses at NYU." He ran his thumb over the CIA logo. "It's okay for now."

Monroe raised a bushy eyebrow. "From sewers to the ivory towers." His mouth twitched as he took in their joined hands. "Sometimes things work out better than expected."

Don't they just, Lindsay thought, as she and Jack walked out into the late March sunshine and down the sidewalk. The last of winter's slush had dissolved into puddles, there was an undercurrent of warmth in the chill air, and people everywhere moved more freely and spoke more lightly. Jack fingered the sunglasses inside his jacket pocket but didn't put them on.

Instead he took her hand in his once more. It was now automatic with him, she'd discovered, as inevitable as the sun rising. And she had come to think that other things about them might be inevitable, too.

"Are you going to accept the job?"

"Maybe," he said absently. "It depends."

Her shoulder nudged his. "Like where you'll stay when you're not traveling?" For several weeks she—and Seline who'd picked up right where she'd left off at age two of her adoration of all things Jack—had laid heavy hints about him moving in with them. Thus far he'd only stayed nights, though nearly every one of them.

"Don't you need to pick up Seline from the shrink?" he asked.

Lindsay allowed him to duck her question. "Soon, and hopefully not too many more times. The psychologist from the Agency is so good she doesn't need pills to sleep anymore. She's planning to return to school, in fact. Start with a couple of summer courses. It's going to take time, but she'll be fine. Not perfect but fine."

Jack gazed into the distance. "I guess sometimes there're happy endings after all."

"If you make them happen," Lindsay suggested.

"Yeah, well, some take a little more work than others. I mean..." he trailed off. Lindsay tugged him to a stop, and stood before him, creating an island of two as passersby bank-ed around them.

"Go on."

Jack steadied his amber eyes on her. "I mean, this isn't over, Linds. I don't know what's going to happen next. I want to be with you, but...if I take this job, I'll have to be away from you and do things, go under again and risk losing...."

Lindsay waited.

"I love you, Linds. I love you and I couldn't bear to lose you. It would destroy me if anything happened to you, and those things know it. They know it would hurt me more than anything else ever could."

She felt his pain and his love, and knew which one she'd seek to drive away and which one she'd keep. She looked him straight in the eye. "To hell with them, Jack. I love you too much to be afraid."

He reached for her bright hair, tugged her close. "Then, I was wondering if you'd share your home with me."

Happiness burst inside her and she broke into a wide smile. "Of course, Jack. My home is your home."

He paused. "How about your life?"

She flung her arms around him, tilted her face to the sun, and to the world above and below them, shouted for all to hear that yes, yes, and of course, her life was his life.

# THANK YOU!

THANK YOU FOR reading *Undertow*. We hope you enjoyed reading it as much as we did writing it.

The next in the series, *Midnight Everlasting*, won't be ready until late Spring 2014 but we've got an opening excerpt ready for you right here, right now. Set in London, it features a tough and tender couple, and rats. We know. What could be more romantic than rats?

After you're done with that, read on for a peek at our romantic suspense novel, *Fox Hunt*.

We'd love to hear from you!

COME SEE US AT OUR WEBSITE.

www.smstelmackauthor.com

LIKE US ON FACEBOOK.

www.facebook.com/SMStelmack

BECOME A FAN OR FOLLOW US ON GOODREADS

www.goodreads.com/author/show/6968150.S_M_Stelmack

Done, and want to get on with reading? Right then. Below is the opening to *Midnight Everlasting*.

# CHAPTER ONE

ZEPHANIE SWEETLY AND her client sloshed through the fetid sewer, their features concealed behind full-faced gas masks, the only illumination the halogen lights in their hands. The heavy boots of their waders pasted to the muck coated on the bottom, making each step through the shallow, sluggish flow seem as if they were caught in an unseen grip.

"Did you know this was once a river? A beautiful one at that," Zephanie commented to her companion, her voice overloud to compensate for the mask. As proof, she aimed her light beam at a pair of iron rings set in the crumbling walls, remnants from when the passage had been a canal, boats moored at its edges.

Her feedback was a Cockney-thick grumble, "Can't imagine a place ma're disgusting."

Zephanie rolled her eyes. Typical criminal. No appreciation of the past.

Long ago, the Tyburn had sparkled in the sun, running from the spring of Shepherd's Well through the green, fertile farmlands that surrounded Roman Londinium. Over the centuries, Westminster Abbey had been built upon an island in its flow, Buckingham Palace constructed along its glittering shore. But as London grew into a smoking metropolis, the waterway had become depleted and polluted, until at last nothing but a reeking trickle of effluent remained—and then even that had been swallowed by the streets.

Today the Tyburn was just a forgotten sewer flowing through a crumbling brick tunnel, but to those in the know it had two claims to fame. The first was that it still ran alongside the royal palace, meaning that they were literally wading through the Queen's shit. The second was their destination: Tyburn Market.

As they slogged onward, the passage abruptly opened into a series of huge galleries, intricate brickwork curving up into grand arches of multi-hued stone. Zephanie shone her light to the left, onto worn stairs leading up.

"I'll go first. Mind your step, though. The way's slippery," Zephanie cautioned, getting a grunt in response.

At the top of the flight was an ancient oaken door, and she banged out a distinct rhythm with the butt of her light. Heavy bolts pulled back, and the door swung open enough to reveal a short woman with a gas mask, double-barrelled shotgun in hand. "Password."

"I think my client had enough shit in the sewers, Leona," Zephanie replied, lifting her mask to reveal her face.

Her aunt let the two angle in, then slammed the door shut, re-bolting it quickly.

"Nervous about something?" Zephanie asked as she stood on a large iron grate, motioning for her client to do likewise.

"Rawheads have been seen again. This time at Stoop's Limit." Leona took hold of a pressure washer and opened up on them. She operated it like a berserker, the concentrated stream drilling into Zephanie and her visitor.

"Agh, sure," Zephanie said and hopped free of the

stinging spray, her client quick to follow. He took her lead as she set down her light and stripped off her mask and thick rubber gloves. "Like anyone even goes there. I swear people tell you stories just to get a rise out of you."

Leona switched off the hose and pushed her mask atop her head, her thin, pale features set in disapproval. "Believe what you want, girl. They're real. Seen them years ago, and not likely to ever forget."

The client's face was flushed and streaked with sweat. "Dere a problem?"

Zephanie wished her aunt had kept her gob shut. It was one thing to spout her tales around the supper table, another to trouble a client. Especially a new one. They had a business to run.

"Only if you believe in the bogeyman, sir," Zephanie answered, shooting her aunt a squelching glare. "Local ghost stories is all. Now if you take off the rest of your gear and give it to Leona here, we can get to the Market proper."

Zephanie escorted her client into the underbelly of a nameless cathedral. The portion above ground had been eradicated centuries ago by pestilence, war and fire. But the hallowed vaults had endured—and long since been converted to a den of thieves. Light fixtures in the arched ceiling illuminated rows of tables, each situated a discreet distance apart. From faded murals, the reproachful eyes of forgotten saints and angels looked down upon the iniquities of the gathering.

Her client spotted his party and, without so much as a nod, walked off to join them. Just as well. Every time his mouth opened it was to belch out a complaint. Zephanie eyed his people, a grinning Mafiosi and a lanky female. Like him, both were new to her, vetted by Leona. Good. Fresh faces meant word-of-mouth was still working as well as ever. Time for her to relax and enjoy a well-earned pint.

She wove her way between the tables, her nose registering whiffs of petroleum and vinegar, the odor of raw drugs; threads of ink and cologne and copper; peaks of scotch and beer; and underlying it all, the smell of sweat and high adrenaline.

She'd crossed the chamber to the bar when her unfailing olfactories detected another smell, stannic and earthy. It was one she'd come across before, while exploring subterranean nooks and crannies, never before in the Market itself. She scanned the room to locate the source. But just like all the other times, she got nothing. She'd do a proper patrol after her drink.

She swung a leg onto a padded stool at the granite-top bar as fancy as anything topside. It was a reflection of its bartender, everything top drawer or not at all.

"All right, Matt?"

He looked up from the drink he was mixing and flashed her a smile. "All right. Saw you coming, cousin. Drink's almost ready. You haven't been about for awhile."

"Been dealing with the city." She sat on a committee that lobbied for the preservation of the eyesore apartment building that stood atop the vaults. "Spent the last month tying things up in as much red tape as I can."

"Think you did enough?"

"Scared off the developers. That's why I'm back." She had convinced everyone, from the committee women with their manicures and spray-stiff hair to the bureaucrats with their big empty desks, that she actually cared about sparing hideous 70's architecture from the wrecking ball. In reality she didn't want a larger building with deeper foundations that might unearth the Market.

He slid over her drink. It was green and had an umbrella. Not the beer she had in mind. "In honor of your victory then. A St. Paddy's Day special."

She took an experimental sip, rolled it in her mouth, swallowed and waited. "Vodka, green crème de menthe, green Chartreuse and a bitter."

Matt looked defeated, then brightened. "Name the bitter."

"Easy. Angostura. The lemon taste gives it away."

He returned to his glum state. "You and that nose of yours. You should be the one behind the bar."

"I can make them but I can't move them. Need a pretty face for that."

Her cousin lined up martini glasses. "You're pretty. Just need to lose the mean look and the goth clothes. And Blackball. How's the little bugger doing?"

Zephanie felt like a proud mum. "Got third place at the Spring Cup last week."

Matt paused, a vodka bottle in each hand. "Only third?"

"I suspect a payoff. Corruption is rife."

He returned one bottle to the shelf underneath and opened the other. "What did you expect from a show for rats?"

She felt herself bristle, even though she knew he was baiting her. "What, you find dog or cat shows strange?"

Matt shot measures of vodka into the glasses. "Oh, here we go."

She couldn't resist. "No, seriously. Rats are just as smart, just as affectionate, just as clean and can eat just about anything. They're the perfect pet."

"No doubt the Queen will be trading in her Corgis any day now. Any rate, I've heard your *rattus uber alles* argument since we were kids. Anything new to report?"

"Nothing from me."

"What? The rat princess not out man-hunting?"

There he was, jabbing away at her buttons. "Would you leave off about that? You're worse than Auntie."

"You don't have to listen to her yabber on about how you're failing to live up to the Sweetly tradition," Matt persisted. "I swear you don't get yourself knocked up soon, I'm hiring you a surrogate."

"Right, and who'll be the sperm donor?"

"Blackball, for all I care."

"That I'd consider," Zephanie said with a lick of her lips, because the mere thought would disgust her cousin. Sure enough, he gagged.

She smirked. "Never mind, Auntie's distracted now. Got herself worked up about those Rawheads. Please tell me you're not the one feeding your mum all that rubbish. You know how she gets."

"It isn't me, I swear," he replied, hand to heart. "She likes to talk with the old tunnel tramps. They're the ones spreading the stories."

"Shock horror. What better source of information than drunks and addicts? I can see why she's so worried."

Matt began placing the completed martinis on a tray, as cautiously and precisely as his next words. "Some of those people go back years, Zeph. Sure they're nutters, but my mum can tell truth from gin goblins. I am not saying there are monsters, but something's up. Be right back."

He took up the tray and headed over to a nearby table where a pair of sleazy heroin dealers were busy chatting up their busty money launderer.

The world assumed that criminals were all about guns and bloodshed, but their business dealings were typically no different than the legitimate kind. Traffickers in cocaine and heroin, smugglers of prostitutes and blood diamonds, cyber-criminals and counterfeiters, all came to cut face-to-face deals at Tyburn Market, the one place in London the police could never find, let alone infiltrate. Terms were negotiated, agreements reached, and nine out of ten times, nothing went wrong. When they did, the Market served as neutral ground where settlements could be made, Zephanie's family acting as impartial arbiters.

The arrangement kept violence between the factions to a minimum, and since war was expensive, the various bosses were willing to pay toshers like her handsomely for the service.

The ethics of her family might be unconventional, but their methods worked. She was lifting her drink to her lips when the lights spasmed and went black. The old familiar stannic smell wisped around her.

Angry protests rang out, and Matt called for calm. "Our apologies, everyone. Generator must have quit. We'll have it back in a minute."

Several lighters and smart phones were flicked on, creating little pools of brightness in the chamber, and Zephanie rounded the bar to fetch the heavy lights stored there. The metallic scent sharpened, and she saw something from the corner of her eye.

She squinted, sure that it must be some trick of shadows, when she saw them. Dozens of them. Inhuman things that crawled from the darkness like panthers creeping up on a kill.

Crying out, she snatched up a light, igniting its powerful beam the same instant the monsters leapt, swarming over the shocked outlaws, slashing and biting.

"Matt!" she screamed as her cousin was bowled over by

the panicked patrons he'd just served. Vaulting over the bar, she shone the light directly into the faces of the beasts, blinding them before they could pounce on Matt. She yanked him to his feet by his collar and together they sprinted for the exit, as a barrage of bullets erupted, their roar and echoes blasting like shock waves around them.

Leona was holding open the door, and bolted it behind them the moment they were through.

Something slammed into the other side so hard a couple of screws popped from the hinges. Leona gave the door both barrels, punching fist-sized holes through the thick wood.

"Grab masks and get out!" she yelled, snapping open the shotgun to reload. Neither Zephanie nor Matt needed to be told twice. In seconds they were splashing through the sewer, making a beeline for the surface. Behind them, Zephanie could hear her aunt running to catch up.

This couldn't be happening. And yet it was.

The Rawheads were real.

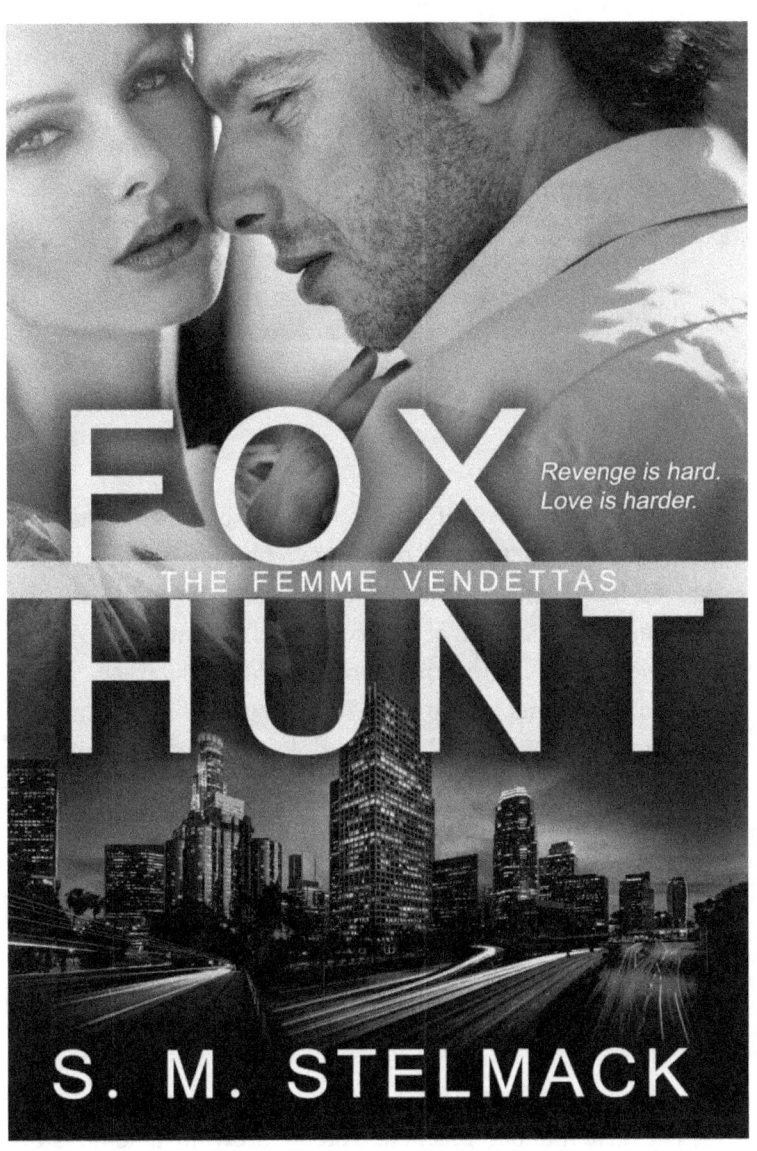

# FOX

**Revenge is hard.
Love is harder.**

## THE FEMME VENDETTAS

# HUNT

# S. M. STELMACK

# PROLOGUE

AKENO SAVORED THE sweet metallic purr of the antique safe as he smoothly spun its dial first right, then back. With the ocean of blood money Matsuda possessed, he could've had something more modern protecting his cash, but Akeno appreciated the crime lord's old-world style. The Swiss precision of the mechanism, the Italian polish of its fittings— he was so glad he didn't have to violate the artistry with the usual drills and picks and pliers, yet part of him also felt denied its deflowering on this, his final take.

So far, everything tonight had gone like clockwork. The mansion's formidable security system had been deactivated with the codes provided, and the key to the old man's office had been hanging right where it was supposed to be. It was shaping up to be a classic inside job—quick, easy and relatively low-risk. The real test was going to be getting away with it afterwards, especially considering who Matsuda was.

The last number reached, Akeno drew in a long, slow breath, and exhaled on a three-count. In a moment, he'd discover if his love really knew her employer's secrets as intimately as his own. Pressing down on the safe's handle, he heard a quiet but distinct click, then slowly swung it open to reveal the prize.

Although he'd paid many uninvited visits to wealthy L. A. estates in his career what Akeno saw before him now made his heart kick like never more: stacks of hundred dollar bills almost filled the safe to capacity. Without a doubt, the biggest single haul of his life sat right before him—even after splitting it with his accomplice.

Well, she'd certainly earned her money. He pulled a large microfiber bag from his pocket and swept the cash into it. Now, to make his escape. So long as there was nothing suspicious to tip off the old gangster, days, perhaps even weeks, might pass before the robbery was detected. By that time, they would be on the other side of the country, sipping margaritas in the Miami sun and living out their fantasies.

As Akeno eased the safe door shut, however, his sensitive ears caught the almost imperceptible turning of the office door handle. He ducked behind the nearby desk, an instant before the door swung open, a dim arc of moonlight spilling in from the hallway.

He rested his head against the hardwood floor to peer under the desk. There was a single pair of feet in black running shoes, and from the shape of the shadow that stretched behind, his visitor was a woman. She slipped inside, shut the door, and a familiar voice spoke in the quietest whisper. "Akeno? Are you here?"

Anger and relief flooded through him as he rose to his feet.

"Susan," he hissed, "what the hell are you doing here?"

She turned towards him in the darkness, and though her face was concealed by a balaclava, he knew she was smiling that devilish grin of hers. She sauntered towards him. "Now is that any way to talk to your Mistress?"

Akeno had no idea how to respond to that. Was she here out of her insatiable need for danger? From the past two months of sex he could believe it. The woman was a handful, two handfuls, actually. And she had a way of mixing pleasure and pain into a cocktail more potent than either.

"What's the matter?" she breathed. "Aren't you happy to see me?"

No, he wasn't, because it meant she didn't trust him, understandable given his profession, but the lack of faith still stung. "You know how dangerous you being here is? This isn't one of your games, Susan."

She gave an amused shrug, slinking around the desk to him. "I like risk, Akeno. I thought you did, too." Her body rubbed against his as she eased up her hood to reveal her mouth, with its hot red lips and perfect white teeth.

He gave her what she wanted because he was powerless to do, otherwise. He yanked up his mask, crushing his lips against hers. To say he was being unprofessional was an understatement, but as her tongue slid into his mouth he had a hard time thinking about anything else. He ran his free hand over the silky fabric of her midnight bodysuit, enjoying the curves sheathed within.

It was she, as usual, who broke off the kiss, tugging her mask down to blank out her face again. Her fingers trailed down his arm to where his hand held the bag. "How much did we get?"

He covered his face. "About a million. Maybe a bit more."

Her dark eyes glinted. "Mmm…with that, we could do a lot of things for a long time." Akeno knew what she meant, and he couldn't help but reach for her, again.

Suddenly, the room was again bathed in dim light, the office door opening to reveal a young man standing in the hallway. Akeno froze. The youth squinted into the darkness. "Jeanelle?"

Akeno spun about, his eyes darting in search of an escape route, but then a gunshot blasted through the room and the boy collapsed like a rag doll. Before Akeno could react, Susan seized him by the arm. "Come on! Run!"

The whole house was awake now, and in a rich neighborhood like this, they had only a couple of minutes before the cops would be on them. There was no time to argue. Leaping over the crumpled body, Akeno felt a spike of sickness drive right through his heart.

The kid couldn't have been older than sixteen, dressed in his robe and pajamas, completely unarmed. There was a neat little bullet hole in his forehead, and from the way he'd fallen, he was clearly dead. Oh God, he thought, sprinting after his lover down the curving stairwell to the front entrance. Oh God, Susan, what have you done...?

# CHAPTER ONE

BRIAN CHANSE WANTED to notch up the speed of his wipers, but they were already going full out. The rain was so fierce they didn't sweep off the water before the windshield was covered again, and the blackness of the New Mexican night didn't help.

"Might as well be driving underwater," he muttered to himself.

He glanced at the GPS. Should have stopped when he had the chance. Santa Rosa wasn't for another twenty miles, though it was still closer than turning around. He rubbed his eyes wearily. There was nothing to do but press on.

At the rate he was going, it was almost one in the morning when up ahead he spotted someone walking the shoulder of the road. He blinked a few times, but sure enough, there was some poor soul slogging through the downpour.

He crawled past to reduce the spray from his wheels, getting a better look. A kid. He pulled his Mustang over and checked his rearview mirror. Yep, it was a kid coming up to his door. A runaway? A druggie? Didn't really matter—he wasn't about to pass anyone by in a storm like this. He lowered his window.

Rain splattered his jacket and cut into his face. It was a teenage girl. She was in hiking boots, jeans and a hoodie, all of which were absolutely soaked, and she swayed before steadying herself against his car.

"Bad night for a walk. Need a lift?"

She studied him, her eyes a shocking blue against the pallor of her skin. Definitely pretty and most definitely not well. She nodded after a moment and circled the hood of his car, while he gathered up the empty fast-food wrappers from the passenger seat and fired them into the back.

She slid in, her short blonde hair matted to her head, her arms wrapped about her in a futile attempt to retain some warmth. He took an extra look where the arms were wrapped, then searched her face. She wasn't quite as young as he'd taken her for, just petite. Probably in her twenties and harmless enough. She didn't seem to have any gear.

"Thanks," she mumbled.

Her face was dead white, even her lips were a dark shade of pale. The desert was a cold place at night, and who knew how long she'd been out there. "I know how this is going to sound, but I think you really ought to get out of those wet clothes. I can get some dry stuff out of the back if you want to change. I'll wait outside."

She stared straight ahead at the rain battering the windshield and shook her head. "I'm fine. I just need to get to the next town."

Stubborn woman. Stubborn and stupid. She was going to catch her death, but what could he do about it? He'd warned her, and he wasn't interesting in arguing with any more people that insisted on putting themselves in harm's way. He'd already had enough of *that* for a lifetime.

Still, he cranked the heat to max, then reached into the backseat and rooted through the mess until he found a beach towel, handing it to her. She took it gingerly, as if it was diseased.

Stubborn and stupid and ungrateful.

He shrugged. "Suit yourself." He shifted the car into gear and continued down the highway, trying to ignore the sound of her chattering teeth.

By the time he parked at a Santa Rosa motel, she was asleep, her chin on her chest. The place was a dump, and by the looks of the peeling paint and flickering neon sign, it was many a year since it'd been anything else. He sprinted inside and rang the night buzzer several times before an elderly clerk came to the grubby counter, watery gray eyes huge behind thick glasses.

"A room, please."

The man took the last key from the board behind him, sliding it over to Brian along with a coffee-stained registry. "That'll be sixty-five dollars. Check-out time is noon. No pets."

As if a dog would want to stay here.

Leaky ballpoint in hand, he scribbled in his name and address, only realizing as he finished that he didn't live there anymore. Then again, he didn't live anywhere anymore. He doled out the money, then picked up the key and headed back to the car. All he had to do now was wake the woman, settle in for a good night's sleep and spend the next day driving to Los Angeles.

Cold rain drumming on him, he opened the passenger door and tapped her on the shoulder. "Miss. We're here. Get up."

She stirred briefly, before slumping back against the seat.

No good deed goes unpunished.

"Come on, miss." He shook her, but she had all the get up and go of a sack of potatoes. He placed his hand on her forehead. Her clammy skin was ice cold.

"Dammit. Why can't people ever just listen?" Unsnapping her seatbelt, he scooped her limp body into his arms. God, not a sack of potatoes but a feather pillow. He hurried up a slick flight of stairs, and managed to juggle keys and her into his room, kicking the door shut and flicking on the light with his elbow.

He laid her on the bed. Her lips had turned bluish-gray and she was shivering harder than a lost kitten. A check found her pulse still strong. She was hypothermic, but not in any immediate peril. The first thing was to get her warm so she didn't get any worse, then call an ambulance.

Brian grimaced at what he had to do next. Him alone in a hotel room, taking clothes off a stranger. Wasn't this just a lawsuit in the making? Then again, a dead woman in his room wouldn't look so good, either.

Peeling off the wet hoodie, his eyes met with a thin white T-shirt, her nipples hard buttons beneath the wet fabric. He reminded himself of the first-aid course he'd taken every year since he was sixteen. This next step was required, that's all.

As he tugged off her t-shirt and sports bra, he tried to keep his eyes to himself, but, oh yeah...she was well-built. He hurried down to unlace her boots. It was then she became conscious. "Don't...please... don't..." she slurred.

"You're hypothermic," he explained, as he slid off her socks and boots. "I'm not going to hurt you, but I have to take off your wet clothes. And then I'll get you some help."

"Don't call...don't call a doctor... please...."

Victims of exposure often made odd requests or even

hallucinated, but she seemed lucid.

"Don't call…" she pleaded. "They'll find… me… please …don't…."

"Who's going to find you?" he asked, but she'd already passed out. He shook his head, then peeled the wet pants over her hips and down her slim, athletic legs. Her panties had come down with the jeans and turning her to her belly, he averted his eyes from her ass. Her firm, squeezable ass. He lost no time in turning down the bedcovers and tucking them snugly around her body. With a bathroom towel, Brian dried her hair as thoroughly as possible. When he was done, it spiked out from her head, and without thinking, he smoothed down its short silkiness. Catching himself, he withdrew his hand. *That* wasn't in any first-aid course.

He pondered getting his suitcase of dry clothes from the trunk, but the rain pounding on the roof and windows settled the matter for him. He next pondered the uncomfortable-looking armchair in the corner of the room, and then the woman's wet mound of clothes. Sighing, he picked them up and hung them over the shower rod in the bathroom.

On his way to the chair, he checked on her. She didn't look good. Her lips still had a bluish tinge and her shivering hadn't ceased. He cursed, shot back into the bathroom and returned with all the towels, right down to the washcloths for her head. He spread them and his leather jacket over her, then flipped the remainder of the duvet on top for good measure, but she kept shaking so badly the coverings trembled.

He hesitated, then took off his shirt and slid beside her. "This had better work," Brian muttered in her ear, "or you're going to the hospital, whether you like it or not." He wrapped his arms around her, pressed his body close, and shared his warmth. Her shivering gradually subsided, her lips flushed a pale pink and her breath blew calmly against his neck. Brian became acutely aware of her soft body against his, and eased himself away before any embarrassing reaction could occur. He'd lie here until she was completely out of the danger zone and then retreat to the chair. He'd just rest for a moment... close his eyes for a while....

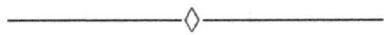

Delta Fox slowly woke, weak, feverish, hungry and... naked. She snapped upright in bed, and when her head stopped spinning, woozily took in her surroundings. The light slanting in told her it was morning, she was in bed, and—oh, shit!— with a man. She recoiled, horrified, but then her leg rubbed against the roughness of his jeans. Reaching down, she tentatively checked herself. Okay, he might've copped a feel but that was all.

She was under a heap of laundry—sheets, blankets, towels, and a man's leather jacket. Her eye on him, she slipped her fingers into the jacket pocket, finding his wallet as she had hoped. She flipped it open, and inside found a respectable amount of cash and platinum credit cards, as well as his California driver's license and a number of other pieces of identification.

The name was Brian Chanse, born thirty-five years ago and a resident of Hollywood. He was a member of the Screen Actors Guild, had a first aid certificate and an organ donor card. She could've fallen into worse hands, but not by much.

Returning the wallet, she laid back, trying to let memories of the previous night solidify in her fevered mind. She'd been hitch-hiking ever since she'd run out of money in Little Rock, and been dumped by a surly trucker out in the middle of nowhere when she'd refused to "pay" him for the ride. Given her luck, it had started raining, and without any real options, she'd been forced to endure the storm. From what she remembered, Brian had been a gentleman and decent enough to respect her request not to call anyone.

She considered taking his cash and car, and heading for the hills. He'd be insured. Except then she'd have the local police on her tail as well. How far could she get sick, exhausted and with an APB on her? Not far enough to avoid either prison or a bullet to the brain.

Okay, first things first. Find clothes.

Her body aching, she draped her legs over the edge of the bed and wrapped a towel around herself. With a steadying hand on the end table, she stood and took a step.

Her legs gave out and she collapsed to the floor with a yelp. From her belly-down perspective, she saw the bed give a bounce, the yank of a sheet and then Chanse was standing above her. Crap, he was hot, all smooth muscles and lean lines. Probably knew it, too. His gaze skittered to her naked backside and Delta grabbed at her towel, doing what she could to salvage her dignity.

He didn't say a word. He bent down, that muscled chest and stubbly jaw up close, and suddenly she was in his arms, the towel twisted between them, and then just as quick, she was back in bed with the covers over her. His hand cupped her forehead.

"You've got a high fever. I'll take you to a doctor."

No, no, no. "No doctors," she said as strongly as she could, but even at that, it came out mewling.

"Look, you were hypothermic last night. You could have died. You really need to at least go to a clinic or something."

"No. I'll be okay. I'll just sleep some more."

His lips in that stubble thinned. "Yeah, but checkout is at noon. I have places to be."

"Listen, I have to get to Los Angeles…I can pay my way…."

"That's nice, but I'm not looking for a traveling companion."

Delta clenched her fists. She needed him. She hated that, hated needing anyone, much less a stranger, much less a gorgeous stranger who probably thought she was some homeless skank. Fighting a wave of dizziness, she forced herself to say, "Then I'll hire you, okay? Get me to L.A. and I'll pay whatever you think is fair."

He snorted. "Sure, and it's because you're rich that you were out hitch-hiking last night. All I want is to get going. If you want to stay here that's fine, but…."

Delta heard his voice fading, his athletic form blurring before her eyes. No, no. She couldn't black out, she had to persuade him somehow. What could she give him…?

FOX HUNT is now available in print and as an e-book!

# ABoUT THE
# AUTHORS

**S. M. STELMACK** IS OUR pen name, short for Serge & Moira Stelmack.

We aim to give what we like in a story— gutsy men and women, high stakes and LOL lines. Serge is the storymaster who blasts out the beginning, middle and end. Moira comes behind, clucking and hemming, as the story undergoes countless rewrites till it meets our vision. She's also the media relations manager, senior editor, marketing VP, director of operations (domestic and foreign), comptroller and the one who makes sure that Serge has a steady supply of cola while he works.

We live with our two kids, and several other strange pets, in a land of wintertime sunshine and snow and summertime mud and mosquitoes. Actually, it's not that bad. The snakes in the local lake aren't venomous.

We really need to move.

Authors, Serge & Moira Stelmack
www.smstelmackauthor.com